LOVE LIES WAITING

Claire Lorrimer

severn
House

This first world edition published 2018
in Great Britain and the USA by
SEVERN HOUSE PUBLISHERS LTD of
Eardley House, 4 Uxbridge Street, London W8 7SY
Trade paperback edition first published
in Great Britain and the USA 2018 by
SEVERN HOUSE PUBLISHERS LTD

British Library Cataloguing in Publication Data
A CIP catalogue record for this title is available from the British Library.

ISBN-13: 978-0-7278-8816-7 (cased)
ISBN-13: 978-1-84751-943-6 (trade paper)
ISBN-13: 978-1-78010-995-4 (e-book)

Typeset by Palimpsest Book Production Ltd.,
Falkirk, Stirlingshire, Scotland.

Sadly Claire Lorrimer died shortly after completing this, her last book, and before she could decide to whom it should be dedicated. Her family therefore wish to dedicate it on her behalf:

To all aspiring authors everywhere, to encourage them to persevere and never give up.

ONE

The footman stood looking down at the sleeping man with an expression of disgust alternating with pity. How could a man drink himself into a stupor when upstairs his wife was dying?

The footman, Jim, knew perfectly well, as did all the staff at Kenilworth Hall, that his master Lord Kenilworth was devoted to his wife Lady Margaret, doting on her as if they were newlyweds. He had married her when she was only seventeen; since then she had given him six children and the seventh infant was about to make its way into the world in what appeared to be dire circumstances. She had nearly died when, after three stillbirths, their first son was born. Lord Kenilworth had promised himself then that he would curb his never-ending desire to make love to her, but his resolve had not lasted long and twice more she had very nearly died in childbirth.

'Lord Kenilworth, Mrs Bains, the midwife, doesn't know what to do. I am instructed to remind you that Her Ladyship has been in labour nearly forty-eight hours and the baby cannot be born without the doctor's help. Mrs Bains is afraid that both Her Ladyship and the baby will die.'

As if he had not been sleeping, Lord Kenilworth jerked into a sitting position and said furiously, 'I ordered Simms to take the coach and fetch him two hours ago. Where the hell is the man?'

The footman cleared his throat, only too well aware that what he was about to say would throw his master into one of his tempers. 'I'm afraid Simms has not returned, milord. It's the storm, sir. Simms said before he left for the village that the horses couldn't abide thunder. And the wind is something terrible . . .'

His voice trailed away as Lord Kenilworth rose shakily to his feet and walked unsteadily to the window. Drawing back the heavy brocade curtains, he struggled to open one of the large windows, but the force of the wind slammed the casement back, nearly knocking him over and bringing with it torrents of heavy rain from the darkness outside, soaking his face and shoulders. The footman hurried to his side and assisted him back to his chair.

Lord Kenilworth remained standing. He was breathing heavily as he grabbed the man's arm with one hand and, with the other, poured himself a full glass of brandy from the decanter on the table. He took only a few moments to down the drink. Then, his voice now slurred, he said, 'Help me upstairs! I must see Her Ladyship!'

Even in his now befuddled state of mind – he had been drinking brandy to calm his fears ever since the midwife had informed him his wife's labour was proving to be a difficult one – he feared that he might lose her.

As they approached the bedroom door, he swore softly under his breath. Where was the confounded doctor? Chislestone village was only five miles away on the perimeter of his estate. The physician was a conscientious fellow and never failed to turn up when he was summoned. Was he himself being unreasonable to expect him to come here in this tempest? Jim was saying it was the worst storm any of the staff could recall.

The scene which met his eyes in the bedroom was far worse than he could have imagined. His beloved wife was lying in a bloodstained bed, her eyes closed in a chalk-white face, the midwife staring down at her parted legs where only the baby's feet and legs could be seen. Aware of Lord Kenilworth's horrified stare, she burst into tears.

''Tis the baby's head!' she whispered. 'Her poor Ladyship's too tired to push no more. We need Doctor Matthews that bad! He's t'only one as can save her . . .'

Lord Kenilworth slumped into a chair at the foot of the bed, his head in his hands as he tried to come to terms with the fact that his wife, his beloved Margaret, was on the point of death and that there was nothing he could do about it. Equally shocked, the footman – who until then had remained by the bedroom door – went over to the now-weeping man and asked gently, 'Do you wish me to send Jenkins to fetch Reverend Phillips, milord?'

Lord Kenilworth looked at him vaguely and then, as his tortured brain registered the man's meaning, he nodded. He himself was not a religious man, although he did attend the village church to read the lesson on occasion as a duty, but he knew Margaret was a devout worshipper who never, as far as he knew, went to bed without saying her prayers, and insisted on even the youngest child attending church on Sundays whatever the weather. She would want Parson Phillips to assist her into the next world.

Suddenly unable to bear the sound of the midwife's sobbing and the shocking sight of his wife and unborn child, Lord Kenilworth stumbled to his feet, left the room and staggered back down the wide staircase to the library where he knew he would find the comfort of another drink. As he slumped down in his chair, the brandy glass safely in his hand, he told himself that he must have fallen asleep and had a terrible nightmare; that if he nodded off again, he would be woken up to hear his wife had given birth to a healthy son or daughter and was waiting for him to go up to her bedside and tell her she was the most wonderful, clever and dearly loved wife a man could have.

Three quarters of an hour later, His Lordship was shaken into consciousness by his valet, Simms. Despite his muttered protests that he wished to sleep, it finally reached his befuddled brain that his wife was literally on the point of death. Simms helped his master to his feet and, holding his arm, slowly led him upstairs and along the corridor to Her Ladyship's bedroom.

Doctor Matthews and Reverend Phillips were both there. The doctor had removed the baby from its mother, who had not survived the ordeal, and Mrs Bains was shaking her head as she stared down at the infant in the crib. It, too, was on the point of death, she announced in a shaky voice.

Lord Kenilworth regarded her uncomprehendingly. On the other side of the crib, the parson stood looking from the baby to its father.

'My Lord, your wife's last wishes were that the baby should be baptized. Sadly, she departed before giving me a name. If you would—'

He broke off, aware that Lord Kenilworth was not listening. He was staring at his wife's lifeless body as the doctor gently drew a sheet up over her face. There were tears pouring unheeded down his cheeks as the parson repeated his request for the dying child to be named.

'Most beautiful of all the girls there!' Lord Kenilworth was muttering, his words so slurred by the alcohol still in his body that they could hardly be understood. 'So young . . . but she married me all the same! Margaret. Margaret Stormont . . . didn't think her father, Stormont, would let me have her . . .'

As his voice trailed into silence, the parson said for the third time, 'A name, milord. The infant is still breathing. I need a name. Your wife said—'

'Should have come!' Lord Kenilworth interrupted, addressing the doctor. 'Should have come . . . wouldn't have died . . .'

'Milord, it was impossible. The storm—'

'The storm!' Lord Kenilworth broke in, his voice bordering between bitterness and anger. 'Hear that, Parson? The storm . . . killed my wife. The child . . . the storm . . .' His voice rose close to a shout before dropping to an almost indecipherable note of despair. 'You wanted a name. Storm. My wife was a Stormont. Beautiful . . . Margaret. Fell in love with her. Storm . . . never forget it . . .' And with tears pouring once more down his cheeks, he fell back into the nearest chair in a drunken stupor.

For a moment, none of the people in the room spoke. Then Reverend Phillips said softly, 'That's not a suitable name. I can't—'

'With respect, Reverend, does it matter?' the exhausted doctor interrupted gently. 'I doubt the baby will last the night and it will be buried with Her Ladyship.'

The parson looked doubtful.

'When Lord Kenilworth has recovered—'

'It is highly unlikely he will remember anything that has occurred,' the doctor said as he packed his instruments into his black bag. 'If necessary, I will assure him that he did himself choose the name. I very much doubt he will care about its oddity. Now, if I may suggest it, can you complete whatever you have to do, as I'm not sure I have the strength to get home to my bed. I expect my surgery will be bursting with patients after this night's tempest. Let us pray for a dry day.'

When, eight hours later, the New Year dawned, it was not only to a dry day but to a cloudless blue sky and sparkling sunshine. Nor was this the only surprise. From upstairs in the nursery came the loud wails of a hungry baby. It seemed that although Lady Margaret had died the infant had decided very firmly that, despite the midwife's and the doctor's predictions, she intended to live after all.

TWO

Late summer, 1854

'Please, please, darling Eloise – please can I miss this afternoon's lesson? You know how boring I find history and art, and it's such a beautiful day. I could take Tiger for a walk and—'

The older of the two girls shook her head. 'That farm dog is not going to be allowed to interfere with your lessons, Storm!' she said firmly.

Lord Kenilworth's older daughter, Eloise, when only ten years old, had taken it upon herself to be a mother to her infant sister after their mother Lady Margaret's untimely death. The baby had survived thanks to the care of an experienced wet nurse and later there had, of course, been nannies and then a governess, but it was Eloise to whom the little girl ran when she wanted kisses or comfort or love. By the time Storm was seven she had become a determined, wilful but sunny-natured child who as often as not was up to mischief. She would play tricks on Mabel, her nursemaid, steal sweetmeats from Cook's larder, trample on the gardeners' prize flower beds when she was chasing butterflies and, worst of all, was cheeky to their governess.

It was several years later, when the last governess had given in her notice and packed her bags, that Eloise suggested to their father, on one of his rare visits to Kenilworth Hall, that he permit Storm to be taught by her own highly intelligent tutor, with whose lessons Storm was unlikely to be bored. Her father had become less and less interested in the estate and spent more and more time in their London house, leaving the management of the estate to his daughter in the absence of his son. Always a heavy drinker, his consumption of ever larger quantities of alcohol was his way of counteracting the depression that had clouded his life ever since his beloved wife's death all those years ago.

After the tragedy of his wife dying, his fondness for his elder daughter increased, as did his avoidance of the company of his younger daughter, whose likeness to her mother grew ever more marked. In the absence of his son, John, he spent a great deal of time driving round the estate with Eloise so that it was almost as familiar to her as it was to John, with its many holdings and their financial management. Finding her extremely intelligent and an agreeable distraction from his endless mourning and the memories of his wife, he managed until she had come of age to restrain his growing need for alcohol to dull his loneliness. But after a prolonged drinking party at his club on one of his visits to London, he started to spend more and more time in the metropolis. Thus it fell to Eloise to take over her father's administrative duties, and it was not long before Jenkins, the estate manager, was bringing anything untoward to her.

It was a strange setup for two young girls to be alone at Kenilworth Hall with only the tutor and the housekeeper to watch over them while their father spent so much of his time in London. The excuse he gave his daughters for his absences was his newly discovered interest in ancient Egypt after reading John's long and detailed descriptions of his travels. He kept all his son's correspondence carefully, forwarding it to Eloise to be stored in his study. One of the few things Mr Carter the tutor managed to pass on to Storm was the ability to paint the national costumes of the inhabitants of the countries her brother visited.

Staring now through the open casement on to the neatly mown, sunlit lawn, Eloise could sympathize with her young sister's wish not to spend the afternoon in the schoolroom. As far as she herself was concerned, she could not wait for Mr Carter to arrive and their lesson to start. A keen, self-taught watercolour painter, she was fascinated by the young man's extensive knowledge of famous artists and their works, and she always regretted it when it was time for him to depart. She understood Storm's obvious pleasure in being out of doors, riding her pony or visiting one of their farms to see the newborn lambs, piglets, calves, kittens or puppies, or in summer watching the haymaking. When Storm was still a toddler,

Mabel had walked her down the drive to watch her two brothers, Andrew and John, climb the huge two-hundred-year-old oak tree by the front gates. Storm determined that she would do the same as soon as she was old enough. She longed to be able to hide there among its leafy branches when she wished to escape some boring activity such as spelling or piano lessons.

Storm's most favoured pastime was visiting her very best friend Cissy. She was a girl her own age, the invalid daughter of their nearest neighbours, the Chislestones.

The two girls, though opposites in many ways, could spend hours together at Chislestone Manor, inventing little plays and acting them out for Cissy's mother Lady Chislestone and her elder brother Hunter. What they were never permitted to do without an adult supervising them was to go down to the lake where Sir Matthew Chislestone and his three sons Charles, Percy and Hunter liked to fish. They were often joined there by Andrew and John. Those happy, youthful, carefree days had sadly come to an end on the death of Storm's eldest brother, Andrew. He had succumbed during an epidemic of scarlet fever at university and John was now seldom to be seen. An inveterate traveller, he was always away, and at the present time he was somewhere in Egypt.

Eloise now turned to look into her young sister's large, hopeful brown eyes, thinking irrelevantly how much like her mother she was. Sometimes she wondered if this was the reason their father took so little interest in his youngest daughter and showed her hardly any affection, although Eloise also resembled her mother and he could deny her nothing on that account. As she grew older she would come upon him from time to time, sitting at his desk in his study surrounded by estate papers with a steadily emptying brandy or whisky decanter at his side, and his eyes would fill with tears and he would send her out of the room. She knew only too well that even fifteen years after her mother's death, he still mourned her. Doctor Matthews, their family doctor, had advised her that this was the main reason for her father's persistent dependence on alcohol.

'Elly, please! I can go out, can't I?' Storm repeated.

Eloise nodded. 'Yes, dearest, but I insist on your taking Mabel with you. Then I shall know you are safe!' she added with a smile.

After giving her sister a quick hug and a kiss, Storm raced out of the schoolroom, nearly knocking over the approaching figure – their tutor. She could not help but be aware that Mr Carter was far more interested in educating Eloise, who shared his love of painting, than Storm herself. She lacked a talent for art and had no interest in it. Boringly, her sister continuously referred to the tutor's ambition to paint in oils, mentioning how he was saving up for oil paints and canvases.

Storm mumbled an apology, stifling a giggle at David Carter's startled face as she ran off along the passage towards the staircase down to the ground floor. Once there she slowed and crept silently along the wall past the dining room and drawing room doors, heading for the small door which led to the garden. Mabel, she knew, would be wondering where she was, but she had not the slightest intention of taking her along as Eloise had requested. She wanted to be free, to have an adventure – any sort of adventure so long as it was exciting. Pausing only a moment by one of the three greenhouses, she remembered the lake and that Jenkins had reported seeing an otter swimming there – stealing Lord Kenilworth's trout, he had complained. Storm had never seen an otter and it now occurred to her to go and see if she could spot one.

Going round to the stables, she collected the long-legged, shaggy puppy. The half-grown stray had been found wandering in the garden by one of the servants and the groom had taken pity on the dog, giving it a temporary home in the stables in a spare loose box where it enjoyed the plentiful scraps Cook provided from the kitchen. Storm had christened it Tiger.

Gathering the folds of her muslin morning frock and petticoat, she ran happily down the drive to the lake with Tiger bounding ahead. The water was sparkling in the bright sunlight and beyond the end of the jetty which led from the boathouse there was a cluster of beautiful pink and yellow water lilies.

Storm, following the excited animal, removed her shoes and stockings and, edging her way to the end of the wooden jetty, sat down and dangled her feet in the cool, shining water. Before she realized what was happening, Tiger pushed past her and jumped into the lake. With a shout of alarm, Storm scrambled to her knees and leaned forward, trying to reach the little dog now paddling away from her. Inevitably, as Storm bent further forward to reach him, she tipped too far and fell in.

At this point, not far from the bank, the water was not deep. Standing up, she was able to grab the puppy and clamber on to the grassy bank. Water streamed from her hair, her face and her clothes. The little dog, quite unperturbed, was shaking itself and rolling in the grass.

Glancing round, Storm could see no other sign of life. Quickly she stepped out of her soaking dress and, after wringing the water from it, hung it over a nearby bush, where it started steaming in the hot sun. Untying the ribbons in her hair, she leaned forward and shook her head, not knowing whether to laugh or cry as several strands of water weed dropped from it. Did she dare remove her petticoat? All at once, horrified, she heard the sound of a horse's hooves and Tiger began to bark hysterically.

As the horseman approached, she saw with relief that it was not Jenkins but Hunter, one of Cissy's older brothers. He was sitting astride his horse, his good-looking face a mixture of surprise and amusement.

'And a very good morning to you, young lady!' he said, his hazel eyes alight with laughter. 'I heard a strange noise as I was taking the shortcut through your woods to the village. I thought I'd take a look in case it was a poacher after your father's trout. Instead I find a half-drowned mermaid!'

Storm was now frowning. 'Hunter, don't just sit there grinning. I'm going to be in terrible trouble when I go home. Elly has no idea I came down here on my own, and by the time I get back her art lesson will be over and she'll be looking for me and—'

'And it was a singularly stupid thing to do to go swimming!' Hunter interrupted her.

'I didn't! I fell in!' Storm's anger replaced the desire to cry, and she explained her attempt to save the silly animal from drowning.

Hunter was smiling.

'Has no one told you that nearly every animal can swim if they have to?' he asked as he dismounted. His voice softened. 'Cheer up! This happens to be your lucky day as well as an unhappy one . . .'

He broke off to reach behind his horse's saddle and lift down a bulky brown paper parcel which he handed to Storm. 'I was on my way to the parsonage to give this to Reverend Phillips for his wife's church sale next week. These are things Cissy doesn't wear any more. Maybe you can find something to fit you. Then you can get out of that rather fetching wet petticoat and hang it on the bushes. The sun is hot enough to dry it very quickly.' He broke off as he took a swift look at the lake and then added, 'In fact, it's so hot I think I might have a quick dip in the water myself!'

He was grinning once more as he removed his jacket and untied the cuffs of his shirt. 'Don't looked so worried, child. I can swim!'

'Hunter, it's the time I'm worried about. It will take me twenty minutes at the very least to walk home and—'

'And I shall get you there in five on the back of my trusty steed!' Looping the reins of his horse over a post by the boat-house, he disappeared out of sight behind it where he removed his waistcoat, cravat and shirt and dropped them on a bench before returning and diving into the water.

For a moment, she stood watching as with strong overarm strokes he all but disappeared down the far end of the lake. She smiled, thinking how much more fun than her own brother Hunter was.

At twenty-six he could behave spontaneously, as if he were half that age, despite the responsibilities he carried. Although she, Storm, was not supposed to know it, Sir Matthew Chislestone was a reckless gambler, seldom at his country seat; he spent most of his waking hours at one or other of the gaming tables in London or in private houses where cards were a priority. Since his two elder brothers were abroad, she knew it fell to Hunter to oversee the management of some of the huge estate.

Her thoughts turned quickly to the bundle of clothes Hunter had given her. In no time she had found a once-pretty lawn nightgown, now lacking its lace trimmings. Wasting no further time searching, she pulled it over her head and stepped out of her wet petticoat and chemise, which she draped over the nearby bushes. She prayed that, made of cotton for summer rather than flannel for winter warmth, they too would dry as quickly as her dress appeared to be doing.

The nightdress fitted her but with little room to spare and, conscious that her breasts, so much fuller this past year, were almost visible, she dived once more into the parcel of jumble and found a faded silk shawl which she tied neatly over her shoulders and round her waist. The now-dry puppy curled up asleep by her feet, she sat waiting for Hunter to return. One day, when she was old enough, she would be married to him, but not for many years yet. He was ten years older than she was and she had a lot of growing up to do before she could be a good wife and manage Hunter's household as well as Eloise managed Kenilworth Hall.

Every once in a while Eloise had had to call upon Hunter to sort out a problem that their estate manager Jenkins had been unable to deal with. The same age as Eloise, Hunter was like a brother to her and, indeed, liked being an older brother to Storm herself. She wondered sometimes whether he remembered that he had once promised to marry her. At one Christmas party he had picked up a tiny gold ring that had fallen from a nearby table ornament into a bowl of nuts and put it on her finger, announcing that he would marry her when she was old enough. She had discussed this many times with Cissy, who said there was nothing she would like more than to have Storm as her sister-in-law, but she was sometimes a little afraid in case one of the many debutantes with whom her brother was so popular might persuade him into marriage. Seeing Storm's horrified expression, she promised to let her know in plenty of time if there were ever a serious rival for Storm to be concerned about.

Hunter now reappeared wearing only his top boots and

breeches, which were clinging to his otherwise naked wet body. Shaking his head to remove the water – much, Storm thought, as Tiger had done – he lay down in the grass beside her.

'You look like a cross between a dairymaid and a Spanish *señorita*,' he said, smiling and rolling over to expose his wet back to the sun.

Storm was about to speak to him but the words suddenly caught in her throat as she stared down at his body. She was reminded in that instant of Mr Carter's beautifully illustrated book of Michelangelo's works. The long, graceful lines of Hunter's naked back and the barely visible curves at the top of his buttocks were identical to those of the artist's statue of David in the book. Seeing it, she had wanted to lean across the schoolroom table and stroke the page. Now she was feeling that same almost uncontrollable longing which seemed to be arousing the strangest sensations in the pit of her stomach. It brought to mind a remark made by Mabel. Many years ago, the maid had been betrothed to a thatcher's apprentice – a young man she had dearly loved – who had been killed falling off a roof. Storm had asked her then how she knew she'd loved him so much; she'd never subsequently married.

'Can't rightly explain, Miss Storm,' Mabel had replied. 'Summat you feel deep down here!' And she'd touched the lower half of her body. 'Summat as happens every time he kisses you, or just smiles. Or even when he's just a-coming across the field to meet you and you hear him singing. Didn't never happen with no one else. Loved my Jim, I did!'

Glancing once more at Hunter's naked back, Storm felt the same strange longing to touch him, to run her hands down to the narrow waist and the start of his muscular thighs.

As suddenly as it had hit her, the moment passed. Beside her lay once again the fond twenty-six-year-old brother of her darling Cissy; the now grown-up little boy who used to race around the garden playing games with her own two brothers. To everyone's surprise, he had failed to propose to the lovely, gentle Eloise, who had turned down many admirers. She had refused to have another season, content to stay at home managing Kenilworth Hall, mothering Storm and enjoying her discovery – aided by her tutor David Carter – of a talent for watercolour painting. She also had what she called her 'work': caring for their farmworkers' families and for those ill or in need in the village.

'I think Eloise is wasted!' Hunter had once remarked to Cissy.

Cissy had told Storm, 'Eloise should have a rich, handsome husband and a brood of beautiful children, and be wealthy enough to travel the world and throw magnificent balls and garden parties which even our Queen and her husband would attend!' Cissy had hesitated, then said wistfully, 'I wish you were ten years older, and then my favourite brother would be married to you.'

With a sigh, Storm turned her gaze away from Hunter and began to inspect her rapidly drying clothes. She touched Hunter lightly on the shoulder and he turned to her, opening his eyes sleepily.

'Hunter, I should be going home.' She stood up.

He yawned, stretched and got to his feet. 'Right, sweetheart!' he said, lifting a strand of dark hair from her forehead and smiling. 'It's nearly dry.' He looked up at the sun high in the sky, turned and went to fetch his clothes from the boathouse. On his return he reached for her dress and underclothes from the branches of the bushes and handed them to her while he put on his shirt and loosely knotted his cravat. Untying the shawl, she pulled her dress over her head. Then, picking up Hunter's parcel of old clothes and clutching her stockings, petticoat and chemise, she twisted round so that Hunter could fasten the buttons at her back. He then put on his waistcoat and hacking jacket and, mounting his horse, reached down and lifted her up on to the saddle in front of him, a grin crossing his face.

'I'm about to tell darling Eloise an outrageous lie,' he said with a twinkle, 'and say that it was my fault you fell in, but I will take you up the back drive and with luck you and that stupid animal will be able to nip in through the garden door without being seen.'

Five minutes later, as they rode up towards the house with Tiger running beside them, they saw Eloise standing on the front doorstep with the tutor, who had overstayed his two-hour tutorial. They were waiting for the groom to bring round his horse. Hunter quickly turned into the back drive and Storm was able to slip away through the garden door in her crumpled dress before her sister could see her. She was laughing with relief as she collapsed on her bed when Mabel came into the room, scowling.

'Don't be cross, darling Mabel!' Storm managed to say. 'I have had such a magical adventure with Mr Hunter and—'

She broke off and at the sound of Hunter's name Mabel's scowl turned to a smile. She tried to look cross as she said, 'I dare say as how you was safe enough with Mr Hunter to take care of you, but I was worried out of my wits. You should've told me . . . sneaking off like that without a word to no one. Time you grew up, Miss Storm, and acted more 'sponsible. Now let's get you cleaned up! Lawks only knows what's happened to your pretty hair. It's got green bits in it!' With these stern utterings she left the room to call for hot water while Storm struggled out of her dress.

Her maid's words reminded Storm of her fall in the lake and Hunter's timely rescue. She must find some way to thank him, she told herself: a present, perhaps a bottle of her father's brandy. There were goodness knows how many bottles in the cellar so he would not miss one. Besides, Eloise said she'd overheard the doctor saying he wouldn't have that much longer to live if he went on drinking so much. Mabel said the poor man was still mourning his wife, although it was fifteen years since she'd died. Storm seldom saw her father. A bottle of brandy would be perfect for Hunter, she repeated to herself. She planned to spend the day with Cissy tomorrow so she would take it with her then.

Outside, the young tutor had mounted his horse and was reluctantly trotting smartly down Kenilworth Hall's long gravel drive.

Storm was unaware that the tutor's heart was beating painfully as he tried to come to terms with the fact that he'd left the young woman he secretly adored in the company of one of the most eligible, good-looking men in the neighbourhood, familiar enough for her to receive his kisses on both cheeks. It was almost more than he could bear, knowing as he did that his birth precluded him for ever from even being a friend to her, let alone a suitor.

In the drawing room, Hunter was declining a second slice of cherry cake and, having reassured Eloise for the fourth time that he alone was responsible for Storm's late arrival home, he kissed her goodbye and was shown out by Roberts the butler. He decided as he rode off that he would take his sister's old clothes to the parsonage the next day. He was smiling as he recalled the sight of the Storm standing in her petticoat, water dripping from her hair as she stood staring at him. It really was a stroke of luck that it was he and not the estate manager, or even a poacher, who had come upon her in such disarray. In a strange sort of way he loved Storm almost as much as he loved his frail little sister who was so delicate, so silently long-suffering, so docile, and Storm . . . well, she had been appropriately named, accidental though he understood the name had been. Most of all he admired her for the time she gave to poor housebound Cissy, who so welcomed her visits. The fall in the lake might have sent another young girl into helpless screams and a fainting fit when she was rescued, but not Storm. She'd actually admitted as he'd taken her home that it had all been tremendous fun.

It's unusual to find a young female with her spirit! he told himself. Meanwhile, he was now looking forward to taking a few days off and going to London, where an extremely flirta- tious actress eagerly awaited his visits, most of which were spent in her large double bed. She was more fun and more understanding than his last mistress, a pretty young widow looking for a second husband who would marry her and be on hand to satisfy her needs.

Perhaps one day he would get married, he promised his mother. Meanwhile, he was happy looking after their estate, making occasional visits to London and enjoying the company of local friends in the surrounding neighbourhood with whom he enjoyed shooting parties, cricket matches and other country pursuits. Ever since they were children and the two families had played together, Kenilworth Hall had been a second home to them, and he knew that although it was a long time since the Kenilworth boys had lived at home, he was still always welcome there. He must talk to Eloise about arranging this coming autumn's harvest festival for all their estate workers, he thought. They held the evening dance in Chislestone Manor's big ballroom, and Storm could help Cissy and his mother decorate it – it was the sort of thing they both enjoyed doing – as long as Cissy was well enough, of course. Storm would involve Cissy with the plans and she'd love that.

With a contented sigh Hunter rode Percy's magnificent horse, Pegasus, into the yard and gave him to the stable lad to rub down and feed.

Tired now, he went into the house and upstairs to his bedroom, where he filled a glass of brandy from the small decanter he kept for such occasions and had a quick drink while Gilbert, his ever-efficient lifelong valet, helped him remove his wet top boots and then prepared him a bath. Downstairs, Cook would be making something special for the family's dinner and maybe making his favourite gooseberry fool for dessert. He was not only a lucky man but a very happy one, he told himself. He must continue to do his best to ensure that all his loved ones were happy, too.

There was only one cloud on the horizon, and that was his estate manager Jackson's concerns about the estate's finances. When he'd spoken to him yesterday, once again the man had drawn his attention to the long overdue payment of several large bills. It would be convenient to see their bank manager while he was in London, he decided. He sank into the steaming water of the bath and reached for the soap placed on the stool nearby with his good humour restored.

Chuckling quietly, he related to Gilbert the story of Storm's unfortunate accident at the lake as his valet fussed over his sodden breeches and boots. He considered, as he so often did now, how lucky he was to have such delightful neighbours as Eloise and Storm Kenilworth. He was not surprised that Cissy doted on the volatile Storm. She was going to be a pretty girl in two years' time when she came out, provided Eloise managed to temper her wild spirit. But not too severely, he told himself, knowing that he admired Storm's fearless, adventurous nature.

THREE

The next day

Hunter looked across the breakfast table at his mother. Lady Chislestone was reading a letter delivered that morning by the post boy. Her thin face was very pale and the lines on her forehead deeply etched, her faded blue eyes filled with anxiety. He felt a sudden sharp pang of concern mixed with pity. His mother's life was not a very joyful one to say the least, he reminded himself.

Last night, Cissy had had one of her frequent asthmatic attacks, which her nurse could do little to relieve other than to administer the medicine which the doctor had recommended, and to burn the dried blotting paper which had been soaked in saltpetre. The resulting fumes had taken until the early hours to be effective.

Although his sister had a nurse to care for her both day and night, his mother insisted upon being at hand during these attacks, knowing that Cissy found her presence reassuring. Lady Chislestone had therefore had very little sleep, but her rigid adherence to the house rules she herself had made did not permit her to have her maid bring her a breakfast tray so she could remain in bed.

'Mama, are you not feeling well?' Hunter enquired anxiously.

He could see she was struggling not to cry – something she would be far too proud to do in front of the servants. Quickly he dismissed the butler and the attendant maid, then turned once more to his mother, enquiring if the letter in her hand had brought bad news. With his father in London, Charles with his regiment in the army and Percy in California, it was possible that any one of them might have met with misfortune of some kind.

Lady Chislestone was now dabbing at her eyes with a lace-edged handkerchief. Hunter waited several minutes while she struggled to reply. Then, abandoning the attempt, she handed Hunter the letter she was still holding.

Fearing that he was quite possibly about to read of Charles's death in the fighting which was raging in Sevastopol, Hunter braced himself before perusing the contents of the letter. It was from a Mr William Ainsworth, seemingly the owner of a flourishing shoe-manufacturing business with factories in both Scotland and London as well as the Midlands.

The letter was addressed to Sir Matthew Chislestone at his country home and enclosed were three promissory notes made out to Ainsworth; all three had been stamped by the bank to indicate they had been returned due to insufficient funds. Mr Ainsworth's covering letter said simply:

> *Sir,*
>
> *I have waited a year now for these to be honoured, and if I do not receive payment by the end of the month, I shall feel obliged to take legal action which I am sure you would not wish me to do.*
>
> *I remain your humble servant,*
> *William Ainsworth*

'I don't understand!' Hunter exclaimed, putting the letter back in its envelope with its enclosures. 'How can the bank possibly insult Father in this way! Of course there are funds to honour cheques. This is a terrible insult and Father must deal with it at once. I will instruct Adam to bring my curricle round immediately and I'll get this sorted out with Father. He promised me he would give up cards in the New Year . . . surely he can't have forgotten to reply to these demands? How could he have been so forgetful?'

As he rose to his feet, his mother put a restraining hand on his arm. 'No, Hunter, no!' she whispered. 'You don't understand . . . your father . . . for the past few years his predilection for gambling has steadily increased. At first it was just for an hour or two's amusement with friends, but then it became like any other addiction and he couldn't stop . . . That is why he spends so much time in London.' She broke off, unable to look at her youngest son's shocked face.

'B-but these!' Hunter stammered. 'Father is a wealthy man. There *must* be funds to meet these demands!'

His mother was now dry-eyed. 'The family wealth is entailed,' she whispered. 'That is to say it comes mostly from investments, shares in companies, many of which are in far-off countries in our Empire, such as India. Of course he receives dividends, money which pays for all our home and living expenses, the upkeep of the estate and so on.' She paused to draw a deep breath. 'Your father once explained all this to me when he was negotiating the purchase of our house in London where we were to spend a great deal of our time enjoying the festivities and private parties. Then, soon after her tenth birthday, my darling Cissy became ill with this dreadful asthma complaint, and as you may recall, Hunter, there were several occasions when she nearly died. I couldn't leave her. I hoped she would recover but . . . but your father and I lead almost separate lives now. If I were with him, perhaps I could divert him from the gambling clubs he goes to—' She broke off and several minutes passed before she said, 'I know Charles was your father's confidant where money was concerned, but it's over a year since he left with his regiment. As for Percy, far away in America with all those people hoping to make fortunes out of the gold they are mining . . .' Once more, tears filled her eyes. Then she added, 'Perhaps you can make your father understand how serious matters have become. For him to be taken to court for non-payment of private loans . . .'

Hunter, too, was horrified. A man's honour was of the utmost importance to him. No wonder his mother was so distraught – she who was normally always so calm, so composed, so serene.

'I am certain this is all some horrible mistake,' he repeated in as calm a voice as he could muster. 'So please stop worrying. Perhaps if Cissy is feeling strong enough now, you and nurse could take her for a walk in the garden. It is a beautiful day.'

Lady Chislestone looked up fondly at her youngest and favourite son. 'Is today not dear Eloise's party for the village children? I thought you were to give the prizes for the sports and fancy-dress competitions, Hunter.'

He frowned. He had in fact been looking forward to the

yearly event that afternoon which, acting as major-domo, he usually made great fun. He hesitated, then said, 'I'm sure Eloise will find someone else to replace me – perhaps that strange, serious tutor fellow, Carter. Never seen him smile! That mischievous scamp Storm thinks he's secretly in love with Eloise, leaning over backwards trying to please her the way he does – bringing flowers pretending they are botanical specimens!'

Lady Chislestone managed a weak smile. 'If the child is right, we should be sorry for the poor man. You know, Hunter, when you were just down from university, I used to think you had a special fondness for Eloise and that you and she might one day get married.'

Hunter's face broke into a smile. 'You were right, of course, Mama. Not that Eloise ever guessed. Of course she had dozens of admirers in those days and, I believe, more than one proposal after she came out, but I've come to the conclusion she has turned her back on marriage so she can continue to take care of her motherless little sister.'

'A very worthy but unwise decision, if it is true,' Lady Chislestone commented. 'How lonely she will be when young Storm marries and leaves home.'

Hunter leaned down and quickly drank his cup of coffee. 'We are wasting time, Mama,' he said, going round the table to kiss her forehead. 'I must go and alert Gilbert to pack me a bag. I intend to leave for London in an hour's time.'

He dealt with his own correspondence and quickly penned a note to David Carter for Adam to deliver. With Ainsworth's threatening letter tucked safely in his valise together with his nightshirt and a change of clothes, Hunter was soon heading for London, which he intended to reach by nightfall.

Over at Kenilworth Hall later that morning, David Carter read Hunter's note informing him he was to deputize for him that afternoon at the village party.

'Don't look so worried, Mr Carter,' Eloise said, smiling. 'I'll be there to assist you.' She was instantly rewarded by his grateful smile.

*   *   *

Hunter, however, was very far from smiling as he stopped briefly at a wayside inn to take lunch and to rest his horses. The bank's refusal to honour his father's debt was inconceivable, he was thinking, as he downed a tankard of ale. When his grandfather had died and the estate passed to his father, there had been many other investments along with the manor house, farms and land. These included shares in the new railways, which had hugely increased in value as further lines were built. His father was an extremely wealthy man and, even if he did not have bank notes readily available, the bank should have had no hesitation in advancing the required amount.

How much was owed? Hunter wondered as he resumed his journey. Before Charles had left for the Crimea, he had warned him that their father had been gambling quite extensively in both gaming clubs and private houses. There was no point guessing, he told himself as he rode through the cobbled streets of the outskirts of London. He would find out soon enough where the problem had occurred.

Sir Matthew was not at home in their London house in Upper Brook Street. He was slumped in a large leather armchair at his club, a half-finished glass of brandy in his hand. Recognizing Hunter, he smiled as he dabbed at his sweating face with a large white initialled handkerchief.

'Order you a drink . . .' he muttered in a slurred voice and beckoned to the attendant.

Hunter hid his dismay at finding his father in such a state so early in the evening. Then he caught sight of a letter headed *The War Office* lying on the table.

'Read it! Read it!' his father muttered, jabbing a forefinger on the crumpled sheet of paper.

Uneasily Hunter picked it up and read the shocking news of his brother Charles's death in Sevastopol. He now understood why his father was so inebriated. He himself had not been particularly close to his brother, but the news still came as an unpleasant shock.

He realized then that he would have to wait until the following morning before being able to discuss the overdue debts. Despite Sir Matthew's protests, Hunter all but forced

him into a hansom cab and on their arrival at Upper Brook
Street ordered his father's valet, Paul, to put him to bed.

Extremely tired after the long day, he too went up to his
bedroom, deciding there was no point in sitting alone brooding.
His unease was exacerbated not only by the growing anxiety
about his father but now by the unhappy knowledge of his
brother's untimely death, so it was some time before he could
relax into a dreamless sleep.

The following morning, he had finished a large breakfast before
his father, now white-faced, made his way to the table. He
nodded to Hunter as the maid brought him a cup of black
coffee and a piece of toast thinly spread with butter. Hunter
was about to recommend the scrambled eggs with anchovies
when his father muttered that the girl knew that toast was all
he fancied when he wasn't feeling too well. His perturbation
increasing, Hunter decided there was no advantage in delaying
his discussion and, giving his unhappy parent no chance to
claim that he would be otherwise engaged, he told him he
wished to have a private talk with him that morning, as soon
as he had finished his breakfast.

Sir Matthew got to his feet, picked up the cane he now
carried and walked slowly out of the dining room. Once seated
behind his desk in the library, he gazed at his son. He listened
silently to Hunter's request for the explanation his son
hoped would be forthcoming, and he pretended at first not
to acknowledge that the letter from his debtor William
Ainsworth was intended for him. Then, avoiding Hunter's
gaze, he muttered that it was Charles who always dealt with
his financial affairs and saw his bank manager – 'Old Porky',
as he called him. If anything was wrong, it would have to
wait until Charles came home.

'No, Father, we know now that Charles will not be coming
home – this cannot wait!' Hunter said quietly but firmly. 'So,
with your permission, sir, I will have a word with Turner and
have him correct this distressing mistake.'

It was a minute or two before Sir Matthew replied. Suddenly,
he smiled. 'Quite right, m'boy – mistake, yes, mistake. You
tell him! Not good enough . . .' He broke off to give a large

yawn, then muttered, 'I suppose I shall have to go home this evening and tell your mother Charles isn't coming back. Think I'll go and have a rest – didn't sleep too well. Tell Paul I need him, there's a good chap.'

Somehow, Hunter managed to extract a note from him to the bank manager authorizing him to discuss his father's financial affairs. Then, his apprehension growing, he summoned a hansom cab to Chancery Lane, his father's note and the threatening letter clasped firmly in his hand.

When Hunter had first gone to university, he had opened an account in a local branch of the bank in which to place the generous allowance his father had given him. He had not, therefore, ever had reason to meet Mr Turner, his father's London bank manager. As the clerk ushered him into a chair opposite the manager's desk, he found himself facing a round, red-faced, bald man wearing pince-nez and an immaculate black jacket and waistcoat. Over his tubby frame stretched a gold chain attached to a large gold watch which he had been checking before Hunter's arrival, and which he now inserted back into his waistcoat pocket.

'A pleasure indeed to meet you, Mr Hunter, if I may call you that!' he greeted him. 'Of course I have met your brother, Mr Charles, on many occasions, but have not had the pleasure of meeting you or Mr Percy.'

Hunter handed the man his father's letter, saying, 'The reason I am here is because it seems your bank has made a very serious error, Mr Turner. Perhaps you should look at this.' He handed him Ainsworth's threatening letter.

As he watched, the man's face turned from red to white and then to red once more. He coughed, took a handkerchief from his pocket and dabbed his forehead. Both his hands were shaking.

'Yes, yes . . . I'm afraid . . . that is to say—' He broke off, sounding close to tears as his voice thickened. He shifted in his chair, quite suddenly cleared his throat and said, 'I am responsible, Mr Hunter. May I beg you to allow me a chance to . . . to confess, to explain? I will try to be brief.' His voice now steadied as he continued, 'Your father and I were at school together. When I was struggling to make my way, he was instrumental in getting me the position I desperately needed – my family was very poor, you see, and I was their only son.'

He paused once more to clear his throat and, as Hunter remained silent, he continued, 'Not long after Mr Charles went off to war, one of my staff brought it to my attention that very large sums of money were being drawn from your father's account on an almost daily basis, the money being made payable to gaming clubs as well as to private individuals. As a lifelong friend of your father's I took the liberty of looking through his past accounts and could reach no other conclusion than that he had been gambling – and steadily losing a great deal of money.'

He removed his pince-nez and silently looked at Hunter.

'Perhaps I should have said a *very* great deal of money. I wrote to your father asking him to pay me a visit but he didn't come. As matters deteriorated to a very serious level, it occurred to me that I must somehow shock him into an understanding of his, er, his difficulties. Mr Ainsworth is also a client of mine and I asked him if he would do me a great favour and delay taking your father to court, as was his intention, until I had had a chance to arrange for the debts to be paid.'

He shuffled uneasily in his chair and avoided Hunter's gaze as he concluded quietly, 'I thought if Sir Matthew actually saw those promissory notes he would understand how disastrous the situation was. Of course, I would be in serious trouble were the directors to hear of my unorthodox behaviour, but your family has banked with me for very many years and I wished to give your father a warning of the danger he will be in if . . . well, if he cannot appreciate how insidious an evil gambling is.'

It was a minute or two before Hunter could find his voice. Then he said, 'I appreciate your concern on my father's behalf and, of course, our family's good name is of the utmost importance. I think you will find that I have sufficient funds in my personal account to clear the immediate debts. I will also speak to my father about the danger of his addiction. I appreciate your intervention, Mr Turner, and my family is indebted to you for arranging this brief respite. Perhaps you would now be good enough to show me the details of my father's account for the past year?'

He then advised him of the added complication of Charles's death, although Mr Turner said that, sad though the news was, it would serve to provide further reason for the creditors to be asked to delay their legal actions.

Half an hour later, as Hunter left the bank and walked back to Upper Brook Street through the warm, late summer sunshine, he struggled to come to terms with the fact that according to Mr Turner his family was not far from bankruptcy. It was inconceivable. When his grandfather had died, the estates were bringing in large sums of money and, as far as his estate manager Jackson had elicited, they were continuing to do so. It was hard to register the size of the cash withdrawals his father had been making – in one case five thousand pounds, which would have been enough to pay for the overdue replacement of the church roof.

As Hunter walked up the steps to the front door of the house, he wondered whether he would find his father in a fit enough state to discuss the arrangements to bring Charles's body home if possible or organize a memorial service for him, and also to recognize the urgency of the family's financial affairs. He realized with a sickening feeling in the pit of his stomach what imminent danger the family was in; unless Charles had left a considerable sum of money to a family member, there was no possible way they were going to honour all the debts.

He must write to Percy to tell him of Charles's death and get him to come home – he needed his support. As far as he was aware, all of Percy's money was ploughed into his and his friend's mining venture – moreover, a letter would take weeks to get to him, and after that it would be weeks before he received Percy's reply. It was many months since the family had received any of his usually regular chatty letters, and this now seemed ominous.

FOUR

A week later, back at Kenilworth Hall, Eloise stood at the window of the schoolroom watching for the tutor who would almost certainly arrive on horseback, bringing him the four miles from the parsonage in Chislestone village, where he rented accommodation.

David Carter was due for their morning tutorial. Eloise had a surprise for him and was eager to deliver it. Storm, meanwhile, had taken the gig over to Chislestone Manor to see Cissy, who had had yet another bad attack of asthma the previous day and was confined once more to her bed.

Eloise smiled to herself as she thought of the happy expression on her darling sister's face when she was told she might miss the morning's tutorial. One thing was certain: Mr Carter would be pleased. He was aware that Storm had very little interest in literature, the arts or painting, his favourite topics, and Eloise knew he preferred it when they were on their own. She attempted not to think about Storm's teasing remarks about David Carter being head over heels in love with her. It was true that she often looked up to find him staring at her and then hurriedly looking away.

'It's just that he is very shy!' she had argued with Storm, but she remembered hearing the intensity in his tone of voice when he had read her one of his favourite passages from *Hamlet* – the declaration of love for Ophelia – when they were studying Shakespeare.

She had never fallen in love, strange though that seemed when she had listened to her contemporaries at the time of her coming out. She had had three proposals of marriage but declined them all, saying truthfully that she was dedicated to looking after her baby sister and widowed father. From time to time, when she read a novel or listened to the tutor quoting a particularly moving story about an artist's love for his model, she would wonder if she was denying herself one of life's greatest emotions. Then she would remind herself that she was now twenty-six, past marriageable age, and was perfectly happy caring for Storm and running her father's household. Such reflections were now hurriedly cast aside as David Carter came into the room.

Apart from the usual saddlebag of books he brought with him, he was also carrying a parcel wrapped in brown paper and tied with a blue ribbon. He handed it to her with a shy smile. He cleared his throat, saying, 'Today is the anniversary of the day that I first came here as your tutor and I thought I should show my appreciation, as I am so much enjoying my employment here!'

Eloise gave a delighted smile and she reached across the schoolroom table and picked up a small oblong box wrapped in white paper. 'I had the same thought!' she declared. 'Do sit down, Mr Carter, and we will open our presents!'

When she had carefully unwrapped the parcel, she discovered the tutor had brought her an embossed, leather-bound edition of Anthony Heath's *Trees of the British Isles*.

'I know how you enjoy identifying and painting the trees on the estate, Miss Eloise,' he said. He now opened the small box she had handed to him. It contained six size-graded camel-hair paintbrushes, and his cheeks coloured in pleasure. 'These will be perfect for the portrait I intend to paint for the Royal Academy. They were impossible to find in the village. I am most grateful.'

'It is such a beautiful day,' Eloise said. 'Shall we take our sketchbooks down to the lake? It will soon be winter, and we shall not be able to enjoy such magical colouring.'

He needed no second bidding and hurriedly collected the materials which they would need.

As they walked down the drive and across the lawn to the path leading to the lake, it occurred to Eloise that this was turning out to be one of the happiest days of her life. Among all the family and friends who came to the house, the dinner parties and soirées, she could not think of one guest who was such an agreeable companion as David Carter.

As he set up her easel beneath one of the silver birches which surrounded the clearing by the lake, she suddenly found herself blushing as she recalled once again Storm's uncalled-for remarks. 'David Carter is head over heels in love with you, Eloise!' she'd said, laughing. 'What a pity he's not a gentleman, although I think he does behave like one. It's a pity you can't marry each other!' With a wave of her hand, she had danced off into the sunshine in pursuit of the exuberant barking Tiger.

Eloise quickly busied herself with her paint box, wishing for distraction from such unseemly thoughts.

When Lord Kenilworth had interviewed him, David Carter had made no secret of the fact that he was the youngest son of a struggling, hard-working and talented potter, who barely managed to feed and clothe his family of eight children. As a young boy, David had shown an extraordinary aptitude for drawing and his father had seen that this talent might perhaps be of some use when he was older and making pots and jugs for the local gentry. However, it was the village schoolmaster who recognized David's potential as a talented artist. The young boy was quick to learn his numbers and wrote imaginative essays in quite strikingly beautiful handwriting. As a consequence, the schoolmaster managed to get him into the grammar school; from there he won a scholarship to an art school. He had only been there for two terms when his father's increasing frailty made it necessary not only for the three pounds' weekly support he sent his talented son to cease, but also for David himself to contribute to the family's survival.

Heartbroken at this sudden end to his hopes of a future as an artist, David nonetheless did not hesitate to resign from the school and apply for employment as a tutor wherever he could. In the meantime, his father persuaded him to use some of his very limited savings to take a working holiday painting watercolours of the countryside, which he hoped he could then sell.

Learning from his local vicar that he could get bed, breakfast and an evening meal for a very reasonable sum at the parsonage in Chislestone village, David wasted no time in going there. Fate played into his hands when the parson declared himself prepared to put his name forward to Lord Kenilworth for the position of tutor, who promptly engaged him.

David was aware that it was not entirely due to his qualifications that His Lordship had employed him, but also because
he had not demanded a high salary and was prepared to live
locally, so as to be on hand at the hall on a daily basis.

Eloise's thoughts turned momentarily to Hunter, and she
smiled at the memory of the occasion when, at her coming-out
dance, Hunter had suggested she marry him. Over the years
they had become the closest of friends, and now she was filled
with sympathy for him, having heard about his brother
Charles's untimely death. If Storm had not already left for
Chislestone Manor she should have taken a note of condolence
with her, Eloise thought. Although older than herself, Charles
had been one of her brothers' playmates with whom she had
always had a happy relationship.

Charles had also once proposed to her, but she had quickly
let him know that she did not return his feelings. Eloise now
found herself doubting whether Hunter would greatly mourn
his eldest brother, to whom he had not been close. It was poor
Lady Josephine who would be suffering at the loss of her
firstborn, and she must call at Chislestone Manor tomorrow
afternoon with flowers for her.

It was to be hoped, too, that poor little Cissy would not be
too adversely affected by her brother's death. No one seemed
to know what triggered the asthma attacks that so debilitated
her. She was very restricted by the illness, and when she did
go outdoors it was in an invalid chair since any form of physical
exertion seemed to trigger her breathing problems. The child
was remarkably patient, seldom complaining in spite of the
limitations imposed by her illness. Storm was wonderful with
her, cheering her whenever she was depressed and finding
things they could do together that would not exert her.

David Carter was now indicating the ripples of sparkling
water left behind the ducks as they paddled across the lake. At
a distance a stately white swan sailed gently towards the south
bank. Eloise dipped her paintbrush in the pot of water her tutor
had given her and with a feeling of utter contentment started
to paint the scene he had chosen for them. At that moment,
there was nowhere in the world she would rather have been.

*   *   *

In the morning room at Chislestone Manor, Hunter was doing his best to console his devastated mother. As he had feared, Lady Josephine had taken the news of her eldest son's death very badly and unfortunately, although his father had returned from London, he had opted to remain shut in his study, leaving all the necessary arrangements for Hunter to deal with.

It was Hunter's hope that Charles had left enough money to cover at least some of the family shortfall; the question of Sir Matthew's massive outstanding debts had temporarily been put to one side. He was awaiting a reply to his request for information from Charles's solicitor to find out if help was going to come from that quarter.

However, the letter he had been awaiting had arrived with the shattering information that Charles had been living up to the hilt and there was no question of a legacy. He himself could not meet whatever further debts his father had incurred from his own resources. Perhaps Percy would be able to help? It was too soon to have received a reply from his brother to his letter, but he thought it was unlikely he would be able to raise the necessary funds. Even if all the immediate obligations were met, and long-term repayments of larger debts agreed, they would certainly not be able to afford to continue maintaining Chislestone Manor, with all its accompanying expenditure. Even with the rental income from the estate, it was inconceivable that his mother should be obliged to leave her home, her whole way of life – nor, indeed, that his darling Cissy would have to do without her nurses. He knew exactly what his father's answer to the problem would be: 'Marry money, m'boy! You'd be a good catch for one of the daughters of these factory owners or railway magnates. They are all set on marrying their daughters into the aristocracy.'

Hunter knew that this was a frequent occurrence; it was not only newly moneyed families who wished for an alliance with the aristocracy, but also rich American girls wanting titles. Such arrangements seemed to him most immoral and objectionable. For two people to have to spend their lives together, to produce children and share a degree of intimacy without any loving relationship, negated the purpose of marriage as he understood it. He would want to love the woman who was part of his daily life.

Through the open window, Hunter could hear the muted sound of laughter. Storm was on one of her regular visits to the manor which, today, enabled Cissy to forget momentarily that the family were in mourning. Cissy had been shocked by her first encounter with death and the inevitable formalities of mourning. She hated the ominous black bow on the front door, the darkened rooms and the obligatory black clothes both family and staff were wearing, and a visit from her vivacious young friend was clearly helping her to come to terms with the family tragedy. Hunter found himself wishing that he was their age, carefree and ignorant of the problems now besetting him.

He turned to his mother and put an arm round her shaking shoulders. One thing was certain: there was no need, at this point in time, to tell Lady Chislestone about the extent of his father's debts. He was hopeful that he would be able to sort it all out before she need be told how serious it was. She grasped his hand, gripping it tightly without warning. The village church bell started to toll, news having reached the parson of Charles's demise. The sound echoed eerily across the lake and lingered in the big house, its mournful message reaching Hunter's ears.

Hunter felt a moment of guilt at his feeling of relief that the bell was tolling for Charles. He had not been close to his eldest brother, who'd been six years older than himself. He hoped now that Percy was having good luck with his gold mine, a childhood dream he had often discussed with Hunter when they were boys.

He would have been horrified had he known that at that very moment, far away in California, Percy Chislestone was fighting for his life in the collapsed gold mine which he had hoped would make him a very rich man. Tunnelling had gone on for several weeks and a certain amount of shoring-up had been put in place when, unexpectedly, very heavy rainfall had dislodged some of the timbers, and a large section of the mine had collapsed inwards. It was two weeks since this disaster had occurred, and hope had now faded that the trapped men could be rescued before their air supply ran out. A letter was on its way to England to advise Sir Matthew that his second son was presumed dead.

Blissfully unaware of the facts, Hunter gently pressed his mother's hand.

'Try to think of happier days to come, Mama,' he said. 'I expect we shall have Percy home soon. His last letter promised he would be back before Christmas.'

He was pleased to see a little colour returning to her cheeks. 'And I have you here to look after me, my dear boy,' she said with a smile.

With an effort, Hunter returned the smile, only too well aware that at this moment in time he was powerless to do anything to avoid the disaster looming over their heads.

FIVE

Autumn, 1854

The summer of 1854 had now reluctantly given way to autumn but there was still warmth in the sunshine, and the family was able to celebrate Cissy's sixteenth birthday party on the south-facing terrace of Chislestone Manor. Sheltered by the lovely stone-built house, the terrace overlooked the lawn and box-edged flower beds which led down to the lake. On its far side was the arboretum, the foliage still clinging to the branches, a myriad of golds and browns.

As the family were still in mourning for Charles, only a small celebration was considered suitable. Sitting round the pretty lace-clothed table were Cissy's parents Sir Matthew and Lady Chislestone, Hunter and, of course, Storm and her sister Eloise. It was, therefore, a quiet gathering. Also, the doctors had warned over the years that too much excitement would set off one of Cissy's distressing asthma attacks. Cissy herself was perfectly content to be enjoying the company of her much-loved family, and had been hugely surprised by the unexpected appearance of her father whom she saw so rarely.

Hunter was keeping them all laughing as he described the mishaps which had occurred during this summer's debutante season. He was much in demand with the mothers, being good looking, single and eligible in every way.

'Another year or so and you will be dancing until dawn when you come out, my sweetheart!' he said, laughing as he gently touched Storm's cheek. 'If I'm not mistaken, your sixteenth birthday is just after Christmas and you will once more be a twin to my precious little sister.'

Storm forced a smile to her lips. In one way she liked it when Hunter called her 'my sweetheart', but at the same time she knew perfectly well that she was no such thing. To him, she was just Cissy's best friend. Her thoughts now turned to Cissy,

who was wrapped warmly in a rug sitting in the miraculous
new chair Hunter had had made for her by the village carpenter.
It was not as long and cumbersome as the bath chair she had
always used when recovering from a serious attack of the
asthma which so often nearly killed her. The local doctor
wanted her to be moved permanently into the new sanatorium
which had recently been opened fifteen miles away but none
of the family would consider it. The conditions there were far
from good and, if Cissy survived the dangers of asthma, she
would be just as likely to contract some other equally
unpleasant disease. Two nurses were employed and Cissy had
always remained at home.

Sir Matthew was regarding his only daughter with a mixture
of love and guilt. He knew she adored him and she made no
secret of the fact that she wished he did not spend so much
time in London – sometimes for weeks on end. Today, however,
he had set aside his grief for the loss of his son in order to
travel down expressly to see her and, as a result, her cheeks
were glowing with pleasure.

'That chair contraption of yours, Hunter,' he was saying.
'Can you wheel the thing?'

Hunter smiled reassuringly. 'Most certainly, Father!' he
replied. 'Shall I give you a demonstration?'

Sir Matthew shook his head and, gathering his now portly
bulk together, he rose to his feet. Smiling at his frail daughter,
he announced, 'I shall take the birthday girl for a perambula-
tion around the lake. Help me get this new toy of yours down
the steps on to the lawn, Hunter, m'boy!'

'I'll come with you, Father,' Hunter said promptly, as he
helped carry the chair down the wide stone stairway.

'Don't need you, m'boy. Stay there with your mother. I can
manage on my own,' his father said petulantly, and set off at
a remarkably fast pace along the stone path edging the lake.
Cissy was smiling excitedly but Storm felt a moment's
apprehension. Was Sir Matthew enjoying himself too much to
be cautious with Hunter's new contraption? He was scarlet in
the face and puffing furiously as the ground sloped and veered
towards the shining waters of the lake.

Storm raced ahead, trying to get a handhold on the basket

chair. Sir Matthew was stumbling as he grasped the handles of the chair for his own safety. In a flash, she realized that Cissy and the chair would within seconds be in the water. Turning, she was aghast to see that Sir Matthew was no longer holding the handles but had collapsed to the ground and was clutching his chest, an agonized expression on his face. In a split second, she turned her attention back to the chair and managed to swing it round so it now tipped over, sliding a few feet sideways before it came to a halt.

Hunter had been watching uneasily from the terrace. Within seconds he raced down to the water's edge and was beside Cissy. He gently pulled her out of the fallen chair and, relieved of the weight, it slid slowly into the lake. He stood up lifting her in his arms, only then noticing that his father had not moved from where he had fallen.

He had been closely followed by two footmen. The shock on their faces was plain to see, which was hardly surprising; Sir Matthew was lying supine with his eyes wide open, and it was instantly obvious that he was dead.

'Cover your master's face,' Hunter said, indicating the rug which had fallen from Cissy's chair, 'and I will send for the dog cart to take him back to the house. I myself will tell Her Ladyship and arrange for the doctor to come at once. Wait here with him. See if you can get the chair out of the lake too.'

Relieved to have something to do, the two servants set about carrying out Hunter's wishes.

With Storm by his side and his sister safely in his arms, Hunter made his way back up to the terrace, where he handed Cissy over to the care of her nurses, whom Lady Chislestone had already alerted, having seen the accident.

'I'll take care of Cissy, Hunter,' Storm said shakily. 'You need to be with your mother.'

He watched as her nurses gently took her into the house, with Storm following close behind, and then strode off to the stables to alert the grooms and order the dog cart. Then, satisfied he could do no more, he went indoors to find Eloise and his mother, who were waiting quietly in the drawing room.

*   *   *

It was Storm's idea that Cissy and her nurses should move into Kenilworth Hall while the funeral and legal matters were being discussed at the manor. Although Cissy had seen very little of her father over the years, when he did come down from London it was never without a hamper of goodies from Fortnum and Mason. Now, her father's death coming so soon after news of Charles's demise, she was only too anxious to have Storm's cheerful company.

At the funeral Eloise and her sister sat in the Kenilworth pew without the support of their father, who had written to say he was not well enough to attend. However, just as the service was coming to an end, there was a loud commotion outside the church door and very belatedly Lord Kenilworth strode unsteadily up the aisle to join his daughters. To Eloise's relief, at that moment the service was at an end and the congregation rose as the coffin was carried down the aisle towards the open doorway. She took her father's arm and gently walked him outside. She was shocked by how puffed and florid his complexion had become and how slurred his speech was as he apologized in a shaky voice to Hunter for being late.

'I am aware that you have not been well, sir, and I know my mother will understand if you prefer not to attend the house for refreshments. I presume you will be spending the night at Kenilworth and with your permission I will call to see you tomorrow.'

With a nod of agreement and a muttered, 'Goodbye, m'boy' under his breath, Lord Kenilworth climbed unsteadily into his coach. Grateful for the respite and believing he had done his duty, he instructed his coachman to drop him at the hall and then go on to the manor. He told his daughters he had no need of their assistance; they should go on to Chislestone Manor without him.

Meanwhile Cissy, who had not attended her father's funeral service, was pushed in her chair to the churchyard where the servants from both houses, together with the entire population of the village, gathered to see the head of one of their major families buried in the area reserved for them.

Hunter looked very pale but he stood upright, his face expressionless as with his frail mother, supported by her maid, he watched his father's coffin lowered into the ground. He wished that his relationship with his father had been as close as that of his two elder brothers. As it was, he felt unable to share his mother's grief and concentrated upon the reception at Chislestone Manor that was to follow the service.

It was a further three hours before all the guests at the 'wake' had departed, with the exception of the portly bank manager, Mr Turner and the solicitor who had arrived together earlier that day to attend the service and now to read the will.

Hunter was aware of the probably disastrous financial situation that was about to be disclosed and suggested that there was no need for his mother to be present since he would be able to show her the necessary papers when she was less distressed.

After his mother had departed Hunter sat at the desk, the only family member in his father's study, listening to the impassive voice of the solicitor as he read the last will and testament. The will was hopelessly outdated. There were generous bequests to Hunter, his two brothers – one deceased and the other, as they were shortly to learn, presumed so – and several of the family servants, along with generous annuities arranged for his wife and young daughter. When the sonorous voice of the solicitor ceased, Mr Turner coughed and, pulling down his waistcoat over his ample stomach, said apologetically to Hunter, 'I'm afraid I have to advise you, sir, that none of these bequests can be fulfilled. As I think you already know, the debts your father incurred far exceed his assets. These will have to be paid before any other outlay.'

It was not the shock it might otherwise have been to Hunter – he was already aware of some of these debts – but hearing the situation so formally announced forced him to the realization that he might have to sell Chislestone Manor, even the estate, to be able to maintain his father's good name.

One thing was certain: he would not allow a member of the family to suffer the disgrace of bankruptcy.

Mr Turner gave him a sympathetic look. 'Maybe when the financial situation is finally resolved there will be sufficient funds for you and dear Lady Chislestone and your sister to maintain a reasonable standard of living.'

'And enough, I hope,' said Hunter, 'to compensate the staff and estate workers who have served the family so loyally all these past years.'

It was not until the following afternoon that Hunter decided his mother had recovered sufficiently to be told a diluted version of the family's shocking financial state. After delivering the unpleasant news he told her that at the wake he had spoken to her close friend Lady Witton, who had kindly invited her to stay and take a holiday by the sea in Lancing.

'It will do you good to be away for a while from these unhappy surroundings,' he said. 'I also spoke to Eloise when I called on Lord Kenilworth this morning and she said that Storm and she would be more than delighted to have Cissy remain at Kenilworth – which, as you know, she would love to do – while you are staying with your friend.' As for himself, he thought he would remove to London for the rest of the winter, in the hope of straightening out some of the family's disastrous affairs.

Lady Chislestone, now no longer tearful but still very distressed, agreed without argument to her son's suggestion. Hunter was relieved by the thought that she would have adequate company to console her and now told the servants that the house was to be closed for the time being.

Although they were far from happy to be sent home on half pay, they were nevertheless pleased to have what amounted to an extended holiday. Only Hunter's valet and a skeleton staff were to go to London with him. Large though the London house in Upper Brook Street was, he intended using only half a dozen rooms until he could make arrangements to reside at his father's club, which might prove to be a considerable financial saving.

Before leaving the manor, Mr Turner had agreed to arrange a substantial overdraft from the bank to tide Hunter over until he could sell Chislestone Manor or any other available assets.

Hunter was now able to tour the estate together with his manager, reassuring him that there would be funds forthcoming for overdue repairs and replacements after he had had time to organize things in London.

He spent a day driving with his mother in the family coach to the seaside home of her friend on the Sussex coast, and on his return he arranged for the care of his horses. He realized that the cost of their upkeep was such that, very reluctantly, he would be obliged to sell most of them.

He paid frequent visits to Cissy at Kenilworth Hall during the week while he and the housekeeper were preparing the manor for its inevitable future sale. He was pleased to discover Cissy seemed unperturbed by his forthcoming departure. Now he had only to say a final goodbye to her and Eloise and Storm, which he would do on his way to London. He would miss them all, he thought, as he watched his valet finish packing his trunk. He had no worries for Storm but was a little more concerned about Eloise. Without quite knowing why, he was uneasy when he recalled some remarks his valet had made about the tutor. Tomorrow, before he left, he needed to reassure himself that his dearest friend was not on the brink of disaster.

It was ten days after the funeral when he called at Kenilworth Hall for the last time on his way to London to bid farewell to Cissy and Storm, and he intended to speak to Eloise about her continuing employment of the tutor. As he rode through the woods to the hall, he realized he had been unconsciously delaying this encounter.

In the normal course of affairs, he reminded himself, Eloise's reputation and welfare would be entirely a matter for her parents. The fact that she had managed so successfully, without parental guidance, to care for herself and young Storm and to keep the huge Kenilworth estate flourishing, had led him, and indeed many others, into assuming she required no masculine guidance. Their relationship was that of affectionate brother and sister, and he now realized he should have paid more attention to her welfare.

It was some time since Carter, a serious young man, had first been employed by Lord Kenilworth as a tutor and, as far as he knew, everyone took for granted his quiet, unassuming presence at the hall each day. Storm left no one in any doubt that she found him dull and the subjects he taught uninteresting. She herself had one main passion in life, other than her love of animals, and that was inventing plays and vignettes which she and Cissy could act out in the music room at the manor, often with the enforced presence of the Chislestones' staff. Neither he nor Eloise nor the tutor were ever invited to or involved in these theatrical activities.

Reaching Kenilworth Hall, Hunter gave his horse to the stable boy and entered the big house by the garden door. As familiar with this house as with his own home, he did not bother to notify the butler of his arrival. He found Storm and Cissy in the morning room, bent over looking at the latest fashions in a magazine, but it was Eloise he wished to see. He would find her in the schoolroom, they told him. Going up the familiar back stairs they all used to climb as children, he knocked on the door of the schoolroom, where he knew the tutorials took place.

Eloise was sitting at the big scrubbed wooden table where they had so often shared nursery meals. A large sheet of white paper was in front of her and behind stood the tutor, Carter, his arm covering hers as he guided her small white hand, in which she held a paintbrush.

The intimacy of their position was undeniable and yet at the same time it could be described as a useful way of guiding a pupil's arm. Carter stepped back so abruptly that he had to grab the back of the chair for support. There was a look on his face which seemed to Hunter to signify guilt. As for Eloise, her usually pale face had coloured a delicate pink, but she was instantly on her feet, greeting Hunter with obvious pleasure as well as surprise.

'I am clearly interrupting your lesson, Eloise,' Hunter said apologetically. 'But I am leaving for London today and wanted to call and have a word with you before I go.'

For a moment he thought he saw an expression of concern, if not fear, cross Eloise's face, but then she was smiling as she said, 'We'll go down to the morning room and Henry shall bring us some tea.'

The tutor now took a step forward. 'There is no need for you to move, Miss Eloise; I will take a turn around the garden.'

Eloise smiled at him. 'In that case, Mr Carter, please ask Henry if he would bring the tea up here.'

David Carter hurried out of the room, his perturbation such that on his way out he knocked over a jam jar containing a sprig of scarlet rose hips, the subject for tomorrow's watercolour painting lesson.

Sitting down on the cushioned window seat, Eloise beside him, Hunter smiled.

'I'm afraid I have frightened the poor fellow.'

Briefly the colour returned to Eloise's cheeks, then it faded once more. She said, 'He is very self-effacing, and when you get to know him you realize how incredibly knowledgeable he is. He has opened a whole new world for me . . .' Her expression now became animated and there was a sense of excitement in her voice as she continued, 'And he has shown me I am actually quite an accomplished watercolour painter. Do you know, last Christmas he had one of my paintings framed by the village carpenter as a present for me to give to Papa?'

For a moment, Hunter was uncertain how to proceed with his plan to caution her about her relationship with the tutor. To do so would seem a cruel way to acknowledge the pleasure Eloise clearly derived from her tutorials. Beside him, she put her hand on his arm.

'Is something wrong, Hunter?' she asked. 'You're not your usual ebullient self.'

Hunter decided it was his duty to warn her, however distressing that warning might be.

'Elly, you and I have known each other our whole lives, and I have loved you like a sister. What I say now is as a brother – you, sadly, having no one here at home to guide you, your father not being here.'

Conscious of Eloise's anxious stare, Hunter rubbed his hand distractedly through his hair. He hesitated and then said gently, 'You and Storm were a great deal younger when your father chose to replace the unsatisfactory governess with a tutor. The household, the village, everyone became used to seeing the fellow with you two young girls on nature walks or in the gardens. It has only been for the past year or two that Storm has been managing to escape the tutorials, leaving you and Carter unchaperoned.' He paused, uncomfortably aware that Eloise's grip on his arm had tightened and that she was trembling.

'Hunter, I do assure you that absolutely nothing untoward has ever taken place between David Carter and myself. He has always treated me with the utmost respect and I . . .' She paused, a strange look now crossing her face as she said quietly, 'I admit to a fond liking for Mr Carter. As I said earlier, he has opened a new world for me, and he seems always to know exactly what I feel about life, art and humanity. He is an extraordinary, deep-thinking man—'

She broke off, colour once more coming to her cheeks as she became aware that she was extolling David Carter's virtues beyond casual praise.

That precise moment was one of huge significance for both Hunter and Eloise, each realizing simultaneously that Eloise had just admitted a very great deal more than she'd intended about her feelings for the tutor. Love was not an emotion that Hunter had ever as yet experienced but the tone of Eloise's voice, the obvious intensity of her feelings and her eager expression when she mentioned Carter's attributes were more than enough to convince him of the truth.

For a moment neither spoke, then Hunter said gently, 'Dearest Elly, do you think in the circumstances it would be advisable to . . . well, to . . .' He trailed off, unable to find the words to tell her to call a halt to Carter's employment before it developed into a more serious relationship.

At that moment, Henry and Daisy appeared with the tea tray. By the time the servants had left Eloise had found the words she hoped would reassure Hunter.

'Hunter, I know what you're thinking. The same thought has gone through my mind several times, but I cannot face what it would be like without this joy in my life. Mr Carter knows nothing of how I feel, and I would never in a lifetime let him know. I do need him, Hunter, insane as it may sound. As you know, I have never wished for marriage or children, strange as that may be, but I understand now that art is the most important thing in my life and Mr Carter provides the knowledge and encouragement I need to fulfil this ambition. That is what I believe fate intended for me and why I have always felt different from other girls my own age.' With shaking hands, she paused and silently poured the tea into two cups, adding sugar and milk to one, which she handed to Hunter. Hunter realized at that moment that he was out of his depth and that Eloise's emotions were hopelessly unfamiliar to him. Had he been mistaken? he asked himself as he sipped his tea. Her obsession with Carter was something about which he knew very little, and it would be better if he did not interfere in the life she had chosen to embrace. At least, he told himself, he must be very careful indeed not to give the staff, the villagers, or anyone in their vicinity the slightest cause for suspecting Eloise's true feelings about her tutor.

SIX

1 March 1855 – 1 January 1856

Dearest Cissy,

Thank you so, so much for your lovely long letter. I hope you and your mother are enjoying the sea air at Lancing despite the cold weather. It seems like a hundred years since you left me here on my own, and now I know you feel the same. I don't think it has ever been so long between our visits to one another and I miss you so much.

We did not celebrate Eloise's twenty-seventh birthday as she insisted she is too old now for her to wish to be reminded of the passing years! This sounds so like my darling sister, does it not? I told her truthfully that I have never seen her look more beautiful than she has done of late. There is no doubt that her painting has opened up a new world for her. I suppose we must thank the dedicated Mr Carter who, Cissy, I swear is madly in love with her, poor man!

Anyway, the birthday passed very quietly, much like any other day here. We did, however, go for the day to visit Eloise's godmother and Petal.

Storm stopped writing as she paused to look out of the morning room window at the white covering of frost on the lawn. A brief sigh escaped her lips as she sat, pen in hand, wishing even more desperately that Cissy was there to discuss her next comment – namely that the poor girl no doubt lovingly christened Petal had grown into an ungainly, clumsy, painfully shy young woman who, like Storm herself, was to be presented next year.

The two girls had managed to find a shared interest in their love of animals but had little else in common. On Storm's return home after her first visit, she had been horrified to learn from Eloise that arrangements were going to be made to send her with Petal to a finishing academy for young ladies in Bath. Eloise made no bones about the truth: her godmother, Mrs Fothergill, was painfully aware of her daughter's shortcomings but, for the first and only time in her life, Petal had refused to obey her mother's wishes for her to go to the academy. That her twin brother, Tom, had gone away to boarding school and loved it did nothing to subdue her near hysterical sobs and protests that she would not leave home.

Shortly after her first visit, a compromise had been reached. Petal would go to the academy on one condition only: that Storm went with her, because Storm had all the self-confidence she herself lacked and she would not be friendless.

This was undeniable, and Storm had felt sorry for the girl but, as she had informed Eloise, there was no possibility of her leaving home while Cissy was staying with her. Eloise had known better than to try to alter her decision, so Storm had made no mention of the idea to Cissy. Then fate stepped in: Lady Chislestone wrote to say arrangements were being made for Cissy and her nurse to join her at the seaside, where the doctors believed the sea air would greatly benefit her lungs.

Mrs Fothergill was ecstatic when Eloise informed her godmother that Storm was now prepared to go to the academy with Petal. Mrs Fothergill then suggested that it would be of benefit both to her and Eloise if she were allowed to present both young girls the following year. She would, she said, have a word with Petal's father and, if he agreed, make all the arrangements for their debut and coming-out dance. It was a welcome suggestion for Eloise, who had been wondering how best to cope with the arrangements that would have been necessary. Mrs Fothergill, although not from society's upper echelons, was the extremely wealthy wife of a retired admiral who spent most of his time in their London home in preference to the country.

Eloise would of necessity have to go to London for the season itself but for the time being she could not bear the thought of having to leave Kenilworth Hall. She refused to admit to herself that it was not her home but the hours she spent with David Carter that she would sorely miss.

Storm's thoughts, meanwhile, were not on next year's festivities but on her imminent start at the academy.

So you see, dearest, with Papa's agreement, I am to go to this school with Petal when the summer term starts on 21 April. Mrs Fothergill heard from Eloise that I would no longer have your company here and, late though it was, used her not inconsiderable influence to book two boarding places for Petal and me at the academy. Petal visited me last week and is dreading it, but I think it sounds quite fun. Not least, I shall be pleased to learn how to dance before my ball next year. We are also to learn French and, the curriculum says, deportment. Eloise thinks that means I'll have to walk round a room with a dinner plate balanced on my head.

Oh, Cissy, you cannot imagine how much I wish you were well enough to come with us! Never mind! I will write and tell you everything that happens.

I'm sending all my love and lots and lots of hugs and kisses.

P.S. Petal brought her brother, Tom, with her when she came to tea last week. He's a really nice-looking boy with a great sense of humour and he kept us all laughing most of the time. He's going up to university shortly. Petal says he is very bright and could get a place wherever he wants. He is Petal's twin and you can see how pretty she could be if she were as slim and agile as Tom. Tom says that maybe the academy will help to make her more graceful as otherwise she will be hard put to attract the young men she will meet at all the balls. (Petal threw a cushion at him when he said that!)

I think you'd like Tom. He reminded me a bit of Hunter. Has Hunter been to see you?

Reading Storm's letters, Cissy always felt a mixture of happiness and sadness. Her friend's big, untidy handwriting was so reminiscent of Storm that the letters brought her closer, at the same time making her realize how their lives were slowly separating. Hers remained the same: long, uneventful days reading, doing jigsaws and tapestry work, with welcome breaks when the weather permitted one of her nurses to wheel her along the promenade, where she would watch seagulls and the waves foaming against the breakwaters. She seldom returned to the big white house on the seafront without thinking how jolly such outings would have been were Storm there to make up stories of shipwrecks and smugglers and finding buried treasure beneath the beach cobbles when the tide went out. Storm's letters were among her greatest pleasures, along with Hunter's fleeting visits from London.

On one such occasion after she had joined her mother in Lancing, she was sitting one day in the spring sunshine which was pouring through the conservatory windows when he appeared unexpectedly. The usual cheerful expression on her brother's good-looking face had vanished and he looked as if he carried the weight of the world on his shoulders. His black cravat and wide black silk armband made him look all the more severe. When she insisted that he should sit down and tell her why he looked so worried, he shook his head.

'It is six months since poor Father died and now Charles and Percy are no longer here to assist me, I have been trying on my own to sort out his affairs. I'm afraid the financial situation does not look a very promising one, Cissy,' he said. 'We may have to make some serious economies.' He paused before adding, 'We may even have to sell Chislestone Manor.'

He broke off abruptly, realizing that he was unburdening himself to an invalid child not yet of age. He quickly changed the tone of his voice and said with an apologetic smile, 'Of course, that's a ridiculous notion. The estate is our heritage . . .'

The frown on Cissy's face vanished as she recalled the most important piece of news she had for him.

'Hunter,' she said, 'Storm said in her last letter that her brother is home. Did you realize John was away on his Grand Tour for eighteen months, if not two whole years! Storm was allowed by the academy to have a week's leave so she could go home to see him. She said he had changed so much it was like being with a stranger. He was only really interested in his father's condition and talked to Eloise of little else but escorting him out to Switzerland, where they have wonderful sanatoriums in the mountains for chronically ill people. He told her he had found one where they sometimes effect a cure for people with addictions such as their father's, although mostly they treat people with tuberculosis.'

It was a moment or two before Hunter could bring himself to speak, as it crossed his mind that perhaps there was such a place that could cure his beloved sister. Then he said in as matter-of-fact a voice as he could manage, 'Yes, I did know John was back in England. We ran into one another at the club and he told me of the plans he had for Lord Kenilworth. He is hoping to be able to move him to Switzerland by the beginning of August.'

Storm's recent letter describing her meeting with her brother John had also informed Cissy that a present was on its way by post.

You must not tell anyone where you got this present! John obviously expected me to be like other girls of my age and enjoy the tasks it involves, the mere thought of which alarm me. Darling Cissy, you are so clever with your needle, and I have to say, the items you are required to make are indeed beautiful, so I hope you will be happy to have the Swiss Lady to dress.

When in due course the parcel was delivered, in the box among the layers of tissue paper was an entire wardrobe of clothes, from the daintiest underwear to a jewelled ballgown – all cut out and ready to stitch for the unclothed Swiss doll. Her long black hair was beautifully braided and coiled round her head. The box also contained jewelled headdresses as well as rings, bracelets and necklaces befitting the various outfits.

It was a very expensive, beautiful toy which, if expertly sewn, would bring double admiration. Cissy had only to look at the picture on the lid of the large box to know at once that Storm would consider this a tiresome task, whereas she herself would take great pleasure in it.

*　　*　　*

If sewing was not one of Storm's accomplishments, she was proving an excellent pupil at the finishing academy. The *directrice* was secretly pleased with Storm's transformation from an unrestrained child to a slim, graceful young girl on the verge of beauty. Although she felt obliged from time to time to curtail Storm's free time when she was found keeping the other girls entertained with stories of her childhood escapades with her older brothers, she admired the child. Moreover, she realized what a huge influence for the good Storm was with the awkward, ungainly girl who had accompanied her to the academy. Miss Petal Fothergill had by the end of that first term lost nearly a stone in weight; she had also learned to walk more like a young lady than a street cleaner and to hold up her head and smile when addressed, rather than screwing up her face in a shy scowl.

Storm, too, was surprised not only to discover how much she enjoyed the companionship of girls her own age, but at the way she was beginning to look. Sometimes one of her companions remarked wistfully that she wished she had eyes as big as hers, a profile or figure like hers, or was as naturally able on the dance floor, and she now half believed it when her admiring shadow, Petal, said she was the prettiest girl in the class. The fact that Storm was far from self-admiring and never tried to curry favour with the teachers added to her popularity. She herself was interested in only two people's opinions of her progress: what Hunter was going to think when he saw her in the summer holiday and, more importantly, her darling Eloise's pleasure in noting the transformation. She was counting on Hunter visiting Kenilworth Hall while she was at home, and planned to surprise him by asking Eloise to invite him to a formal dinner party, when she would wear one of the pretty new gowns Eloise was having made for her.

To her intense disappointment, Storm's planned surprise never once showed even a glimmer of hope of materializing. Hunter had on the spur of the moment accepted John's invitation to travel out to Switzerland in August, at his expense, to examine the sanatorium in greater detail. They wished to reassure themselves that there was genuine hope of a cure for Lord Kenilworth's dependence on alcohol and, possibly, a cure for Cissy. By the time they returned travel-weary to London, Storm had perforce gone back to the academy for the autumn term. She wrote to Cissy at once.

> *I was so, so disappointed. I so wanted Hunter to see that I had grown up and was not to be treated like a child any more. Now I shall have to wait until Christmas. We were invited by the Fothergills to stay with them for a few days during the Christmas holiday, but Eloise does not want to leave Kenilworth Hall any more than I do. She says we could give a Boxing Day party and invite Petal and her family. This would be good because then Hunter might come down from London to celebrate with us, especially as it's almost my birthday. Petal says Tom and her younger brother Daryl really enjoy Christmas and, somehow or other, always make family parties fun. Cissy, do you think there is any possibility the doctors and your dear Mama would let you come and stay for a few days? Maybe you could ask Hunter to persuade them to let you come. I know you would like Petal and Tom and it would all be quite perfect if you were there.*

Almost unbelievably, this time the majority of Storm's hopes did materialize. A radiant Cissy was driven to Kenilworth Hall in the Chislestone coach with her nurses, and was settled back in her old rooms until the start of the new year. Petal and her family arrived in time for a festive lunch on Boxing Day and planned to stay until New Year's Day, thus encompassing Storm's birthday dinner party, to which their near neighbours had also been invited. As Petal had predicted, Tom was a wonderful house guest. He kept everyone smiling with his jokes and riddles and was always ready with ideas for their entertainment – charades which included the grown-ups and noisier card games like Racing Demon and Chop-Off-Your-Thumb. Tom flirted outrageously but harmlessly with Storm, whom he vowed he would marry as soon as he attained his ambition to become Prime Minister. Since that remote possibility was at the very least twenty years ahead, Storm replied laughing that she would have accepted his proposal had she not wished to be married before she was an old woman.

It was light-hearted banter, and sometimes Cissy would join them in quieter pursuits. It was altogether a very happy seasonal visit with only one major disappointment for Storm – it was not Hunter, but the coachman, who had brought Cissy to Kenilworth Hall.

SEVEN

Spring, 1856

'You look really beautiful, darling!' Eloise said as she sat on the edge of Storm's bed in Kenilworth House, Mount Street, watching her try on the lovely ivory lace-trimmed gown she was to wear when she joined the other two hundred who were to make their curtsey to Queen Victoria in two weeks' time.

Storm smiled happily, her eyes dark with excitement as she viewed her reflection in the cheval mirror in her bedroom. She reached up to touch the tiny white feather Eloise had fixed in her shining dark hair and felt her heartbeat quicken as the thought struck her: Hunter might not even recognize her when he came to her coming-out ball next month. When she and Eloise had written the invitations, he had been first on her list. His reply had been both informal and disappointing: that he was having to deal with some difficult legal problems concerning the winding up of his father's and brothers' estate, and that there was a possibility he might have to go to America shortly. However, he would do his very best to be back in London in time for her ball.

Storm's heartbeat slowed as she carefully removed the head-dress, telling herself that Hunter would surely know how much his presence meant to her and would organize his affairs so that he would be able to attend her ball. There would, of course, be many more dances at the houses of the other debutantes, but she could no longer be sure that he would even be back in England for the rest of the season.

Mabel assisted her in removing the lovely gown and covering it with its cambric protector, then hung it on the side of the wardrobe. Storm surveyed her unclothed body, tiny-waisted but with perfectly rounded hips and breasts. She had changed so much during that year in the finishing academy. Although at the time she had not wanted to go to such an establishment, she now blessed Petal's parents for instigating it. She could see quite clearly what a rapscallion she had been, virtually running wild with only Eloise to control her. As for the tutorials with Mr Carter, she must have missed as many as she had been obliged to attend.

Storm's thoughts now turned to her sister as Mabel helped her back into the pale yellow muslin dress decorated with tiny blue silk flowers made for her by Mrs Fothergill's French dressmaker. It was stylishly fashioned and her figure was envied by Petal, who remained plump, although she had managed to lose a considerable amount of weight. With her improved looks, Petal had gained a great deal of confidence, and though she was still shy she was now happy to share all of Storm's activities, even looking forward to the presentation at Buckingham Palace.

Admiral Fothergill had taken a house for his family in Eaton Terrace for the duration of the season and Tom, awaiting the start of his first term at Oxford University in the autumn, had taken it upon himself to escort the girls to all the exhibitions and accompany them to soirées, musical evenings or whatever delights the season's hostesses held for those looking for enjoyment.

Tom made no secret of the fact that he was, as he put it, 'wildly in love' with Storm. Of course, there was no question of her ever marrying him because she was going to marry Hunter. Now she had grown up enough to be of marriageable age, there was no reason why Hunter should continue to treat her as a child; moreover, looking at herself in the mirror and seeing herself as he would see her, she knew he would have no further need to behave as if he were her elder brother.

Thinking of her real brother, Storm frowned. On one of the very few occasions she had seen John after his arrival home from his travels he had arranged to go abroad again, taking their invalid father. He had said he would be back from Switzerland within a month at most, so would be home to assist Eloise in their London house when it was Storm's turn to have her ball – something each of the families hosted throughout the long summer season. Storm was not interested in these other invitations which came pouring in. It was extremely doubtful that Hunter would attend many of them. Unless he was going to be present, there would be no pleasure in any of the evenings.

Although Storm confided her feelings to Petal, she was reluctant to do so with Eloise who, she knew very well, looked on Hunter's obvious affection for her as no more than that of an indulgent brother. Whenever Storm had let drop in casual conversation that she expected to be Hunter's wife when she grew up, Eloise had smiled and said, 'Yes, dearest!' as if speaking to a youngster who had announced he wanted to be a train driver or fly a hot air balloon like Signor Lunardi.

It worried Storm knowing that while her sister was living in London for the season she was missing the pleasure of her painting lessons and the congenial companionship of their tutor. Thoughts of David Carter and his somewhat unusual place in their family life concerned Storm. When she would return home from an outing with the Fothergills she would often find her sister standing by the drawing room window staring out at the carriages, carts and hansom cabs not as if actually seeing them but as if she were dreaming of being elsewhere – home at Kenilworth Hall, no doubt, sitting beneath the shade of the chestnut spinney with Mr Carter and their easels and paints, seemingly without a care in the world.

It crossed Storm's mind now that the long, companionable hours her sister spent with David Carter and the undeniable progress Eloise had made with her painting were really the only important aspects of her sister's life. Although a charming and excellent hostess, popular with their neighbours, it was only at home, wearing her painting smock and hurrying off to greet the tutor on his arrival in the mornings, that Eloise ever looked truly animated.

A sudden wave of anxiety swept over Storm. In the past, she had even teased Eloise about her liking for Mr Carter, saying jokingly, 'You're captivated by him, aren't you, Elly – and look at you, you're blushing!' Eloise had turned quickly away, telling her not to be so silly. Well, of course, it *was* silly. Mr Carter had never tried to hide the truth about his background. In fact, he had sometimes related stories about his childhood – how they could only have a bath once a week, all eight children using in turn the big tin bath of water taken by their mother from the copper in the wash room and from the big kettle on the range; how, being the youngest, he never enjoyed clean water. He told them how sometimes at the end of the week when there was no money left for food, he and the brother closest to him in age would go down to the market and request any fruit, vegetables or pastries which would otherwise be thrown away. He told them how he had never had a new piece of clothing until he went to grammar school and had to have a uniform, otherwise always wearing his brothers' outgrown clothes and boots.

After such stories, when he had returned on his horse to the parsonage, Eloise would shake her head, saying how remarkable it was that despite this upbringing he had such a wide knowledge of botany and the history of art.

Was it conceivable that Eloise could ever marry this man? Storm asked herself. She did not think so, however much affection she might have for him. Although he never spoke a word out of place he could not hide the expression in his eyes when he gazed at her, nor the tone of his voice. Storm could not see a way in which the future could end happily for Eloise, who had never shown any romantic interest in the young men who had courted her in her youth. If Mr Carter were now to disappear from her life, Storm could see no ultimate happy marriage for her, only a solitary spinsterhood with perhaps her father's company, should he return from the foreign sanatorium cured of his addiction to alcohol.

Storm sighed again, her thoughts now turning to her brother, John. He was almost a stranger to her though closer to Eloise, who had shared his childhood. He had said he would return to England in good time for her coming-out ball. Perhaps he would know what, if anything, could best be done about Eloise and her strange relationship with the tutor.

Storm's face now broke into a satisfied smile as her eye caught sight of the lace flounces peeping out from under the dust cover hiding the dress hanging on the door of the cupboard. Despite Eloise's protest that its figure-hugging heart-shaped bodice and tight waistline made Storm appear far older than a young debutante should look, the French dressmaker had insisted that 'Mademoiselle looks so charming, so innocent that the seductive lines of the dress will not be noticed.'

They were words Storm had treasured ever since the dress was finished and hanging in her bedroom. More than anything in the world she wanted Hunter to be 'seduced', as madame had put it; to be amazed by her transformation from the urchin he had known to a young woman now ready for marriage.

In a conscious effort to curb her impatience, Storm turned to tell Eloise, who was sitting attaching ribbons to her new bonnet, that she was going to Eaton Terrace to take tea with Petal and Tom. She then fetched Mabel, after which she ran downstairs to instruct Roberts, the butler, to call a hansom cab for them. Although the visit would not be exciting, she told herself as the cab rattled its way down Mount Street towards Eaton Terrace, even a childish card game of Rummy or Black Maria would be preferable to counting the days, even the hours, until Hunter came into the ballroom and saw her waiting for him in her beautiful new gown.

Petal and Tom came running downstairs to greet her. Dispatching Mabel to the servants' hall, she followed them upstairs to the schoolroom where, for the next hour, she forgot both Hunter and her ball while the three of them enjoyed themselves in a companionable game of Black Maria.

EIGHT

Spring, 1856

I t was now a month since Mrs Fothergill had presented Storm and Petal to the Queen at Buckingham Palace, and tonight Storm was to wear her presentation gown at her coming-out ball at the house in Mount Street. Petal was not having her ball until the following week.

'Will you just stop fidgeting, Miss Storm!' Mabel said as she tried for the second time to tie the laces of the corset to be able to fasten the row of tiny buttons on her dress. 'That could be a coach arriving and you not downstairs to receive your guests!' she said as she pulled the full skirts down over the layers of petticoats, her hand smoothing the soft cream silk.

Storm's face flushed with excitement as she darted over to the window and looked down to the driveway. Her expression changed swiftly to one of acute disappointment as she recognized the carriage: it was the Fothergills' coach, not Hunter's, as she had hoped it might be. He had, of course, been the first person on her list of the guests she wished to attend the dinner before the ball started, and he had promised to do so.

Mabel was scowling as she waited patiently for her young mistress to return and sit at her dressing table so she could fix the star-shaped clasp, studded with seed pearls and rubies, in Storm's hair. After doing so, she then placed a pearl necklace round her throat, which had belonged to Storm's grandmother, and handed her the long white kid gloves.

'No matter who that is, you should be down in the hall with Miss Eloise to receive your guests. Didn't you learn nothing at that academy of yours? You hurry on down now, quick as you can.'

To Storm's relief, she did not have to face Eloise's disapproving glare on the stairs. Instead she met the parlour maid

conducting Mrs Fothergill and Petal upstairs to a guest room
set aside for the ladies to see to their toilette.

Mrs Fothergill smiled at Storm. 'I'm afraid we are early.
Tom was determined that we should arrive before any other
guest so he could put his name on your dance card while there
was space to do so!' Her glance now went to Storm's dress.
'You look quite beautiful, dear child,' she said, as they walked
towards the guest room. 'You will most certainly be the belle
of your ball!'

She had grown very fond of Storm this past year and she
now kissed her affectionately on both cheeks while the maid
divested her of her velvet cape.

'You look lovely, too!' Storm said to her friend with genuine
approval, after Petal had removed her midnight blue velvet
cloak and turned towards the glass to 'fluff out' her skirts.
Aware that Eloise would be waiting impatiently for her downstairs, Storm now linked her arm through Petal's. Together
they hurried along the corridor to the top of the wide staircase
behind Mrs Fothergill.

'Your mama was absolutely right; that rose pink and ivory
lace really suits you, and . . .' Storm added in a whisper, '. . .
the style shows off your perfect figure too!'

They smiled at one another, recalling the efforts Petal had
made this past year to lose her unflattering plumpness.

Mrs Fothergill chatted happily as they descended the stairs,
and Eloise came hurrying towards them. For once, she was
not smiling.

'Wherever have you been, Storm?' she said reprovingly. 'You
should be beside me to receive our guests. Please excuse her,
Mrs Fothergill!' She turned to Tom, who was waiting behind
her. 'Take your mother and sister through to the dining room,
Thomas, dear!' she said. 'Storm, I have a message for you.'

As the Fothergills moved away across the hallway, Eloise's
voice softened slightly and she put a hand on Storm's arm.
'Darling, I'm sorry to have to tell you that Hunter's footman
came round a short while ago with a note from Hunter saying
he was unfortunately delayed and would not be able to arrive
in time for the dinner party. He was most apologetic and
promised to come to the ball later.'

Seeing the expression on Storm's face, she added quickly, 'You really cannot let this spoil your evening, darling. It's very tiresome of Hunter but his absence is no good reason for you not to enjoy yourself. You look quite beautiful and, with so many admirers, I doubt you will have time to miss him.'

There was no time for Storm to reply; Roberts was holding the front door open for a further group of guests. Knowing how much time and effort Eloise had put into arranging this special evening, Storm did her best to appear indifferent to the news of Hunter's apologetic note. She even managed to feel angry with him and determined not to forgive him when he did arrive later, unless he could assure her there was a very good reason for his delay.

Eloise was right, Storm thought. Hunter had no right to absent himself at this last minute; no right to disappoint her. She had not tried to hide from him how important a guest he was on this so special night. She would, of course, relent, if only because it was his company she wanted, his admiration – yes, and his arms round her as she partnered him for her first romantic waltz.

Tom, with his usual adeptness, had managed to persuade Eloise to substitute his own name for Hunter's by the place next to Storm at the table. He behaved towards Storm as if he were far older than his eighteen years and flirted with her amusingly. He referred to Hunter – and he knew all about him from his sister Petal – as if he were of no importance to Storm.

'I expect the fellow thinks himself a bit too old for debutante dances,' he said casually. 'Petal says he's nearly thirty!'

'That's not true!' Storm protested. 'Well, Hunter's only twenty-eight.'

Tom tactfully replied, 'I suppose that still allows him to be called eligible. I wonder he has not yet found a wife.'

It had been on the tip of Storm's tongue to reply that Hunter had been waiting for her to grow up so he could marry her and now, tonight, at this very important moment in her life, she intended to show him that she was not a schoolgirl any longer but a young woman.

Only to Petal had she confessed that it was not just as a loving companion that she wanted to belong to Hunter, but

as a woman. But she had not confided her more intimate
desires: that she wanted him to hold her in his arms, to
kiss her, to take her into his bed where she could feel his
naked body.

It was because of these thoughts that Storm realized she
had left childhood behind and Hunter, who knew her so well,
could not fail to be aware of it when they met. Almost unbelievably, it was half a year since she had confided in Petal.
While she had been ensconced at the academy, Hunter had
been in London looking after his late father's affairs. Even
Cissy had seen him only once during that period. That was
why his attendance at her ball was so very important.

After the dinner party, a six-piece orchestra that was
situated in a corner of the ballroom on a raised dais started
the evening's dancing with a lively polka. Grinning and not
a little breathless, Tom told Storm that she was at her most
beautiful when she was laughing, and that if ever her mood
was sad she was to seek his company so he could restore
her happiness.

Of course Hunter would come, she reassured herself. At
any moment he would come into the ballroom and she would
see him by the door, searching for her. She would not let
him see how anxious she was. She would be smiling happily
as she danced the quadrille or a Highland reel. Perhaps she
would pretend she hadn't seen him. Possibly she could bring
herself simply to nod casually and quickly start conversing
with her partner so he would know she was cross with him
for turning up so late.

However, although Storm's attention rarely strayed for long
from the ballroom door, as the evening went on there was still
no sign of Hunter. Fully aware of Storm's ill-concealed anxiety,
Tom did his best to keep her smiling with his amusing anec-
dotes whenever his name came up on her dance card. Several
of the other young men present were now objecting that Tom
had claimed five dances on her card, but he cheerfully ignored
them and swept her back on to the dance floor.

When the time came for the supper dance Storm did not
need Tom to tell her that she was being unreasonable in
supposing that Hunter would arrive at this time of the evening.

Either he had forgotten his promise to be here or whatever had detained him from the dinner party was serious enough to prevent his leaving wherever he was.

It helped her come to terms with this reality that she was so much in demand. Eloise had whispered to her that she was unquestionably the prettiest girl in the room. The young men crowding round her between dances all had requests for further meetings in the days to come. With a huge effort she managed to return their flirtatious comments with 'maybe' and 'perhaps', not wishing to tie herself down in case Hunter suddenly turned up with a plausible explanation for his absence.

The first streaks of dawn were in the night sky when the orchestra leader announced that the dance following this one would be the last of the event and would be a waltz. Tom hurried across the room to claim Storm for the polka which the orchestra was just starting. They had barely circled the room once when Tom said quietly, 'There's a tall, good-looking gentleman standing in the doorway scanning the dancers. Could it be the fellow you were expecting?'

Storm's heart was thumping fiercely as she looked across the crowded room. Her instinct was to rush over and greet Hunter but the pressure of Tom's hand on her arm detained her. 'He doesn't need to know his tardiness has spoilt your evening. Just give him a smile and wave as we go past.'

Knowing instinctively that Tom was right, she managed a friendly smile and did not look in Hunter's direction again while they circled the room to the rhythm of the music.

Hunter was waiting for her as Tom led her off the dance floor.

Storm's heart and mind were so full of conflicting emotions, nearly a full minute passed before she could bring herself to speak. Then, in as casual a tone as she could manage, she said brightly, 'Hunter, you managed to get here after all. Have you met Thomas Fothergill, Petal's brother? Tom, we have the last dance, don't we? So I'll see you shortly.'

Tom did as he knew she wanted and disappeared among the crowd without disputing her claim to the last dance, which wasn't true.

Hunter, meanwhile, had been unable to take his eyes off

Storm's appearance. 'My beloved little duckling has grown into the most beautiful swan!' he said, his voice husky as he tucked his arm intimately through hers. 'Storm, I am just so sorry about this special night of yours. I tried to extricate myself but—'

He got no further before the orchestra leader announced the last waltz. Without hesitation and ignoring what Storm had said about having the last dance with Tom, Hunter led her back on to the crowded dance floor. She felt the warmth of his gloved hand on her back through the thin silk of her gown.

Storm wondered for one minute if she were going to faint with the enormity of the emotion which now engulfed her. Hunter's body, although not quite touching hers, was near enough for her to feel an overwhelming wave of excitement at his proximity. Her heart was like that of a wild bird caught in a trap. All she could think about as they circled the room with the other dancers was that Hunter was holding her in his arms, that he thought she was beautiful. He was now murmuring the words from the waltz.

Suddenly his arm tightened and she heard his voice, almost a whisper in her ear, saying, 'I will love you always . . . always . . .'

Storm's heart was singing as he led her off the floor when the music ended, her hand resting lightly on his arm. It no longer mattered that he had arrived so late. All that mattered was that he loved her.

Suddenly a loud American voice overrode the general murmur of conversation. 'Hunter! Wherever have you been? We were supposed to meet in the hall ten minutes ago. You're a very naughty boy!'

The woman who had spoken appeared at Hunter's side. She reached up and touched his cheek intimately with her white-gloved hand which, Storm noticed irrelevantly, was encircled with diamonds and other ostentatiously beautiful bracelets. Her face was heavily powdered and rouged and her large, dark eyes seemed to Storm to glitter like those of a bird of prey. But for the overall impression of harshness, she would have been beautiful.

She now linked her arm possessively through Hunter's,

saying in her strident voice, 'We've gotta go, honey, so don't bother to introduce me.' She looked directly at Storm without smiling and said, 'We have two whist tables in progress at my house, and I promised we wouldn't be gone more than half an hour at the most.'

'But I thought . . .' Storm said, looking up at Hunter, '. . . you had planned to spend the evening here. I don't understand—' She broke off, realizing she was on the point of bursting into tears.

Seeing how shattered she was by the discovery that it had never been his intention to attend the ball after all, Hunter tried to take hold of her hand, but she hid it in the folds of her dress. She realized suddenly that no matter how fulsome his compliments, she was still his sister's little girlfriend, running wild in the woods surrounding Chislestone village. She should have known she would always be a child to him. It was only to be expected that he would have female admirers of far greater sophistication than herself. This American woman now blatantly claiming Hunter – well, he was welcome to her. As far as she herself was concerned, she never wanted to see him again.

As if by some sixth sense, Tom suddenly appeared at Storm's side. 'I do apologize for interrupting you, but Petal is looking for you everywhere and I promised to try and find you. I gather it is quite urgent.'

With a rush of gratitude, Storm laid her hand on Tom's arm and said, 'Hunter and his friend are just leaving, so I am sure they will excuse me.'

Without glancing at Hunter she gave a curt nod to Hunter's American woman friend and allowed Tom to conduct her quickly back to the drawing room.

When Storm finally fell into bed at six o'clock that morning, she was too tired to reflect on the gamut of emotions she had experienced during the past night. There was one thing she was determined about – Hunter would never be more to her now than just Cissy's brother. When he called shortly after breakfast, she sent the footman back saying she was still asleep and did not wish to be disturbed until the evening.

Among the many beautiful floral tributes that arrived after the ball by way of thanks, there was one from Hunter with a note saying, *Please don't be cross; I can explain. It was not my fault.*

Bitterly, Storm reflected that it couldn't be anybody else's fault. If he had really intended to be here with her, nothing should have stopped him. Nothing would have stopped her. She buried her face in the beautiful display of flowers and tried not to cry.

NINE

Spring, 1856

It was just after Easter, when Eloise, Storm and the household servants had departed for London in anticipation of Storm's presentation and coming-out ball, that David Carter had decided to pay an overdue visit home. He found nothing changed and his adoring mother was really pleased with the small painting he had had framed for her of her favourite garden flowers. His father was concerned about the low state of his son's bank account, David having spent far more than he should have on a large linen canvas and a selection of oil paints from Winsor & Newton.

It was with a feeling of relief, he realized, that he left behind the almost claustrophobic atmosphere of his childhood home and his parents' love.

On his return to the parsonage, David had covered a table with sketches outlining Eloise's beautiful face and figure. He couldn't wait to start work on the portrait that he was determined to produce. With both Eloise and Storm away in London, he was no longer required for tutorials and was able to work unhindered, passionately, furiously, sometimes into the early hours of the morning in the old conservatory the parson had kindly allocated to him for a studio. It was hugely frustrating when he had to wait for yesterday's paints to dry before he could continue portraying his beloved. When he looked at his painting, it was almost as if she were there in person. He had placed her seated by a window, with the light shining on her hair and her enigmatic smile touching the corners of her mouth as she stared out of the picture. It was not a *Mona Lisa* smile, but one full of the promise of pleasant days in warm summer sunshine and the sweetness of her happy expression.

His own fiercest critic, he was really pleased with his work; he seemed to have caught the very essence of her.

His judgement of his portrait was to be endorsed by Reverend Phillips's cousin, an art lover from London, whom his landlord had insisted upon his seeing.

A few days later the man was shown into the conservatory by Reverend Phillips, who introduced him to David, quietly engrossed in cleaning his paintbrushes. David stood up, went over to his easel and pulled off the dust sheet covering the picture. The visitor stood, staring closely at the portrait. David realized he was holding his breath in anticipation of the man's reaction, then slowly the visitor turned to David.

'It is worthy of attention,' he said enthusiastically. 'You should enter it into one of the competitions open to those who submit work to the Royal Academy.'

David Carter was shocked. 'I am not a professional,' he said to the two men. 'I could not possibly be considered good enough for the Royal Academy. Surely you know they only exhibit really famous artists such as Mr William Holman Hunt and Sir Edwin Landseer, not amateurs like me?'

The two men ignored David's words of reluctance and continued to stare, absorbed by the picture before them.

'Apart from anything else, Miss Kenilworth might not like it,' David said quietly.

Mr Phillips waved this protest aside. 'I myself shall write to her,' he said. 'I cannot believe she will withhold her permission. You must hurry now, Carter, and finish the portrait to meet the deadline. I will lend you my carriage to take it to London so it will not be damaged once completed.' He smiled at his protégé in a friendly fashion. 'My wife tells me you have been the most trouble-free paying guest we have ever had, Carter, and I must say I agree. It was a fortuitous day for all of us when Lord Kenilworth hired you to tutor his daughters, although I do have to pass on a word of warning. Local people do not understand your working relationship with Miss Kenilworth, and my wife tells me rumours have been circulating that the two of you have been seen together unchaperoned quite frequently. I'm sure there is no harm whatever in this association, but you know what village gossip is like, so I think that when the family returns from London you should be a little more circumspect in your outings together in the woods and the fields.'

David had tried to subdue the tide of anxiety that overcame him every time he thought about a life in which he did not see Eloise practically every day of the year. At least while she was in London he had no opportunity to spend time with her, and he wondered whether there were moments when she actually missed his company. It was far too presumptuous to imagine that Miss Eloise had any kind of sentimental feelings for him. Her nature was kind, sweet, thoughtful and caring, but it had crossed his mind more than once that their solitary painting excursions might be misconstrued as being outside the strictures of propriety.

Only occasionally, when by chance his hand might accidentally touch hers, would he see a faint blush of colour in her cheeks, but he put this down to embarrassment rather than reciprocal feelings. Even if he were a man of considerable wealth and impeccable background there was no reason why Eloise should find him attractive. By comparison with Mr Hunter Chislestone, who was a constant visitor to the house, he was neither tall, robust nor handsome, none of which might have mattered so much had he not been the son of a potter.

After the art lover had said his goodbyes and Parson Phillips had taken him off to enjoy refreshments with his wife, David was left alone once more. On the spur of the moment, he decided that he too would write to Eloise and ask her permission to submit his portrait of her to the Academy. No matter how praiseworthy Mr Phillips and his cousin might think it, he would not blame Eloise if she should object to having her image on view to the public.

Two days after tearing up his previous attempts at writing to her, he took out yet again a new sheet of paper and finally succeeded in composing what he felt was a suitable letter. Not without many misgivings, he took it to the postmistress in the village and posted it to Kenilworth House in Mount Street.

Since Storm's ball, letters of appreciation, flowers and invitations had flooded in all week. Hunter had called in person each day. Finally one morning, extremely relieved, he found Eloise alone in the morning room busy arranging one of the many bunches of flowers in a vase. He told her that he was desperate to explain to Storm why his delay at her ball had not been his fault, although she had steadfastly refused to see him.

'For all she has been presented, this is her first season, and Storm is still a child, Hunter.' Eloise explained her sister's stubbornness as, sitting down in a chair by the fireplace, she gestured for him to sit. At that moment a maid entered carrying a tray of coffee which she placed on the table beside Eloise. When she had left the room Eloise continued, 'And she has hero-worshipped you ever since I can remember. Perhaps this is a good thing to have happened and she will start to make closer friends with young men of her own age, such as Tom Fothergill. Of course, he is still too young to be considered a suitor, but in a few years' time . . .' She poured cups of coffee for them both and waited for his reply.

Hunter declined the cup with a shake of his head and his voice was husky as he said quietly, 'I have loved her dearly, Eloise – as much as I love my darling Cissy. I suppose I always knew I was Storm's hero but I never took it seriously when Storm and Cissy giggled together as they planned our wedding!' He grimaced. 'I suppose this would be an appropriate moment for me to bow out of her life. She clearly believed that I cared more about that tiresome American woman's wishes than I did about being at the ball with her. Perhaps it would be best for everyone if I just stayed as far away as possible.' He stood up abruptly and paced across the room and back again. Then he drew a deep sigh. 'You know, Eloise, I am finally having to concede that soon I will no longer be an eligible bachelor useful for making up numbers at dinner parties. I hate to have to tell you this, but our family is insolvent and the London house goes on the market shortly. Chislestone Manor will follow later. I haven't yet told Mama or Cissy but I am praying that they will be able to remain in comfort by the seaside with Mama's friend.'

Eloise rose to her feet. Setting down her cup, she quickly put a gentle hand on Hunter's arm. 'Hunter, I'm so sorry, so very sorry!' she said, shocked by Hunter's confession. She'd known things were bad, but not how bad. The Chislestone family had lived at the manor for at least eight generations and it was inconceivable that the beautiful old family house would in future be inhabited by strangers.

They talked quietly for a few minutes, but Hunter could not settle, and finally excused himself without trying to see Storm.

After Hunter had left, Eloise sat stunned on her own in the morning room trying to fathom a way in which poor Hunter could be helped. She thought perhaps her brother John would be able to lend him some money to tide him over, although it was unlikely he would have such a considerable sum of money set aside. John, meanwhile, was still in the Swiss Alps, where he was supervising their father's care in the sanatorium and enjoying the opportunity to do some mountaineering with the local guides. She and Storm received the occasional letter from him, but he was not at hand to offer his opinion.

The next morning at breakfast, however, when the post was brought in, there was nothing from John but, to Eloise's heart-thudding excitement, she saw David Carter's beautiful italic writing among the letters. Her fingers were trembling as she drew the letter out of its envelope. It was two pages long.

Dear Miss Eloise,

I understand from the parson that you will shortly be receiving a letter from him, and possibly another from his cousin, a Mr Algernon Scott, an art collector. They want your permission, as do I, to submit the oil portrait I have painted of you to the Royal Academy.

Dear Miss Eloise, I am sure you will understand that no artist is ever fully satisfied with his work but, although my portrait is far from perfect, I think I may have been fortunate enough to capture that sweet, caring nature of yours in your expression. I would not, therefore, be ashamed for art lovers to see it, as I think they would understand why I felt compelled to capture you in all your beauty on canvas.

Should you have even the slightest feeling of reluctance for your portrait to leave my possession, I shall not

hesitate to keep it safely with me until I see you, when I
will present it to you for your safe-keeping.

I am trying to curb my impatience, but August, when
you return home and we can resume our painting days
together in the woods and fields, seems too far away. I
think of such days often but expect you are too busy to
do so.

From your devoted servant,
David Carter

Tears filled Eloise's eyes but did not fall as she read the letter
a second time and then clasped it to her fiercely beating heart.
Although the writer had not once used the word 'love', she
could read behind the formal phrases the emotion he was
feeling when he wrote them. For years now she had suspected
that his affection went deeper than that of tutor for pupil, but
she had always tried to bury such thoughts because they so
impossibly mirrored her own. She knew only too well that
marriage between them was not even to be thought about and
that, if her father were well and directing operations at home,
David would have been dismissed long since.

As it was, Hunter had warned her that there was a certain
amount of gossip in the village about the number of times she
was seen alone with David, including their afternoons together
in the countryside. People were only too ready to assume the
worst when there was something to gossip about, despite
the fact that she was now twenty-eight years old and no
longer a young girl in need of a chaperone. Retrospectively,
she thought now, it was short-sighted of her not to have paid
more attention to what others' reactions might be when they
caught sight of her alone with David.

Her mind turned to the request in David's letter for her
permission to enter his portrait of her and have it displayed
to the public. She had had no idea he had been working on
it, so it must be something he had decided to embark upon
when she and Storm had left for London. Momentarily she
caught her breath, realizing that the painting must have
very considerable merit if Reverend Phillips and his art-loving
cousin thought so highly of it. She would not stand in David's

way if its public viewing would be to his advantage. As to whether she would approve the likeness or not, she really did not mind, certain as she was that David would not portray her as ugly or objectionable in any way.

She finished the piece of toast she had been eating and, getting up from the table with her coffee cup in her hand, she walked over to the window and looked down at the busy street below. A knife grinder had stopped next door and a scullery maid was offering him a bundle of kitchen utensils to sharpen. Further up the street she could see a coalman shovelling coal into one of the chutes. A horse-drawn omnibus rattled past the window, two excited children waving from the upper deck.

It was strange to think that life was continuing exactly as it always had, whereas she herself knew she would never feel the same again. It seemed that David's letter, with its undeclared revelation of love, had opened a cage in which her heart had until now been carefully guarded and set it free to express the devotion she felt for him.

Those rare moments of euphoria were of shockingly short duration. A few hours later Eloise was sitting sewing quietly when the door of the morning room opened and Roberts came in carrying a tray on which lay another letter, and this time she recognized Hunter's sprawling handwriting.

'Mr Chislestone delivered this and said he would be calling round to see you in an hour's time, Miss Eloise. He asked me to tell you he is trying to find out more details and to confirm these facts are indeed correct.'

Clearly the butler did not know the contents of the letter, but he hesitated, instinctively guessing there was some urgency. The letter contained the dreadful news that both her father and her brother John had been killed near the Alpine village of St Moritz in a devastating freak late avalanche that had occurred high up in the mountains in May. Further details would become available once the rescuers had managed to get there with their equipment.

Seeing the colour of Eloise's cheeks, Roberts said gently, 'Can I get you anything, Miss Eloise? Cook has made some fresh lemonade, or tea, perhaps?'

Eloise shook her head and dismissed him. Her heart beating

furiously, she clutched the piece of embroidery on her lap and
tried to stem the tears she felt creeping down her cheeks.
Glancing at the pretty French clock on the mantelpiece, she
saw that she must wait another half an hour before Hunter
arrived. She picked up the letter and reread its shocking news.
They had arranged between them that he would cease calling
so regularly to see Storm and, as far as possible, would stay
out of her sister's life until she had faced the fact that Hunter
was far too old for her. But now he had obviously concluded
that the seriousness and urgency of the news about her father
and brother swept aside such considerations, for the sisters
were now certain to need his assistance. She and Storm were
on their own, without male relatives to care for and advise
them, and he was the closest possible lifelong friend and could
act as substitute for one of the girls' brothers. Eloise felt a
rush of gratitude for Hunter's unexpected involvement in this
terrible family tragedy. How, she wondered, had he received
the news of the avalanche before she herself had been advised
of it? Might John, who had been his friend in childhood, have
considered that if anything untoward should happen it would
be better if Hunter broke the news to Eloise, rather than that
she should hear it from official sources? Eloise searched for
a handkerchief, trying to regain her composure.

At that moment the door of the morning room opened again,
and Storm came in looking very pretty wearing her new straw
bonnet tied with a big silk bow under her chin and a periwinkle
blue walking dress with a stylish matching jacket trimmed
with a deeper shade of blue braid. Mabel was not far behind
her carrying a parasol and Storm's gloves.

'I'm off to meet Tom and Petal. Tom has managed to get
tickets for the theatre this afternoon. Mrs Fothergill will be
accompanying us with their widowed aunt,' she told Eloise
excitedly. 'Will you be all right without me?'

The smile left her face as she saw her sister's expression.
She hurried towards Eloise.

'What's wrong, Elly?' she asked anxiously and, seeing the
tears gathering in Eloise's eyes, bent down and put her arms
round her. In all the years she could remember, the only time
she had ever seen her sister cry was when news had arrived

of their brother Andrew's death. Wordlessly, Eloise handed Hunter's letter to her.

She was still doing her best to console Eloise when Hunter was shown into the room. Where an hour earlier her heart would have filled with joy, she now felt an overwhelming feeling of gratitude that he was there to help them cope with this dreadful news. Throughout her life her father had played only the smallest part, his devotion being to his elder daughter. He'd had an instinctive aversion to the baby whose birth had caused Lady Margaret's death, so Storm had grown up taking his lack of interest for granted. Her father's death, therefore, however gruesome, did not really touch her heart. And she had barely had any contact with John, who spent most of his time abroad.

On the rare occasions John had been at Kenilworth Hall it was to talk business with his father, and Storm had seen him only at mealtimes. He was, therefore, all but a stranger to her. Such had been their relationship that his death now, along with her father's, did not affect her greatly although, as she told Hunter, she was horrified at the thought of an avalanche smothering people to death. When Hunter attempted to put an arm round her, supposedly to comfort her, she shook him off, saying in a tightly controlled voice, 'Thank you for your concern but I'm perfectly all right. Who told you about . . . about the accident?' She broke off, hearing her voice tremble a little.

Hunter, sensing her aversion, removed his hand from her shoulder and took Eloise's hands in his. 'The Swiss authorities notified me because a half-written letter was discovered addressed to me, saying how well your father was. The avalanche was too vast to be cleared by hand and the survivors were waiting for rescue workers to reach them. The victims had not yet been identified but one of the survivors found the letter, which he gave to the authorities. They then forwarded it to me along with a note telling me of the disaster. Of course I notified Mr Arbuthnot, your solicitor, and he will call to see you tomorrow morning, if that arrangement suits you.'

Storm now forced herself to look up and meet Hunter's

sympathetic gaze. 'What will happen now? Will they bring
Papa and John home to be buried, or will—'

'I think it may depend on how long it takes for the rescuers
to identify all the victims. You are not to worry your heads
about anything – Mr Arbuthnot and I will arrange whatever
is necessary.'

Instinctively, Storm wanted to throw her arms round Hunter
and let him hug her but at the thought of how terribly he had
let her down over the false promise to be present at her ball,
she stiffened and drew sharply away.

Hunter had wanted to see Storm to explain that it had not
been his fault. The day before the dance he had been in Bath,
where he had been introduced to Mrs Caroline Metcalf, an
extremely wealthy American woman who had shown an
interest in buying land in or near Chislestone. Sensing a
possible purchaser for Chislestone Manor, Hunter had accepted
her invitation to dinner and whist, a card game which he
enjoyed and played well.

That evening, she had insisted upon a continuation of the
game next day in London, where she would organize two
tables. Hunter, she declared, must go to London with her and
they could continue discussing the possibility of her purchasing
some, if not all, of the property.

Retrospectively, Hunter realized that her proposed purchase
of the land was no more than a means of getting to know him
better and, before the first evening was over, of starting a
serious flirtation with him. To her friends, she introduced
him as her 'gorgeous boy' or referred to him as if he were
not there with remarks such as, 'Isn't he just a honey?' And
then she would say with a loud laugh, 'Of course I'm taking
him back to America with me, am I not, honey?'

When Hunter had tried to explain that he could not be one
of the eight whist players she had invited to her hotel rooms
because he was dining elsewhere, she'd taken matters out
of his hands, writing a note for his footman to take round to
Mount Street saying he was detained.

'I'll drive you round there later in my new carriage,' she'd
said. 'Promise!'

But later had turned out to be far into the evening with only the last dance left to be played. Hunter had been stunned by Storm's transformation from child to very attractive young woman, but there had been no opportunity for him to explain matters to her before Mrs Metcalf had made her appearance. Her grip on his arm as she dragged him away was such that, short of creating an embarrassing scene, he'd had no alternative but to go with her.

Now, his thoughts returning to the present, more than anything in the world he longed to take Storm in his arms and hold her. He took a step towards her but, as he did so, the morning room door opened and Roberts announced in his butler's stentorian tones, 'Master Thomas Fothergill is waiting in the hall, Miss Storm. I understand you are due to meet Miss Petal.'

For a split second, Storm stood as still as if she herself were a statue, her eyes fixed on Hunter's face. And then Eloise said gently, 'You run along, my darling. There's nothing you can do here. Hunter will help me take care of everything. We shall be in mourning long enough.'

With a loving but brief hug for her sister, Storm managed to withhold the tears that were about to engulf her and hurried as fast as she decently could from the sight of Hunter's tall, upright figure and the enigmatic look on his handsome face.

TEN

T hree months after the death of Lord Kenilworth, Daniel Collins laid down on the kitchen table the copy of the English newspaper he had been reading and, in a loud voice with a heavy Australian accent, shouted for his wife to join him. He could faintly hear her chattering to the woman next door and his mood changed from excitement to irritation.

When Mildred finally arrived a few minutes later, he banged his fist on the table and shouted, 'I don't expect to sit here waiting while you and that senseless old crone talk your silly heads off, and don't just stand there gaping at me, Mildred! Sit down and read this page of *The Times*.'

Mildred had arrived at the Collins' household as a nurse many years ago when Daniel's mother was dying, had stayed on as housekeeper and eventually, for convenience sake, as his wife. She had been fond of his mother and continued caring for her self-centred bully of a son for her sake. There had never been any children, nor had they been wished for by either of them.

Daniel grabbed the arm of the grey-haired, tired-looking, much-bullied domestic drudge and pulled her closer to the table. The column of print he wanted her to read was a rather dull obituary of an elderly British gentleman by the name of Lord Kenilworth. It also referred to the death of his last surviving son, John, in the same accident in the Swiss Alps some months previously.

'So?' she asked in her quiet, tired voice. 'How is that important? I don't get it!'

Daniel's good humour was now restored and he said eagerly, 'Kenilworth! That's James's father . . . you know, the one he's always telling me about! Bet he hasn't seen the paper . . .'

Mildred gave a derisive laugh as she sat down on the wooden chair by the table. 'James the son of a titled gentleman? You must be joking. I don't know much about gentlefolk but I do know they have clean hands and clean-shaven faces or tidy beards, and look decent. And James is no more gentlemanly than you!'

Daniel pushed back his chair and made as if to rise, his face purple, but as he lifted his arm to strike his wife he caught sight of his hands and stopped as the realization hit him that Mildred was absolutely right. He looked a right mess – just about as unlike a real gentleman's son as he could possibly be.

He put his hands on his knees and did not reply, his eyes thoughtful, his mind working furiously. The last surviving son . . . That meant there wasn't a male heir. In the obituary it said that Lord Kenilworth had left his entire estate to the elder of his two daughters; they would be James's half-sisters if he really was Lord Kenilworth's son. But as it was eldest sons who inherited, the daughters didn't matter. All that mattered was that Lord Kenilworth did not have any male cousins or other such relatives who might have a stronger claim than James did.

He had known James Smithers since they had met at the age of eight at the school where Daniel's father, Mark Collins, was headmaster. James was a rather shy, sad child with a bad stammer, almost certainly caused by the fact that his stepfather, the mathematics master at the school, constantly berated him for being almost innumerate.

Daniel was also an outcast, his schoolfriends believing that his good marks were due to his relationship with his father. As a result, the two eight-year-olds had become close friends and supported each other.

Now in their forties, they still saw each other but only occasionally. He had no real affection for James, but he had always been intrigued by his stories about the titled family from which he was an outcast. James showed him his birth certificate, which named a baron called Lord John Kenilworth as his father, and a marriage certificate. He also recalled an old variety theatre programme James had kept, in which his mother had been listed as one of the performers. On the inside page was an image of a pretty chorus girl. Scrawled across the foot of the dog-eared page had been the words, *From your precious Lily to her adoring JLK.*

At first, when he was a boy, James's accounts of his birthright were limited, but when he was grown up he had been told by his mother, on her deathbed, the full story of his origin.

When she was a beautiful young actress, the wealthy bachelor John Kenilworth, who had not yet inherited his father's title, had set her up as his mistress, his youthful adoration continuing for several years. Then, suddenly, he had met Lady Margaret Stormont, the most beautiful debutante of her year, and fallen in love with her. It was, James's mother had related, the most terrible moment of her life when her lover had told her he was going to be married to Lady Margaret, because she also had news for him: she was pregnant.

Tearfully, as she lay on her deathbed, James's mother informed him that his father, by then Lord Kenilworth, had done the honourable thing and married her in Scotland, where he'd ostensibly taken her for a holiday. On their return south, he had bought her a ticket to Australia and given her a very large sum of money to support herself and the child for the foreseeable future. He had made her put her hand on the Bible and swear never to try to contact him again unless she were in the direst of circumstances. In that case she was to write a letter addressed to him but signed by an invented male friend living in Australia, inviting him to visit.

His mother, James had told Daniel, had never had occasion to do so. Soon after his birth she had married his stepfather Roger Smithers, a mathematics master at a new school run by the Jesuits, and this meant there had been no necessity for her to ask for financial support. True to her promise to John Kenilworth, she had forbidden James ever to make contact with his real father or his family.

Daniel toyed with a wooden spoon on the table as his mind sought to find a way in which he could capitalize on James's extraordinary relationship with the English aristocracy. He was in little doubt that James was indeed Kenilworth's child;

James had shown him both his birth certificate and his mother's marriage certificate some years ago.

He banged his spoon noisily, causing Mildred to start as it flashed through his mind that, if he were in possession of both documents, he could impersonate James Smithers and claim to be Lord Kenilworth's legitimate heir.

The enthusiasm at the prospect of possible wealth and prestige which had lit up his face soon gave way to uncertainty. James would surely notice if those certificates went missing, and would quickly discover that he, Daniel, was impersonating him. It would be naive to suppose that James himself would claim his rightful inheritance and be willing to share the kudos and financial benefits with him. He sighed as it crossed his mind that if only James had died recently he might have been able to impersonate him without danger of discovery.

Daniel sat up suddenly and gripped the arms of the kitchen chair. Did he really care as much for his friend as Mildred thought? In fact, he and James were two loners who had always found it extremely difficult to form friendships with other men of their age. James had left school with few qualifications and had started a sheep farm some miles out of town, where he lived an isolated life with which he always seemed content. Daniel himself had reluctantly followed his father into the teaching profession but had recently retired early from his position as a somewhat unsuccessful English teacher in order to pursue his woodworking hobby, and from that he scraped a living.

He had few other friends, and it had become a habit to ride out to James's farm from time to time, more to get away from Mildred's nagging than because he actually enjoyed James's company. There was not and never had been any genuine affection between them.

His hands tightened their grip on the chair as he stared unseeingly across the room. Could he . . . dare he . . . cause an accident of some kind that would paralyse James? Do something that would make speech impossible? Do something, anything, that would enable him to impersonate James and claim the inheritance?

Mildred had started her daily mopping of the kitchen floor. Needing time to think quietly away from his wife, Daniel got up and, with a muttered curse, went out into the garden, to his woodworking shed. It contained a worm-eaten old rocking chair where he would sit to escape Mildred's endless complaints about the poor conditions in which they lived, which she knew he could afford to improve were he not set upon adding to his savings. He had married her for convenience rather than love, and her increasing nagging had turned his weak affection to dislike. Settling in the rocking chair, he thought with a grimace that if ever he were to get to England in James's place, he would certainly not take Mildred with him.

He sighed and tried to think of a way in which he could get hold of the certificates and get James out of the way. Obviously, he should not draw his attention to the obituary in case his friend realized he had a fortune at his fingertips. Was it possible, he asked himself, that somehow or other James could be made to fall off his horse and suffer a blow to his head that would render him unconscious? A blow heavy enough to damage his brain?

Even as the possibility occurred to him, he realized that it would be impossible to guarantee that James would not recover from such a fall, and that he would have to think of some other way to get rid of him.

Suddenly Daniel's heart rate trebled as a shocking thought flashed into his mind: James must be killed. It was the only way. He must be silenced for ever.

Daniel's heartbeat slowed; his instant attraction to such an idea gave way to doubt. Could he really be contemplating the death of the man who had been his lifelong friend? Would he really not care if he never saw James again? Would it not concern him to think that he was actually a murderer? Momentarily he did feel fear, but then the prospect of what he could achieve if he had the nerve to put an end to James's life swung his thoughts back to the possibility of doing so. Not a fall from his horse, but a single blow to the back of his head, and then he would push him off the roof of his farmhouse, from which he would remove a couple of tiles.

Daniel's excitement now consumed his whole body and the possibilities raced through his mind. He would tell Mildred that he was going fishing. He would have lunch with James as planned and somehow get possession of the certificates. Then he would leave, spend the late afternoon and evening fishing and, when it was dark, return to the farmhouse, smother James and throw him out of the bedroom window so that it appeared that he had fallen from the roof. He would then go up to the roof, remove two or three tiles, disturb the guttering over which James would ostensibly have fallen and return home in the early hours. If Mildred remarked upon his late return he would simply tell her that the fishing had been bad and he had stayed on hoping to catch more in the light of a bright moon which had lit up the waters of the river – all to no avail.

Daniel got up from his chair and went out into the garden, where he tried to come to terms with the thoughts racing through his brain. Was such a crazy scheme as he had been considering possible? Was he strong enough to lift James's unconscious body and throw it out of the window? Might he be seen by one of James's farmhands – who were billeted in a shed not more than fifty yards distant – returning to or leaving the farmhouse in the dark? There were a great many 'ifs', not least whether he could persuade James to show him the two certificates again, thus affording him the opportunity to find out where they were kept. Even supposing it all worked out in his favour, he would be ill-advised to leave Australia too quickly.

Bending down absent-mindedly to pull a large weed from Mildred's vegetable bed, his mind racing, he thought further that the safest course of action would be to write to the Kenilworth estate manager. He would say that he had read the obituary and, realizing he must be the legitimate heir, was arranging to sail to England as soon as possible; upon his arrival, he would take the necessary action to establish his relationship with Lord Kenilworth's daughter and produce the necessary documents to prove his case.

First, of course, he would have to think of a safe way to kill James.

England, 1856

It was a beautiful sunny morning, so warm that David Carter suggested the York stone terrace outside the dining room window of Kenilworth Hall would be the perfect place for him and Eloise to do their painting. The chestnut trees lining the drive were displaying canopies of green leaves and the grass verges below were still awash with wild flowers.

Storm had left soon after breakfast to spend the day at the Fothergills, where she and Petal were to play a morning game of shuttlecock on the newly cut grass. It had taken Petal quite a lot of time and feminine cajoling to persuade the gardener the day before that the grass was dry enough to be cut with the newfangled mechanical mower. Storm was, of course, in mourning for her father and brother and her social activities were limited. She had lately spent a few days with Cissy at the seaside, and during the visit she had learned that Hunter was on the verge of selling the family home.

'To a rich American woman!' was all Cissy could relate, tears filling her eyes as she did so.

Just for a fleeting second, Storm had wondered if the prospective purchaser could be the same woman who had so rudely turned up at her coming-out ball and claimed Hunter as if he had been her property! But that had been weeks ago and the last letter she had received from Cissy said that there had been no further news from Hunter of the sale.

Bitterly, Storm concluded that he was probably having an affair with the American and that it had been entirely wishful thinking when, during the few brief moments that he'd held her against him in the waltz, she had imagined that he'd actually fallen in love with her. She'd mentioned none of this to Cissy or, indeed, to Petal, and had been happy to continue the flirtation with the happy-go-lucky Tom until he had to return to university for his examinations. As for the death of her father and brother, she had shed no false tears and, unlike the weeping Eloise, was dry-eyed when Mr Arbuthnot, the solicitor, read Lord Kenilworth's will to them.

No one, of course, had dreamed that the wealthy land-owner might conceivably leave his worldly goods to a female member of the family. However, as there were no surviving male relatives, it was natural that he should have left the estate to his elder daughter. With Andrew's death all those years ago and John abroad for such long periods, it had been Eloise who had sat with him and with their estate manager each week going through accounts and future activities. In fact, as alcohol had got the better of her father, it had always been Eloise who made the final decisions on what should or should not be done.

'Miss Kenilworth, you are now a very rich and eligible young lady!' the solicitor had cautioned, adding that she must be wary of unsavoury suitors. At first his remark had made Eloise smile, but then it had occurred to her that he might have been warning her against David Carter, and she had felt deeply worried and upset.

She now faced the fact that it was only a matter of time before she would have to call a halt to David's daily visits. She no longer denied to herself that they loved one another and that both were behaving unduly stiffly lest they give the truth away by some thoughtless look or touch.

She followed him out now on to the sunlit terrace and silently set up her easel alongside his. They had barely arranged their sketch pads, jars of water and paints when a horseman came cantering up the drive. It was the parson's groom. Dismounting, he bade Eloise good morning and then tied the reins over the hitching post, walked up the side steps leading from the drive to the terrace and, crossing the terrace, handed the tutor a package. Hurriedly opening it, David found two letters inside which he read silently: one from the parson himself congratulating David, and the other a letter from the Academy saying that David's portrait of Eloise had won the prize.

Congratulations, Carter, the covering letter said.

This has just arrived addressed to me as your sponsor. The authorities are anxious to get in touch with you as soon as possible, and The Times *newspaper wishes*

*to interview you prior to the presentation of the
award.*

*I am delighted for you but never had the slightest
doubt as to your ability as an artist. If Miss Kenilworth
can spare you, perhaps you would return to the house
and we can discuss your journey to London.*

'Reverend said as to waste no time bringing this to you,'
announced the groom with a broad smile. 'Said as how it was
splendid news.'

David remained where he was, the letters in his hand.
His face was white with shock, but quickly suffused with
colour when Eloise held out her hand and asked gently if she
might read the news.

'Of course, you must go to London straight away,' she
told him once she'd read the contents, her eyes shining. 'If I
were not in mourning I would accompany you. How kind of
Reverend Phillips to send word so quickly!' Her cheeks glowing,
she added, 'You can stay at Mount Street. Most of the servants
have returned here with us but the under-housekeeper, Miss
Hibbert, is still there with a skeleton staff. I will give you a
note for her saying she is to prepare one of the bedrooms for
you and to see you have hot water and food. You must take
the carriage as I shall not be needing it. Oh, dear, I do so wish
I could come with you. I haven't even glimpsed this portrait
of me yet!'

David had been silent until now, but when Eloise stopped
talking he said quietly, 'It's very kind of you to offer the
accommodation and the carriage, but I have no wish to go to
London. Of course I am proud and delighted my portrait of
you has been so well received, but I painted it for my own
pleasure and I'm sure there must be many other submissions
as worthy as mine, if not more so.'

For a moment, Eloise all but forgot the presence of the
parson's groom and reached over to David in order to take
his hand in hers. Remembering in the nick of time that such
intimacies were not the done thing and might have disastrous
results for them both, she merely held out her hands in
supplication. 'Of course you must go, Mr Carter. You will

now be one of our famous English artists. People will want to meet you, talk to you. Maybe they will want you to paint their portraits. You cannot hide away from the world now! Why, if you will not go to London to see them, they might come down here to see you!'

David's voice was quite calm as he said in a quiet, controlled voice, 'I want neither recognition nor riches, Miss Eloise. If I am to forgo any part of my present life as a result of this painting, then I shall be forced to wish I had never put brush to canvas in order to commemorate your likeness for eternity.'

He broke off and turned to the groom, who was staring at him open-mouthed. 'Please thank Mr Phillips most kindly for his letter and its enclosure, and tell him that I will not be going to London and will return at supper time as usual. Now, Miss Eloise, we have already wasted enough of this beautiful morning, and I suggest that we start work without further delay.'

When Storm returned at teatime and heard news of the morning's events, she was shocked. There could be only one reason why David Carter would not have jumped at the chance of fame and fortune, and that was his desire to remain close to Eloise. As for her sister, Eloise was glowing with pride, as happy for David's success as if he were her child – or her husband! That afternoon, disregarding her own vow to treat Hunter as if he did not exist, Storm wrote him a letter telling him that he must somehow find a way to protect Eloise.

> *She is falling deeper and deeper in love and I fear that*
> *it will not be much longer before my darling sister*
> *commits some dreadful folly. As it is, her indiscretions*
> *are becoming ever more noticeable and I fear for her.*
> *I hope there is some way you can help. Storm.*

She gave the letter to the post boy when he called with the afternoon mail, and extracted a promise that it would be on its way to London in the mail coach later that day. At the same time, she feared that there was very little Hunter could do to prevent her darling Eloise from slipping into any further danger.

It would be a while before Hunter could conclude his business affairs in London, by which time Storm and Eloise had gone down to Lancing to spend a seaside holiday with Cissy and their mother. He would have to discuss Eloise's situation there.

ELEVEN

Lancing, Sussex. December, 1856

I t was an unusually fine December afternoon and Cissy, Storm and Eloise were sitting together on the beach in the shelter of the bathing machines enjoying the winter sunshine and out of the cold wind gusting from the sea. The beach at Lancing was conveniently situated at the foot of Lady Clarice Witton's house, where Cissy and her mother were still living. Negotiations for the sale of Chislestone Manor were dragging on with no firm decisions made, and Hunter had thought it best for his mother and sister to remain where they were until they knew what was to happen to their home. Lady Witton, a widow too, was pleased to have their company.

Storm was currently enjoying a visit to her best friend, and Eloise had accompanied her. Storm was, she had told both Eloise and Cissy, bored to tears with the mourning restrictions – the more so, as she admitted to Cissy, because she could not bring herself to grieve over the deaths of two relatives who had been almost strangers to her throughout her childhood.

When suddenly Cissy lifted her arm and pointed to a tall male figure approaching, Storm looked up without interest – and then caught her breath. It was Hunter, looking incredibly handsome in a caped greatcoat and breeches and gleaming hessians, striding purposefully across the beach towards them, turning many a female head as he did so.

'Lady Witton said I'd find you all here!' he said, bending to kiss Cissy's cheek. Quickly, Storm turned her face away and bent to pick up a pebble and lob it towards the sea, lapping the sand a dozen feet away.

'Storm!' Hunter's voice was quite sharp. 'I've come down to see you and Eloise – as well as Cissy, of course – because I have something I feel might be quite important to discuss with you. To have your advice – may I have your attention?' Then he turned to Cissy, and in a softer voice said, 'This won't interest you, dearest, so why don't you go back to the house?'

Cissy, unwilling to be parted from her beloved brother so soon after his arrival, nevertheless reluctantly did as he bid. She gestured to her nurse, who was sitting on a bench nearby with her knitting chatting to one of the maids, to bring the chair, and after she was safely installed they disappeared up the beach. Eloise looked up at Hunter and said anxiously, 'What is it, Hunter? It sounds serious.'

With an effort, Storm looked up at him. For weeks now she had been telling herself that not only had she stopped loving him, she actually hated him. Now she had only to hear his deep baritone voice to realize that nothing had changed. He was the only man who could ever affect her in this way. She steeled herself to look at him. 'So what is the problem, Hunter? I must say I am surprised that you are asking for my advice!'

Hunter concealed a sudden smile. 'No, my sweet, not really your advice, but your memory. Can either you or Eloise recall whether at any time in your childhood anyone in the family ever mentioned someone called James – possibly a relative – who came from Australia?'

Storm forgot about her relationship with Hunter and shook her head. 'Not that I can think of, although there was an occasional foreigner – schoolfriends of our brothers. Eloise, you would remember better than me as you were allowed to mix with the grown-ups.'

Hunter now sat down beside them on the steps of the bathing machine and stretched out his long legs. He was silent for a moment before he spoke. 'I must tell you both that I am not a little concerned. You see, your housekeeper in London informed me that a stranger had arrived there, purporting to be a close relative of yours. Miss Hibbert gave him my name as a family friend, and at his request I met him at Brown's in Albemarle Street for a drink. He told me that he is your half-brother. He says that your father married his mother, an actress, and when your father fell in love with your mother, his mother was shipped off to Australia where, he claims, he was born.

His mother apparently then married a schoolmaster called Smithers, so he grew up with that name. He professes to be, legally, James Kenilworth. On seeing your father's obituary in *The Times* and reading that he had no male heir, he set off for England to assume responsibility for the family.'

Both girls gasped, too shocked to speak. Then Storm caught her breath, saying, 'But that's ridiculous. How could Father have married our mother when he already had a wife? I never heard a more unlikely story. Anyway, ever since the beginning of Father's illness, Eloise has managed our estate, haven't you, darling? As a young girl I used to find you in Father's study going through the account ledgers with Jenkins. Father willed the estate to you, didn't he, Eloise?'

Hunter nodded but remained silent. He did not feel able to recount to these two innocent girls that if, by any chance, the story was true, Lord Kenilworth would have been a bigamist and his children illegitimate. He certainly did not divorce his first wife; that would have entailed huge publicity in the High Court, where the case would have been heard, and afterwards he would not have been allowed to marry Lady Margaret. He supposed that Lord Kenilworth might have felt obliged to marry the chorus girl after he had made her pregnant.

Hunter glanced anxiously at the girls' faces as he recalled that the man calling himself James Kenilworth had declared that he had in his possession the certificates for both his mother's marriage and his own birth, which would prove his claim if he were obliged to take it to court.

'He intends to come and see you at the hall, Eloise,' he told her, 'and I would like to be there when he does so.'

He had known Lord Kenilworth since boyhood and found it impossible to believe that the man was a bigamist. Was it possible, he wondered, that Lord Kenilworth could have obtained a divorce elsewhere? In another country? Lord Kenilworth had been such an upright man, respected by all who knew him. Drink had ultimately been his downfall, and so it was possible that the man had been trying to drown the memories of his illicit past as he neared the end of his life.

Hunter had taken a strong, instinctive dislike to the Australian and believed him to be an imposter. If the fellow took his claim to court he must ensure that Eloise had a really first-class barrister.

He picked up a pebble and threw it towards the waves as Eloise now hesitantly confessed the news that she had already received a letter from the Australian, just before she left home with Storm to spend a few days with Cissy at Lancing. He had referred to himself as a distant relative, she told Hunter, and made no mention of his actual relationship to the family.

'So I had no reason not to invite him down to lunch at Kenilworth Hall in two weeks' time,' she continued quietly.

Hunter was shocked. 'Eloise, I don't believe the fellow's story, and I have insisted he shows me his birth certificate and his mother's marriage certificate, which he claims to have in his possession. He knows I am staying at my club so he can bring them there. We met at Brown's but I do not know where he is residing. He must have taken lodgings. I would very much like to be present at the luncheon.'

Eloise clasped her hands together and shook her head, insisting that there was no need. 'I cannot believe that he is claiming to be our half-brother. You must have misunderstood him, Hunter. That would be impossible and it is far more likely that he is a distant cousin. I shall find out the truth when I meet him. There really is no need for you to be there. He may have realized you didn't believe his story and he will speak more freely if you are not there. Storm and I can come to no harm hearing what he has to say.'

Ignoring Hunter's unspoken protest, Storm said, 'In any case, of course, it is quite ridiculous. I think you are right, Eloise. Father never mentioned that he had another son.'

Eloise's eyes were thoughtful. 'Those babies listed in the family tree, the ones who died at birth before John and Andrew were born – maybe one of them did survive after all. Perhaps he was a "black sheep" of the family, banished by Father for some serious misdemeanour, which is why we never knew about him before. But this is being fanciful,' she added, 'and I am not prepared to refuse to meet him. It would not be fair.'

Storm opened her mouth to speak again but, seeing the expression on Hunter's face, she closed it. Hunter was very, very far from being stupid. If he believed this man to be an imposter, perhaps he might indeed be so. Eloise was so sweet-natured and trusting that she must make certain that her darling sister was not duped.

It was only when the three of them had returned to Lady Clarice's house for tea that Storm had a chance to draw Hunter to one end of the large drawing room and talk to him alone. Standing by the open casement, she said quietly, 'I know you are worried about this man, Hunter, and I will ensure that I am with Eloise when he comes and can hear what he has to say. Eloise is too trusting; I fear her judgement may be undermined by the fact that she thinks of little else but Mr Carter and the success of his portrait of her. I wish that she had agreed to have you there too, but I shall of course advise you of what transpires.'

'I heard someone mention her portrait at my club last week,' Hunter replied.

'It seems more and more people are going to view it,' said Storm. 'And he even received a letter from an art lover who wanted to buy it. I have not yet been to London to see it. Have you seen it, Hunter?'

Hunter's expression changed as he said, 'Yes, I went to look at it last week. It is quite remarkable. Somehow he seems to have captured the . . . the inner essence of your sister. I can't quite explain what it is – sort of the epitome of femininity. If one were not already aware that the artist who painted her was in love with her, it would be obvious, just from seeing the portrait. I have read your letter.'

After a brief pause, Storm said, 'I'm so afraid she is in love with him, Hunter, and there is no doubt that he loves her.'

Hunter nodded. 'Yes, I agree! However, I am hoping that the success of his painting will eventually necessitate his moving elsewhere. If he is to establish his career he needs a proper studio and the time and money to travel, if he so wishes, to paint whatever takes his fancy. Artists need freedom.'

'I hope you're right,' Storm replied. She grimaced and continued earnestly, 'Meanwhile, do you think that the Australian really is my father's eldest child? Would that mean we would have to welcome him into the family?'

Hunter hesitated. 'According to the story he told me he is

the eldest, and he says he can prove it. If the certificates are indeed genuine then I am afraid we do have a serious problem to deal with.'

He added, 'One thing is certain: I told the fellow that before his claim goes any further, the two certificates will have to be validated. I advised him against the expense of employing a lawyer at this point in time as I feel it is my responsibility to undertake these checks on behalf of your family. I may be quite wrong but I had the impression that he was very far from being a man of wealth or of aristocratic background. I know Australians have a different accent to ours, but he seemed to me to be lacking in refinement. Far from being a wealthy landowner, he spoke of having a farm with some sheep on it.'

Storm turned her eyes away from Hunter's patrician face. She felt a sudden, violent desire to hurt him as he had hurt her. Without stopping to reconsider her remark, she said, 'Should we hold it against him, Hunter, that he doesn't own a big estate? Do you not think that now you are having to sell your family home, you might have become slightly obsessed about the loss? Surely no one will consider *you* unrefined when you no longer own Chislestone Manor.'

Hunter was immediately aware of the sting behind Storm's words, and understood that she had still not forgiven him for failing to turn up at her party. Holding her beautiful, slender young body in his arms during that last waltz, he'd been very aware of her feelings for him and seriously conscious of the effect that this newly adult young woman was having on him. He had always loved her – as a little sister – but that was different. Seeing her now in the simple primrose yellow muslin dress, however, her eyes darkening, her voice bordering on unfriendly, he saw her once more as the little girl who was Cissy's best friend, stamping her foot because he would not take her up with him on his horse.

Ignoring her remark, he referred to the matter more immediately disturbing him, namely that Eloise had been surprisingly adamant in saying she did not wish him to be present when she had the Australian to luncheon. He now asked Storm if she thought she could get Eloise to reconsider her decision.

But Storm was no longer sympathetic to his wishes. 'I really can't see what you are bothering about, Hunter!' she interrupted in a cold voice. 'Apart from the fact that Eloise is not stupid, she has Mr Carter hanging around most days. It's perfectly obvious she is in love with him, so she is not likely to give this so-called relative much of a welcome.'

Hunter accepted what he understood was his dismissal without argument; nevertheless, he was determined to keep his eye on this James Kenilworth's activities. He turned back towards the others.

Aware of the sudden tension between the two people she loved most in the world, Cissy called to him. 'Have there been any developments regarding our home, Hunter? It must be nearly four months since you told us the rich American lady said she wanted to buy our estate.'

Hunter walked across the room and sat on the sofa beside his sister. Glad he was no longer facing Storm, he hid his embarrassment at the mention of the American woman Mrs Caroline Metcalf. He could recall all too clearly, as doubtless could Storm, her strident voice reproaching him for keeping her waiting while he danced with Storm. There was no denying that the continuing delay over the purchase of his home was due to the fact that she was hoping he would come with the property. Quite blatantly, she told him that she was 'crazy about him', as she put it, and wanted him to stay on as her husband and master. She had even gone so far as to say, one evening when they had been in her hotel lounge drinking cocktails, that she had not at first been all that enthusiastic about living so far out in the country and that Chislestone Manor was not sufficiently modernized for her taste. But on her first meeting with Hunter, when his agent was showing her around the house, she had instantly made up her mind to go ahead and buy the property provided Hunter went with it.

His eyes turning towards the two older girls, Hunter debated how much of the truth he could tell them. Innocent as they both were, it was unlikely they had ever before come across a predatory woman – in Mrs Metcalf's case, a widow – who was prepared to spend such a fortune simply to acquire the presence of a man she was physically attracted to but who showed no reciprocal feelings. When challenged by Mrs Metcalf, Hunter had admitted that he was not in love with any other female but was committed to marry his sister's best friend, Storm, when she was old enough. Needless to say, Mrs Metcalf had been indefatigable – embarrassingly so – and refused to take such a promise seriously, dragging on the negotiations for the manor in the hope that Hunter might yet agree to her terms rather than allow the sale of his estate to fall through.

He turned back to his sister, who was sitting quietly beside him. 'You are quite right, Cissy,' he said gently. 'The prospective buyer has really had long enough to make a decision, and it is my intention to tell the good lady that I will be asking my agent to put the estate back on the market if she has not made up her mind to purchase it by the end of the month.'

Cissy felt considerable distress whenever the sale of her home was mentioned, but her love for her brother was more important than anything else, so she hid her deepest feelings from him. 'I'm sure someone else will turn up soon,' she said gently. 'Meanwhile, Mama and Lady Clarice seem to be getting along very well together.'

She made no mention of the tears her mother shed whenever the sale of the house was mentioned, or her still more sorrowful tears when her late husband or sons were spoken about. She grieved mostly for Percy, whose body had never been found and who had died so young in that horrible gold mine in California, his last treasured letter saying joyfully that there was every indication the mine was about to reveal two gold seams which would make him and his partner both millionaires. Cissy hated to think of her brother's body lying among the dirt and ruins of his dreams.

She looked lovingly at Hunter, always her favourite and mercifully in splendid health. She just wished he were not so worried, not just about the family financial situation but also about Eloise, and about his current relationship with Storm. She wished she could persuade Storm to forgive him his absence at her ball.

Belatedly his mother came into the room with Lady Clarice, apologizing for the fact that they had been delayed.

Hunter, standing up, said, 'I have to return to London shortly, Mama. I wanted to see you and Cissy and assure myself that you were both in good health, but I hope to be returning very soon with more positive news. I imagine you and Lady Clarice are enjoying this lovely weather and I am happy to see Cissy looking so well.'

He turned to look at Eloise and Storm, commenting that they, too, were apparently benefiting from the seaside breezes. 'I will see you both at Kenilworth Hall when I meet Jenkins about estate affairs next week.'

For the fleetest of seconds Storm nearly turned to face Hunter, her expression no longer rigid. With every fibre of her being she wanted to catch hold of his hands, beg him not to go so soon, to stay, if only long enough to tell her that he did love her – that the American woman meant nothing to him and that it was she, Storm, who mattered to him in the same devastating way he mattered to her. She loved him. She always had and she always would. There was no point in trying to believe otherwise.

Eloise got up from her chair and put her arms around him. 'You are always welcome, Hunter, as you know,' she said fondly. 'Is he not, Storm?'

Nodding briefly, Storm turned quickly away as if something had caught her attention and stood staring unseeingly at the bleak sea in the distance. She was actually hiding the telltale tears stinging her eyes.

It really was ridiculous that he felt so perturbed by Storm's hostility, Hunter thought when he climbed into his curricle half an hour later. Although now he understood that he had let her down badly by not turning up as she had hoped the night of her ball, he did not see this as a valid reason for her continuing antagonistic attitude towards him. And yes, he told himself, it was natural that he should be upset, but it disturbed him to such a degree that he was impatient with himself.

Storm turned hurriedly away before Hunter's curricle disappeared at the end of the promenade. Then, forcing a smile to her face which belied the searing pain that was engulfing her heart, she returned to Cissy's side.

TWELVE

December, 1856

'Elly, darling, please don't cry! It will be all right; you can write to each other . . .'

Storm broke off as she realized how inadequate her efforts to comfort her sister were. How could words on paper replace the hours of companionship Eloise and their tutor had shared these past years? Their separation was almost as poignant as if they had been a married couple.

She drew a long sigh. There was, she knew, no solution to Eloise's distress. David Carter had been obliged to leave Chislestone and Kenilworth Hall for ever when Reverend Phillips, David's sponsor and friend, had felt obliged to banish him. The rumours about Eloise's relationship with her tutor, who spent most of his waking hours at her side, had gathered momentum as news of David Carter's fame as a portrait painter had spread. Eloise's reputation would shortly be in shreds, the reverend had said, and he had to put the moral welfare of his parishioners first. David Carter must leave.

Storm had not been present at their parting a few days previously. Eloise, at first dry-eyed, had informed her that she did indeed love David, and he her, but she could not have gone away with him to get married, and anyway he would not even consider such a thing, virtually penniless as he was. The fact that Eloise had more than enough money to keep them both in comparative luxury made no difference.

As far as Eloise knew, if he had not already done so, he was moving up to London to a residential college which had offered him a job as a teacher. So far she had had one letter from him, which ended with protestations of his undying affection, and it was this which had caused Eloise's tears.

'Elly, you must stop crying. Our visitor will be here in half an hour.'

Eloise dried her eyes with her handkerchief and smoothed back her hair. 'I don't see how it is possible that Father married anyone else but Mama.'

'He might have done so, Elly,' Storm said. 'He might have fallen in love with someone before he met Mama, when he was very young. People can fall in love before they are old enough to realize they are making a mistake.'

The way she had fallen in love with Hunter, she thought bitterly. She might even have married him if he had asked her. There was no likelihood now of that ever happening. The possibility was a ridiculous pipe dream, and had of late become a hundred times more improbable. Eloise had told her that Hunter had been seeing even more of the American Caroline Metcalf, who might solve his financial problems if she were to buy his estate. In that case he would not lose his precious Chislestone Manor and his mother and Cissy would retain their home.

With an effort, Storm dragged her thoughts back to the present and the Australian stranger who was expected at any moment. He was coming down from London by train to lunch with them. Hunter had described him as a somewhat rough character, lacking the refinements of a gentleman. She and Eloise had agreed that they would not hold that against him if he were indeed a relative. If that was so, Eloise declared, he deserved their friendship.

As the Kenilworth coach drew to a halt at the steps of Kenilworth Hall, Daniel Collins's heart increased its pace. The house was even more imposing than he had imagined and, armed with the knowledge that only the older of the two girls stood between him and ultimate ownership of the magnificent estate, he felt close to euphoria as he walked up the steps and knocked on the front door.

A stiff, upright figure – presumably the butler, he thought – opened the door and took his coat, hat, gloves and walking stick before advancing slowly across the hall to an open double door and announcing his arrival to the occupants. When he entered, the large drawing room fire was ablaze, and the room was filled with vases of winter pine and witch hazel, producing a beautiful smell of the country. The two young women who stood up to greet him were elegantly dressed in frocks of grey and violet velvet, which were stylish in spite of their sober colours; the sisters were obviously still in half-mourning and the elder was wearing a black lace cap. Everything in the room exuded wealth and good taste, from the huge pictures on the walls depicting garden scenes to the thick rug in front of the magnificent marble fireplace, and Daniel was conscious that, before long, all this might be his.

During luncheon, he told the girls that although they had known nothing of his existence, he had been aware of theirs. He had badly wanted to get in touch with the family of half-brothers and sisters ever since he was a young child, he told them, but his mother had forbidden it. She had been devoted to their father, he related, and had promised him that she would never get in touch with him or permit their son to do so.

Eloise felt sympathetic towards him; this explained why they had not known of his existence until after their father had died.

What Daniel did not mention was the date of the marriage, or that of his birth. Mr Chislestone, that fellow Hunter who professed to be the girls' guardian, had forbidden him to refer to the dates on the two certificates.

At first, his reaction had been to disregard any interference from Hunter, unrelated as the man was to the Kenilworths, and he had considered withholding the two precious certificates from him. Then, realizing that they would undoubtedly be checked by anyone verifying his claim, he decided that Hunter was less likely to be as thorough as a lawyer might be. Moreover, the man had explained that he wished to protect the two girls from realizing that not only was their father a bigamist but they were illegitimate. Hunter was obviously hoping that he would turn out to be an imposter. Daniel was confident that the two certificates would verify his claim and it was only a matter of time before he supplanted Miss Eloise Kenilworth as Lord Kenilworth's rightful heir.

Ever since Hunter had first mentioned the Australian and his claim to be a family member, Eloise had pondered on the situation. The more she thought about the man's birth, the more she realized that this whole unhappy situation was not of his making. If his unlikely story turned out to be true, there was no reason why he should not be welcomed into the family in the same way as an unknown distant cousin.

'It appears you have extensive gardens,' Daniel was saying. 'I would so love to see more of the English countryside. I have never been to England before and I have only seen London, so I had no idea of the beauty of this area.'

Eloise smiled. 'Then you must come and stay if you can prolong your visit, or if you do not have the time now you could visit us in the spring. We could show you the estate and you could meet our neighbours.' She smiled at him again. 'Shall we call you Cousin James for the time being? It would avoid a lot of questioning by the servants and our friends, should you meet them!'

On his arrival Daniel had, without prior thought, given his name to the butler as Mr James Kenilworth, as he now told Eloise, but he was quite happy to be called 'cousin' for the time being. With some difficulty he ignored the expression on the younger girl's face. Her name fitted her very well, he thought wryly.

Storm asked bluntly, 'What is the purpose of your visit now, Cousin James? Were you simply curious to meet my sister and me?'

Daniel leaned forward in his chair, ignoring the unfriendly tone of Storm's voice, which was bordering on impertinence. 'I can assure you there have been many, many times when I longed to meet my real family. My stepfather was a good, kindly man who provided me with an excellent education, but from time to time there would be a brief reference to the Kenilworths in the English society columns and I would be filled with longing to meet you all. But as I said, my dear mother would not allow it.'

'Yet you have come all this way to see Eloise and me now – the only two remaining members of our family,' Storm said.

Daniel was unperturbed. 'My dear, it was a matter of the sad circumstances of your father's death, along with your brother's. I knew my presence could no longer be an embarrassment to him. I felt compelled to come and see for myself whether you two orphaned daughters were finding it difficult to manage so large an estate without male guidance.'

Before Eloise could reply, Storm said quickly, 'Did Mr Chislestone, our close friend and neighbour, not tell you that he is always on hand if my sister needs help or guidance?'

Daniel quickly recovered. 'Yes, of course, a charming gentleman. I understood from your coachman, who met me at the railway station, that your neighbour has to sell his property; that the estate is in financial difficulties. How dreadful for him to lose his birthright! Tell me, do you know if there are any small cottages which might be sold with the land, as I do not wish to impose on you? If so, I would seek to purchase one where I could come and stay during your summer months. I do so dislike our Australian winters, although they are not as extreme as yours.'

Having finished the meal, Eloise and Storm stood up, and as he rose to follow them from the dining room he looked at Eloise, who was showing none of Storm's negative reaction. His earlier impression of her as a sweet, gentle young woman was justified. Although she was past the usual age for marriage (but not yet with the spinster's 'life-has-passed-me-by' look) she was, in fact, bordering on beautiful – sad, but beautiful. Unhappy love affair? he wondered. As far as he could ascertain, she would be in her late twenties – still very marriageable. It was to be hoped that there was no immediate possibility of a husband. If she were a married woman, his aim to supplant her as the heir might be jeopardized, were his claim to go to court.

Moving back to the drawing room, he went to look out of the window overlooking the garden and said, 'Where I live, there are no beautiful trees like those I saw lining your drive on my approach to the house. Of course I have read many books about England, its history and geography, but I now see that words can never do justice to the beauty of your countryside. It must be such a joy for you living in these lovely surroundings.'

Eloise's face lit up. 'I'm so pleased to hear your compliments, Cousin James. Until quite recently, my sister and I enjoyed the company of a tutor who is also an exceptional artist. Mr Carter taught me watercolour painting.' Her face now lit up as she continued, 'We used to choose a different outdoor venue every day when the weather permitted.'

Ignoring Storm's expression at the heightened tone of her voice, she said, 'Perhaps you would care to take a turn around the garden if there is time before you have to return to London?'

It was a moment or two before Daniel replied. Astute as he was, he had noticed Eloise's tone when she had mentioned the tutor fellow, the blush on her cheeks and the younger girl's scowl, and quickly put two and two together . . . there was a liaison of some kind between the elder Miss Kenilworth and the tutor.

'You'll come with us, Storm, will you not?' Eloise was saying, but Storm shook her head.

'I have letters to write which cannot be delayed,' she said. Then she added in a sharp tone of voice, 'As Cousin James is a relative you don't need a chaperone, do you, darling?'

Eloise tried to hide her surprise, although she had guessed that by her silence Storm had not taken to their visitor. It was, of course, an extraordinary account he had related concerning his birth, but since he had proof of his mother's marriage to their father and of his own parentage, she saw no justification for disbelieving him. Moreover, he was proving to be not only tactful about their father's secret wedding to a chorus girl, but also quite charming. She was delighted when he showed himself eager to see the garden.

Their sortie was even more enjoyable than she had anticipated because he was so interested in the chosen locations where she and David had had such wonderful hours together. He expressed admiration for David and eagerness to see the portrait of Eloise.

'Your tutor must have come to know you very well over the years he taught you and your sister,' he said. 'I doubt very much if any artist could reproduce the exact likeness of a person he did not know intimately.'

For a moment, Eloise did not reply. Then she said, 'Although Mr Carter did not have a privileged background, he was exceedingly well educated and' – despite herself, her voice trembled – 'we became very good friends.'

She means she fell in love with him, Daniel surmised, and a slight sneer twisted his lips. He would remember that. Meanwhile, he had discovered an excellent way of obtaining her approval and, with a bit of luck, she might invite him to stay. It could be useful in future, when he took over the ownership, to see how this young woman managed this estate so efficiently on her own.

His claim must succeed! he told himself fiercely. He turned his attention back to Eloise, who had found one of the tutor's sable paintbrushes caught on a bush and was holding it in both hands as if it were a precious ornament.

'I must post it to Mr Carter without delay!' she exclaimed.

'Or maybe I could deliver it to him in person?' Daniel suggested. 'I would be so pleased to have an excuse to meet him, and, of course, to tell him I have had the great pleasure of meeting the subject of his portrait. I can refresh his memory of all these delightful spots where you and he painted together.'

Eloise's face was filled with pleasure. 'What a kind thought, Cousin James. As you know, we are still in mourning for Papa and John, so I have not been up to London, but please tell Dav— Mr Carter that I shall visit the Academy as soon as . . . as it is appropriate.'

She means as soon as she possibly can, Daniel thought with an inward smile.

'Tell me, Cousin, what chance do you think there might be of my finding a cottage to rent near here where I could relax for a few weeks before I go home? It's so very agreeable here and it would mean I could get to know you and your sister better.' He shook his head sadly. 'Although I fear she is finding it difficult to believe I am her half-brother.'

'Storm, my sister, is not long past childhood, Cousin James, and very impulsive,' Eloise replied. 'I'm sure you will find her a great deal more agreeable once she gets to know you. As to your finding a cottage to rent, it is not necessary. We have a dower house on the estate which is unoccupied and you are more than welcome to make use of it for your holiday. I will have no difficulty getting a cook, maids and groom for you from the village. You have your own valet, I presume?'

'Yes, of course!' Daniel lied, thinking that the first thing he would do when he returned to London to collect his belongings would be to hire a manservant, and, of course, he would accept the offer of the dower house for his use. Although he would have to pay the servants from his dwindling savings account, he should be able to live here more cheaply than if he were in London. He had already made severe inroads into his savings and if the tiresome Mr Hunter Chislestone took too long to get his certificates verified he would soon be running out of funds. Not only that, he had told Mildred he would be away six months at the very most, and had left her sufficient money to live on while he was absent. After six months, he had gauged, his right to the Kenilworth estate would have been established and he would have all the money he needed.

A cynical smile lifted the corners of his mouth as he recalled Mildred's assumption that she would join him in England as mistress of the manor – something which he had not the slightest intention of allowing. He would give her enough money to lead the kind of life she wanted, which, as there was little affection between them, he was reasonably sure she would be content with.

As Eloise turned and started to walk back with him to the house, he forgot Mildred as his spirits soared. Not long now, he told himself jubilantly. Soon he would be master of this magnificent estate.

For a fleeting instant the memory of James's body lying crumpled on the cobbled yard beneath his bedroom window shot into his mind and he remembered the frightening moment when he feared he would not be able to lift the lifeless man. After he had killed James he'd had frequent and terrible nightmares of those green eyes staring up at him in terror as he held the chloroform pad over his mouth and nose. Gradually he was comforted by the thought that in the remote area where James lived there would be no likelihood of the chloroform being identified; his suicide, or accidental death, would be taken for granted. Nevertheless, when it was at last proclaimed as such, his relief had been enormous and only very occasionally, as now, did the memory of that night return.

It was all a huge risk. The odds were against him, and he knew it, but he also knew that he could not live without having made the attempt to transform his life. Now that he had seen Kenilworth Hall and part of the estate, and had met his supposed half-sisters, he was delighted. To own such a property was to be master of a kingdom.

Watching the two figures approaching the house from her bedroom window, Storm's anxiety increased and, with no justifiable reason, every instinct in her warned her that this man was indeed an imposter and that her darling Eloise was being duped. When Eloise came to her room and told her of her offer of the dower house, she felt still more concern.

Refusing to join her and their visitor for tea in the drawing room before he departed back to London, Storm went to her late father's study and, sitting down at his desk, wrote to Hunter. She had promised herself that she would never be the one to contact him, and that when from time to time he came into her orbit she would be as cold and distant as possible. But she now felt so violently mistrustful of the man professing to be her half-brother that she felt compelled to appeal to Hunter to find a way to protect Eloise. Her sister's nature was far too trusting, too kind, too naive. One had only to think of the danger in which she had put herself in befriending David Carter – even allowing herself to fall in love with him.

Dear Hunter,

Eloise has not only seemed to accept the Australian's unlikely story about his relationship to us, she has offered him the use of the dower house for a holiday while he is here in England. This surely is madness when she has only known him for half a day.

As a lifelong friend of my sister, I hope you will consider doing something to protect her since I cannot do so and there is no one else.

Yours sincerely,

Storm

Having read it through, she crossed out the 'Yours sincerely', which she feared might make Hunter laugh and, writing the letter a second time, signed it simply 'Storm'. Finding Mabel in the kitchen, she asked her to go to the village to post it in time to catch the last post.

Hunter received the letter the following day and, reading it for the second time, sat back in his chair, wondering why he felt so disturbed. It was not simply the possible danger Eloise might be in: it was something else, something he could not at first grasp. Then it came to him – Storm had described him as Eloise's lifelong friend, which was, of course, true, but why had she not written 'our lifelong friend'? Had he really hurt her so badly that now she felt compelled to hurt him?

Even as the thought struck him, Hunter realized with an ache in his heart that it was true, and that the loving young girl who had once adored him was gone for ever.

THIRTEEN

January, 1857

Daniel had returned to his London lodgings and Eloise had prepared the dower house for his return. He was now comfortably installed there and seemed very happy with the accommodation. Meanwhile Storm was anxiously awaiting Hunter's response to her letter. She was far from sure what he could do to get rid of the fellow or, come to that, that he would be willing to do so.

She and Eloise now barely conversed unless it concerned an essential household matter. Mabel had told her that her sister had received a letter from Mr Carter, whose beautiful italic lettering on the envelope she had recognized. For the past few days Eloise's eyes had been red-rimmed from constant crying, and Storm's resolve to show her mistrust of the Australian by her silence now weakened. Finding Eloise in the schoolroom, looking out of the windows into the bleak winter garden below, Storm sat down at the old wooden table where she and her sister had done so many of their lessons as children and said quietly, 'Tell me what has happened to distress you, Elly. I know it has something to do with Mr Carter.'

It was several minutes before Eloise replied. Then, without turning, she said in a husky voice, 'He's not going to write to me any more . . . he thinks I would be happier if we both accepted that we can never be together. He said he is thinking of going abroad – he has had an invitation from a possible client in Italy.' Tears muffling her voice, she turned her back on the grey winter scene and whispered, 'He said that he'll never forget me or stop loving me—' She broke off and covered her face with her hands as the tears now poured down her cheeks.

Storm sprang out of her chair and hurried round the table to hug her sister. 'Don't cry, Elly, darling. Please don't cry!'

She handed her handkerchief to her sister. 'Perhaps Mr Carter is right and it would be best if you tried to forget each other.'

Eloise's tears stopped and her cheeks flushed. Taking the handkerchief and mopping her eyes, she said fiercely, 'I'll never forget David, never, never . . .' And then she burst into tears again.

When finally Eloise was calm, she blew her nose into the handkerchief she was still clutching and said in a quiet voice, 'I shall not try to stop David going abroad if that is what he wants to do. You know, Storm, much as I am hurting now, I am not sorry – and never will be – that I knew David for so long and grew to love him. I'd never loved anyone before, and although I now have to grow old without him, I have no regrets.'

For a moment, Storm longed desperately to confide in her sister that she knew exactly what she meant; that she, too, had discovered what it was to love a man with every fibre of her being, yet know that there would never be a happy consummation of that love. In Hunter's eyes she would always be a child, his sister's little friend who hero-worshipped him; often untidy, often unruly, a trial to her governesses, least of all a pretty little girl on the threshold of womanhood. Only once could she have believed that he saw her as someone he loved, and that was when they had danced close to one another at her ball.

Remembering now how Hunter had failed to arrive in time for the dinner at the start of her ball, and how the sophisticated loud-voiced American woman had laid claim to him, she reflected bitterly how naive she had been. The fact was that she had no more hope of a happy loving marriage to Hunter than Eloise had of marrying their former tutor. It was not so bad for Mr Carter, Storm thought. The Academy still had his portrait hanging in their gallery and according to Eloise he had continued to receive huge praise for it and even an unprecedented offer to buy it. He now had this astonishing success, in complete contrast to his former uneventful life, to distract his thoughts from Eloise. Her sister had nothing but the management of the estate to occupy her mind.

It now suddenly occurred to Storm that this might have been the reason why Eloise had given such a friendly welcome to the man they were calling Cousin James; why she had gone to the extraordinary lengths of offering a complete stranger the occupancy of the dower house. He was a distraction – someone to think about other than the man whose company she missed so terribly. Maybe she should not have asked Hunter to intervene and should get word to him quickly not to come down to Kenilworth.

She had not yet done so when, after luncheon, she decided she would go out for a walk. As she crossed the hall to fetch her padded velvet mantle and gloves, she saw Hunter's curricle draw up unexpectedly at the open front door. He jumped down and handed the reins to his groom. As he strode into the house he did not stoop to kiss Storm's cheek, as had once been his custom, but held her hand for a brief moment in greeting. Eloise was downstairs in the small room adjacent to the kitchen where she was arranging boughs of winter jasmine, freshly picked by the gardener that morning, Storm told him.

'I'll ring for Daisy to bring tea to the morning room,' she said non-committally, 'and she will inform Eloise that you have arrived.' Hunter was dressed warmly for the country in his greatcoat and a muffler, both of which he handed to Roberts along with his tall hat and gloves, but he still looked incredibly handsome, if a trifle tired.

'Was the journey tedious?' Storm enquired formally as they went into the welcoming comfort of the drawing room and sat down opposite one another on either side of the fire, which was burning brightly.

'Not too bad!' Hunter replied. He added with a slight smile, 'My curricle nearly collided with a young boar which ran across the road in front of the horses. I went to Chislestone first and had a word with the caretaker to make sure there were no problems, then I came on here.'

Storm's face remained expressionless. 'Have you managed to effect a sale yet?' she asked.

Hunter shook his head. Stretching out his long, booted legs towards the fire, he drew a deep sigh, and clasped his hands together as if for comfort as he replied, 'As a matter of fact,

that's something I have been intending to tell you and Eloise:
the reason why I have been delayed since receiving your letter
is that my potential buyer has decided not to purchase the
estate.' He broke off and frowned. 'The wretched woman has
returned to America.' He continued huskily, 'Frankly, I'm far
from sure now that she ever meant to go through with the
transaction.'

Storm's instant reactions were twofold: relief that Hunter
was not romantically interested in the woman and sympathy
for him, for the months wasted while he was led to believe
he had a buyer.

'I'm sorry!' she said, meaning it. 'Spring is on its way and
it's a lovely time for Chislestone to be shown to potential
buyers. I'm sure someone will soon come along who falls in
love with it.'

'That may not be soon enough!' Hunter replied, his voice
grim as he raked his hand through his hair. 'Our family debts
have been outstanding far too long, and although the banks
have been very considerate they too are beginning to wonder
if Chislestone is worth what we need to get for it.' He gave
a wry smile. 'One cannot blame the banks for refusing to take
the property as security against the vast amount of money
outstanding.'

'I heard what you said, Hunter!' The voice was that of
Eloise, who had come into the far end of the room. 'I am
really sorry to hear of your difficulties. Has your American
lady backed out?'

'Afraid so!' Hunter replied, rising to his feet and crossing
the room to kiss Eloise's cheek. 'If things go on as they are,
you will soon be sending me cakes to eat when I'm in the
Fleet.'

Briefly Eloise smiled. The debtors' prison he was referring
to had closed years before. She went to sit down on the sofa
beside him. 'It's lovely to see you. What brought you down
here?'

Taking care not to meet Storm's anxious stare, he replied,
'Just thought it time I caught up with your news. Have you
seen the Australian again since he came to lunch?'

'Yes! He is living in the dower house,' Storm broke in

quickly. 'Eloise is letting him use it for the next few weeks for a holiday here.'

'I'm really sorry to hear that,' Hunter said sharply. 'Despite the fact that the two certificates he gave me look genuine enough, I find myself highly suspicious of the man himself. I can't account for it. Call it an instinct, if you like, but I really do think it would be better, Eloise, my dear, if you kept the man at arm's length until we are sure he is the person he professes to be.'

'Oh, no, Hunter, I don't agree with you,' Eloise replied quickly. 'I found him quite charming. He was so pleased to be shown round the estate and was quite genuinely complimentary. I don't know why you and Storm have this mistrust of him. He has told me that when it is proved that he is Father's firstborn son he will be more than happy to help run the estate. As he said, he is after all our half-brother. Frankly, Hunter, I like him!'

'Well, I don't!' said Storm fiercely. 'And I don't think Eloise should have let him have use of the dower house. I hope that now you are here, Hunter, you will talk some sense into her. She hasn't been able to think rationally ever since Mr Carter—' She broke off as she realized she was going too far.

At the sound of David Carter's name, Eloise's eyes filled with tears. Storm, too, was on the verge of crying as she realized how tactless she had been. What she would never do, though, was cry in front of Hunter. Fortunately, at that moment Daisy came in with the tea tray and a plate of scones that Cook had hurriedly warmed when she had seen Hunter arriving.

Fearing that she might be unable to stop the threatened tears from falling, Storm said, 'I'm really not very hungry, besides which I am late already. I promised to take some flowers from the greenhouse down to the church.'

Before Eloise could protest, Storm turned and hurried out of the room.

FOURTEEN

January, 1857

Seeing the look of concern on Hunter's face, Eloise said apologetically, 'I am afraid Storm is going through a somewhat difficult phase. I think she is finding this period of mourning rather trying. I took the decision that we should go into half-mourning until the winter is over while we are here in the country. Storm was enjoying the season so much and now the only entertainment is with Admiral and Mrs Fothergill, who are an unconventional couple and don't bother applying any of society's rules of behaviour which don't suit them.'

Hunter grimaced. 'And I'm afraid I didn't help the situation with my failure to meet her expectations at the ball.'

Eloise nodded. 'She was still very much a child then, Hunter. She wanted to surprise you by showing you how grown up she had become. My darling sister has always been impetuous, as well you know. It's why we could never keep governesses for long. We had three . . .' her voice faltered and became almost inaudible, '. . . before Father employed Dav— Mr Carter.'

The distress that Hunter had felt at Storm's behaviour now suddenly gave way to anger.

'Storm is behaving like a spoilt child!' he said. 'When I told her that Mrs Metcalf was a potential buyer, she should have understood that this was far more important than a few dances!' His face drawn, he said with a look of disgust, 'I should never have agreed to Chislestone being taken off the market while that woman made up her mind. She sounded so positive, Eloise, so keen to—'

He broke off, a cynical smile replacing the frown on his forehead. 'I realize now that she wanted me to be part of the deal!' He sighed. 'You would have thought that at my age,

I should have realized sooner that the wretched woman's flirtatious manner was not simply the normal friendly way American women behave, and put a stop to it then.'

Eloise did not speak while he related his misfortunes. After they had each eaten a third scone and enjoyed a second cup of tea, she said, 'Your potential buyer's change of heart must be very worrying for you, Hunter, but while we have been having our tea a sudden thought has occurred to me. Last week Mr Arbuthnot, our solicitor, came down to see me to discuss our accounts. He told me that probate had been granted so he was now able to advise me that my father's estate is worth far more than was thought. Also that John owned a large share of it, the proceeds of which he drew upon only frugally. He took care of Father's affairs when Father became ill.'

Hunter nodded as Eloise continued, 'Years ago John told me so before he went on his travels. He was concerned lest anything dire should occur in his absence, but was going to keep in touch with Mr Arbuthnot and our bank, letting him know where he could be contacted in an emergency.'

She paused to ring the bell for Daisy to collect the tea things. When the maid had gone, she said, 'Hunter, it only occurred to me just now that I could buy some of the cottages and a parcel of your land! I'm sure we can afford it. Mr Arbuthnot said we would have to find somewhere to invest the money that is now lying idle. He suggested the railways or shipping, but I would be more than happy to invest locally. If I did so, you could keep Chislestone Manor for your mother and Cissy.'

Hunter's face had changed expression several times, at first to surprise, then hope and finally regret. 'Dearest Eloise,' he said, his voice husky, 'I cannot think of a more generous and thoughtful suggestion, but of course I cannot allow you to come to my assistance in that way. Don't you see—'

'No, I don't see any reason for your refusal!' Eloise interrupted. 'Of course, I am only aware of the value that your land agent has put on your estate, but would that sum be sufficient to repay your father's debts?'

For a long moment Hunter did not speak. Then he said, 'If – and I do mean only if – Mr Arbuthnot, or a financial adviser perhaps, were to agree that such a transaction would be of genuine benefit to you . . .' He broke off before saying in a quiet tone, 'My dear Eloise, I do so wish I could likewise solve your problems.'

Eloise hesitated, looking down at her hands. Then she said, 'I love him, Hunter. I love David, and some weeks ago I was bold enough to tell him so. He is planning to go and live in Italy, you see, and I cannot bear the thought of not seeing him.'

She leaned forward in her chair and said in a shaky voice, 'While I saw him every day it was bearable that we could never get married because of our social positions. Does it shock you to hear that I would have married him had he been willing, had it not been for Storm and what it would do to her chances of making a suitable marriage – and, I suppose, to the family name. But David – well, he can barely afford to pay for his needs, and I understand that he would not want to be kept by me.'

Eloise was now close to tears. She whispered, 'We were so happy living here, seeing each other every day. Sometimes his hand would touch mine or he would gently lift a strand of hair from my forehead, and he would hold my arm when he helped me up from my painting stool.' Her voice was now stronger as she added, 'Oh, I know it was so very far from what our love demanded but we were happy, Hunter. That is to say, until the gossip started. I suppose it was inevitable because I was frequently unwise enough to go off to the woods with David to paint without my maid or Storm as chaperone. You yourself warned me about it and finally Reverend Phillips told David he must leave the village if he did not want to ruin my reputation entirely. That's why David stayed up in London, where we cannot meet at present.'

'I am truly sorry, Eloise. I'm afraid our hearts do not always follow the dictates of our brains.'

Eloise's eyes were full of tears. 'I don't need to be married to David in order to be happy! I *was* happy. We both were, Hunter, wonderfully so, but now I am to lose even the chance of seeing him when in future I go to London.'

Hunter's brows were drawn in thought. He asked, 'Do you

think Carter would share your belief – that you could each live happily simply seeing each other every day?'

Eloise regarded him with a puzzled frown. 'Yes! Yes, I do!' she acknowledged. 'In David's last letter, he said exactly that; but you know that's not possible any longer.'

Hunter nodded. He said quietly, 'A thought has come to me, Eloise, which might make it possible.'

Eloise stared at Hunter, her eyes narrowed questioningly. Hunter explained, 'As you have suggested making it possible for me and my family to remain at Chislestone Manor, I, in return, could employ your Mr Carter as a tutor for Cissy. Unable as Cissy is to lead a normal life, it would be lovely for her to have the mental stimulus he could give her. The entire east wing is unoccupied and he could live there, not as a servant but as someone I have befriended. You could visit Chislestone whenever you wished and he, Carter, could come here whenever Cissy or I visit which, as you know, is frequently.'

Eloise was staring at him. 'But your mother, Hunter – would Lady Chislestone agree to such a plan? And would you really wish to befriend David?' She hesitated, then said haltingly, 'And Hunter, suppose you fell in love with someone . . . wanted to marry them . . . have children? Your wife might not like the idea of a stranger living in what would be her home. Nor can I be certain that David himself would agree to such an arrangement.'

'I shall not get married,' Hunter said flatly. 'I am approaching thirty now, and too well accustomed to my freedom from marital responsibilities. Besides, I have my mother and Cissy to love and care for, and,' he smiled, 'I have you and Storm as my very dear friends.'

Eloise's expression became thoughtful. 'I wish I could feel more certain that this extraordinary idea of yours was feasible! You know, don't you, Hunter, that even if we cannot carry out your plan for David, I will still purchase the cottages, farms and any other land or woods you don't wish to retain. Although you do not believe you might fall in love with someone you would like to marry, it could happen.'

Hunter paused as he asked himself whether his impetuous

proposal was possible. Would it put an end to the unfortunate gossip among the servants and villagers? There was, too, the question of the unfortunate Carter himself and whether he and Eloise, so much in love, would be happy with the proposed solution for their relationship.

He had a sudden fleeting thought of Storm's ill-concealed antipathy towards her tutor, which was almost certainly due to the fact that she felt he was responsible for jeopardizing Eloise's reputation. She was still so innocent; no doubt she would be scandalized if she knew he had a mistress in London who made him welcome whenever he chose to visit her.

One thing he could be certain about was that it would be a vast relief to know that he, his mother and Cissy would be able to continue living in the family home if his father's debts were indeed settled by Eloise.

He turned to her. 'Would you like me to put the proposition to Carter when I return to London?'

After a moment's thought, Eloise said slowly, 'No, not quite yet, Hunter. David said in his letter that he had always longed to go to Italy because of the importance that country placed upon art and artists. And I would not want my need of him here to deter him from what is important to him. Do go and meet him, though, so that you can form an opinion of his state of mind. You must make him feel quite free to make a new life for himself. When you know how he feels, we can discuss your idea again.'

'You must write down his address for me,' Hunter agreed.

After she had walked over to the small writing table by the window and done so, she handed him the note and said emphatically, 'Whatever we decide, Hunter, I meant it when I said I would like to purchase the cottages, the farms, the land. It can all continue to be managed by your man Jackson – and your tenants will pay their unchanged rents in the same way they always have. Everything will remain as it has been under your care.'

For a brief moment, Hunter's throat constricted as he realized that there was now a real possibility for Chislestone Manor to be absorbed into the neighbouring estate. It was a solution he had not dreamed possible. It would not have to be sold to strangers. The villagers, cottagers, farmers, inn-keeper, carpenter and blacksmith would not have to deal with a new landlord in place of Jackson, the one they had almost certainly known since childhood. His mother might not like a stranger living in the house, but perhaps she would be won over by Carter's charm and excellence as a tutor – assuming that Carter himself would approve of the scheme. One big advantage for Carter would be that he would have adequate space for his painting. As far as Hunter was concerned, Eloise's offer was an overwhelming relief. His mother had dissolved into tears when he'd told her she might never be able to take up residence at Chislestone Manor again. Then Cissy had cried because their mother was so distressed, and he had diffused the threat by saying that of course nothing was definite as yet and Chislestone Manor was still unsold. He'd failed to mention the mounting pressure the banks were putting on him. Now, he thought, the future might well be secure again for his mother and Cissy.

'I have a meeting tomorrow morning with Old Porky the bank manager – that's Mr Turner,' he told her, smiling, 'so I must be on my way. I will let you know as soon as I have spoken to Carter.'

Eloise looked at him anxiously. 'But it will be dark soon, Hunter, and our coachman Harry told me two days ago that a gentleman who had stopped at the Pig and Boar for refreshment was robbed within an hour of his departure for London.'

Hunter shrugged dismissively. 'It does not surprise me, but you need not worry, Eloise. I shall have my groom with me and we will both be armed. The horses are well rested and we will make good speed.'

Storm did not rejoin Eloise in the morning room until after Hunter had left. Her face flushed, she announced, 'I got back a few minutes ago and waited upstairs until Mabel told me she'd seen Hunter leaving. I really don't want to have anything more to do with him, Eloise. I know we can't stop him coming here when Cissy is visiting, but must you go on making him so welcome?' Removing her mantle and bonnet and throwing them on to a chair by the door, she dropped down into the larger of the two sofas and added, 'Do you know, Eloise, Hunter gets away with murder! Just because he's so good looking and knows how to be charming to everyone, they all fall for his smile. I did! When I was a silly young girl, I thought he was . . .' Her voice trembled and she coughed quickly and continued, 'I used to think he was the sort of man I'd like to marry.' She gave a hard little laugh. 'Thank goodness I saw his true colours. I can't think of any greater disaster than being married to a man you can't trust.'

Eloise turned away from her sister's flushed face as she tried not to hear the angry little voice, so full of hurt pride. In one way, she could not help but be pleased that Storm no longer held Hunter on a pedestal and hero-worshipped him, but the degree of her sister's dislike at this moment in time was very disturbing.

Worried by her thoughts as she was, Eloise decided to say nothing for the time being of her offer to buy the Chislestone properties, or of Hunter's suggestion for David's future. Storm's reaction would be something they would both have to deal with if these plans proceeded.

Eloise's heart doubled its beat as she thought of David and how he would react to the idea of living at Chislestone Manor. There was no question of them being able to get married, but the prospect did not bother her. She had never known physical passion nor needed it. Simply holding David's hand, feeling his breath on her cheek or the touch of his arm on her shoulder, was enough.

Dreamily, she did not question whether it would remain so. All she was praying was that if Hunter put his plan to him, David loved her enough to agree to the strange way of living it proposed.

Storm, meanwhile, ate her evening meal with Eloise in silence, retiring to her room afterwards and burying her head in her pillow, vowing never to speak to Hunter again. Then, agonizingly aware that she loved him as much as ever before, she finally gave way to tears.

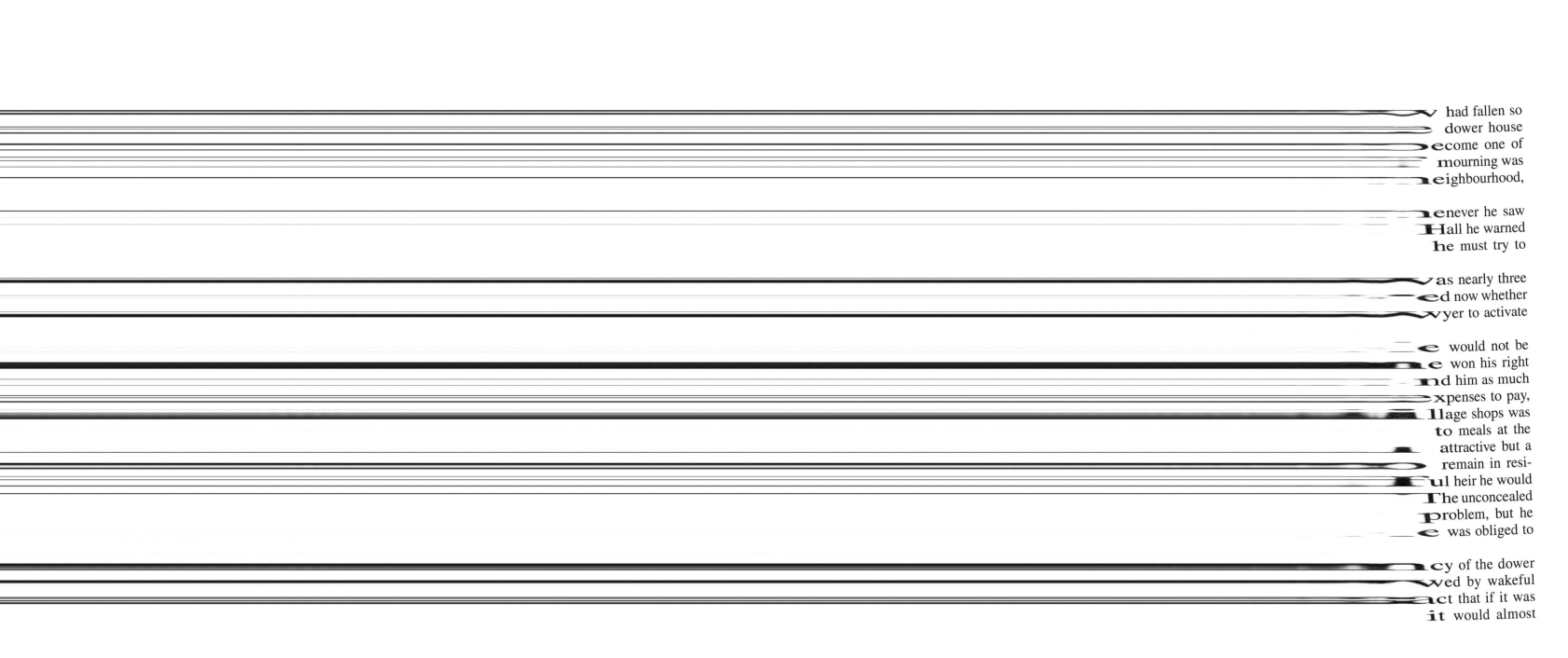

had fallen so
dower house
ecome one of
mourning was
eighbourhood,

enever he saw
Hall he warned
he must try to

as nearly three
ed now whether
vyer to activate

e would not be
e won his right
nd him as much
xpenses to pay,
llage shops was
to meals at the
attractive but a
remain in resi-
ul heir he would
The unconcealed
problem, but he
e was obliged to

cy of the dower
ved by wakeful
ct that if it was
it would almost

he had always had for
deepened to something
was that her apparent d
see more of her when
Eloise in managing the

Hunter tried now to
he knew, the Australian
his claim. However, if t
Australian, what was the
to disinherit Eloise? His

The man whom Eloise
accommodated in the d
his way into her affect
encouraging her to talk
intelligence, his sensitivi
in love with the fellow a
so too. Eloise seemed to
birth ever since he had
had in his possession.

Turning his attention
outskirts of London, slow
they encountered in the
was. He'd travelled dow
was nearing midnight by
installed in their mews
had returned to his club.
into bed, he determine
Chislestone, Kenilworth
himself that he was not
highly unconventional beh
He had the uncomfortable
objected if her Scottish ad
he asked himself, should
got up to?

FIFTEEN

February, 1857

T he weather was bitterly cold but no snow had fallen so far. Daniel was enjoying his stay in the dower house and his relationship with Eloise had become one of easy friendship. Now that the family's period of mourning was over Eloise took him for sorties around the neighbourhood, introducing him to the local community.

Hunter still had the two certificates and whenever he saw Daniel on one of his brief visits to Kenilworth Hall he warned him that checking old records took time and he must try to be patient.

How much time? Daniel asked himself. It was nearly three months since he arrived in England. He wondered now whether he should have handed the certificates to a lawyer to activate for him in the first place.

His savings were beginning to run low. He would not be concerned about his financial position once he won his right to inherit because he knew any bank would lend him as much money as he needed, but meanwhile he had expenses to pay, although the cost of food from Chislestone village shops was moderate, and Eloise frequently invited him to meals at the big house. She was, he thought, not only an attractive but a likeable young woman, and if she wished to remain in residence once he was acknowledged as the rightful heir he would have no objection to her remaining in the hall. The unconcealed dislike of the younger girl was more of a problem, but he patently ignored her, as she did him, when he was obliged to be in her company at mealtimes.

Despite his satisfaction with his occupancy of the dower house, the pleasant days were often followed by wakeful nights as he contemplated the horrifying fact that if it was known that he had stolen the certificates it would almost certainly lead to the discovery that he had killed James.

As the days passed, he took every opportunity to increase Eloise's friendliness towards him. He encouraged her to give way to her desire to talk about the artist who, she informed him, was now in Italy but would be coming back to England at Easter. Unknown to Daniel, Hunter had not yet mentioned to Carter the idea that he should live at Chislestone Manor and tutor Cissy, because events had overtaken him. Apparently Carter had been persuaded by an Italian countess who had seen his portrait of Eloise to travel to her castle near Florence and paint a portrait of her. She had offered him accommodation at the castle, where he could paint the portrait and live as her guest.

Although, despite his birth certificate, Eloise was finding it hard to accept that James really was her father's firstborn son, she did not doubt that the poor man genuinely believed he was. Meanwhile, she found him a charming companion and was prepared for the time being to give him the benefit of the doubt. She tried not to consider how her father would have felt about the son he had never recognized taking her place as heir to the Kenilworth estate, or, indeed, why he had never spoken of his existence.

On Hunter's next visit he suggested, with Storm's emphatic agreement, that their visitor had spent enough time at the dower house and should be asked to leave, but Eloise, with unusual vehemence, refused to contemplate Hunter's proposal. She pointed out that she and Storm had no plans to take up residence in London at the moment and country life and the running of the estate suited her. Cousin James was company for her with Storm spending so much time at the Fothergills, where she was always made welcome.

Unable to bear the sight of the man purporting to be her half-brother, Storm did indeed escape as often as possible to the Fothergills.

Although Tom Fothergill was at home on vacation, he had brought with him from university a young American girl of his own age. Not only was she pretty, amusing and an excellent sportswoman, she openly flirted with Tom. Storm liked the girl, Mary Lou, and did not mind that Tom's attentions were no longer centred on her. During the onset of spring the Fothergill house was filled with their friends and she enjoyed their company.

Glad to be away from Kenilworth and Cousin James, and to be absent during Hunter's ever more frequent visits to discuss her sister's inspired idea to purchase his land, which Eloise had now shared with her, she would ride over to the Fothergills and stay several nights there at a time. She could have remained longer, diverted as she was by the company and their activities, but her conscience would not permit her to desert Eloise any longer than she was already doing. Her sister had also told her of Hunter's plan to employ Mr Carter as a tutor for Cissy, and although he had not yet put this to the young man, she was concerned at the idea of Eloise becoming close to him again.

In an attempt not to think of Hunter so continuously she flirted with one of Tom's older friends, a Scot called Douglas McKillock, a handsome young man who was obviously taken with her. One evening, she had allowed him to kiss her. In the soft, starlit evening air on the terrace outside the drawing room where they had been dancing, he became very passionate. Storm, only slightly aroused by his kiss, wondered whether she would be better able to forget Hunter's beautiful naked body by the lake the day she had fallen in if she allowed her passionate admirer to touch her breasts, which he clearly wished to do. Ever since the night of her ball when Hunter had held her so close against him during their dance, she had known that her body belonged to him, that she'd wanted him even closer, wanted the new and wonderful sensations inside her to go on and on . . . But in the darkness of the Fothergills' garden, Douglas's tentative fondling of her breasts did not excite her; it evoked the longing to be in Hunter's arms. The need to feel his hands, his body, was more intense than ever.

When Storm returned home the next afternoon, she found Hunter ensconced with Eloise in the drawing room, a map of Chislestone village and the surrounding countryside on a table in front of them. They both rose to their feet, Eloise to cross the room and give Storm a welcoming embrace.

'I wasn't expecting you until tomorrow, darling,' she said. She added happily, 'Will you ring for Daisy to bring in some fresh tea?'

'Thank you, but I think I will go to my room and change my clothes,' Storm said, avoiding Hunter's outstretched hands and moving quickly aside.

'Can you not change your clothes later?' he asked. 'I have to return to London presently. It must be more than three weeks since we last saw each other and I want to know what you have been up to, spending so much time at the Fothergills.'

Storm did not return his smile and muttered, 'Some other time, Hunter – I really must go now. You will have to forgive me but I have a slight headache.' She hurried upstairs without bidding him goodbye. Mabel was waiting for her in her bedroom. Close as her maid was to her young mistress, she was well aware of the present family situation and, like all the servants downstairs, had overheard their mistress Eloise offer to buy Mr Chislestone's estate.

'Oh, Mabel!' Storm exclaimed as her maid helped her out of her travelling clothes and started brushing her hair. 'Do all the servants always know everything we do?'

Mabel smiled. 'Well, Mr Roberts sends the young ones out of the kitchen when it's something private-like,' she said, referring to the kitchen and scullery girls and Jed the boot boy. 'Mr Roberts knows he can trust us not to gossip, except between ourselves!'

'I suppose I did know!' Storm said, then added, 'So I suppose you know about Mr Hunter's offer to employ Mr Carter as Miss Cissy's tutor and accommodate him in the east wing at Chislestone when he returns from Italy?'

Mabel nodded. 'Can't see as it will do no harm, and if it makes Miss Eloise happy . . .' She paused. 'Weren't good, that gossip as was going about, despite us all knowing neither of them two would ever misbehave.'

Storm gave a deep sigh. 'I just wish Mr Hunter would stop telling us all what and what not to do. He is not our brother and if he must interfere, he should be trying to keep Mr Carter out of Eloise's life. What is more, he just demanded to know what I was doing at the Fothergills, as if it was any of his business!'

Mabel regarded Storm's unhappy face thoughtfully. 'If you want my opinion, Miss Storm, and I dare say you doesn't, you's feeling the way you are because you fancy Mr Hunter and you're peeved 'cos he sees you like the little girl you was and he don't fancy you the same way.'

For a moment Storm was speechless; she had been unaware that her maid was so perceptive. Before she could speak, Mabel said, 'If I were you, Miss Storm, I'd go back down-stairs all jolly-like and tell him what fun you was having at Miss Petal's, and how Master Tom was flirting with you the way he always does!'

A smile spread over Storm's face. 'It wasn't Tom!' she told Mabel, who was now fastening a tortoiseshell comb into the back of her mistress's smoothly coiled hair to try and control its thick curls. 'He has a new American girl he is fond of, and I had a Scottish friend of Tom's called Douglas vowing he'd fallen in love with me at first sight! Actually, I quite liked him, and he's very good looking. He wears a kilt, and I gath-ered his family owns an estate in the Highlands with a castle and grouse moors, and a forest with deer, so they go stag hunting every year.'

'Well then!' Mabel exclaimed happily. 'You go down and tell him what you just told me. It won't do him no harm to know that you be a grown-up young lady now.'

Her face serious, Storm nodded as she turned and hugged the old woman. Mabel had taken care of her ever since her mother died when she was born, sharing her upbringing with Eloise. It had been Mabel, not her sister, in whom Storm had always confided her childish problems; Mabel who had wiped her tears and put things right. The only secret Storm had ever kept from her was how her childish adoration of Hunter had changed that day she had fallen in the lake and she'd realized she really did want to be married to him and longed for him to love her.

As she went downstairs to rejoin Eloise and Hunter, she knew Mabel was right and she should take her advice. She could understand Eloise's offer to help Hunter repay his father's debts; she could also understand Hunter's desire to show his gratitude, but she disliked intensely the idea of the tutor's return to live at Chislestone Manor.

Hunter was on the point of leaving to return to London when Storm arrived in the hallway. Somehow, she managed a smile. 'Oh, don't go yet, Hunter. I've so much to tell you.' Seeing the look of surprise on his face, she continued quickly, 'It was all quite exhausting at the Fothergills and I really must apologize if I sounded grumpy when I got back. Mabel has just given me a wonderfully refreshing bath and I feel myself again. Do stay a little longer.'

She took his arm and, after the briefest hesitation, Hunter went back with her into the drawing room. Eloise crossed quickly and hugged her. 'You look lovely, darling!' she said. 'That dress really suits you so well. Hunter, are you staying?'

'For a few minutes,' Hunter replied, smiling at Storm. 'Your sister is quite right!' he said warmly. 'The dress does suit you, Storm. You really are quite remarkably pretty these days, isn't she, Elly?'

The compliment had sounded genuine and Storm's effort to retain her nonchalant smile was all but undone. Quickly, she launched into an account of her visit to the Fothergills' house and how she and Douglas had won the family archery contest arranged by Admiral Fothergill one afternoon, and how they had gone skating together on the frozen lake and danced and played games of hide and seek in the evenings.

'Needless to say, we played Douglas's version,' she said, 'in which not one but two people were sent off to hide, and the rest had to find us.'

She broke off as Eloise, her face shocked, interrupted. 'But darling, are you saying you were without chaperones?'

Storm nodded. 'Mrs Fothergill is very modern and Admiral Fothergill is so easy-going. She said she knew she could trust us all to behave like adults, even though we had chosen to play childish games.' Storm managed a laugh. 'I don't think it crossed her mind how simple it would be for two people hiding in the broom cupboard to steal a few kisses.'

Eloise frowned and Hunter said sharply, 'You should be careful of your reputation, Storm. A stolen kiss in the manner you describe may well seem harmless to you, but your companion may boast to others of his conquest.'

Storm's hesitation was only fractional. Then she said airily, 'I doubt that, Hunter. Douglas comes from far too well bred a family, as Mabel would say. I believe his father is chief of their clan and Douglas was very strictly brought up. I really can't imagine he would indulge in tittle-tattle!'

Hunter's eyes narrowed. 'I still think you should be more reticent,' he said.

Hearing the tone of their voices, Eloise felt it was time she intervened. 'Should you not be leaving, Hunter? It will be dark before you reach London.'

'Yes, indeed, you're right. I should be on my way,' Hunter said, putting his arms round Eloise and kissing her forehead. Storm moved quickly away to the window, knowing that if he were to kiss her, her body would betray the intense longing she was feeling for his embrace.

'It looks as if we will have rain.' Storm turned with a fixed smile. 'Do not delay, Hunter.'

Half an hour later, as Hunter and his groom were well on their way back to town, his thoughts were not on the dark highway but on his encounter with Storm and Eloise. Eloise's offer to buy part of the estate was, without question, a solution to his immediate problems. But whether his suggestion to employ Carter was a workable solution for the tutor and Eloise was questionable. Now, suddenly, he wondered whether it would prove to be a terrible mistake. Could Eloise and Carter maintain a chaste relationship living at such close quarters? Even if they could, would their neighbours and the villagers accept that Carter was his friend rather than Eloise's? That it had been his idea to install him in the family's house?

Even more worrying was Storm's behaviour. There were moments when he felt that she was close to disliking him, or at least that she had lost all the affection she'd shown him as a young girl. Thinking back to her coming-out ball when they had danced the waltz and he had held her unconventionally close to him, he had wondered for a brief moment if she actually loved him. He had even wondered if the brotherly love he had always had for the untidy, unconventional child had deepened to something more adult. One thing he was sure of was that her apparent dislike of him hurt. Inevitably he would see more of her when he was using his experience to assist Eloise in managing the Chislestone estate.

Hunter tried now to regain his former optimism. As far as he knew, the Australian had not decided to go to law to prove his claim. However, if the case did go to law and favour the Australian, what was the likelihood of the man being allowed to disinherit Eloise? His own lawyer thought it highly unlikely.

The man whom Eloise had (unwisely in Hunter's opinion) accommodated in the dower house appeared to be worming his way into her affections in a very subtle way. He was encouraging her to talk about David Carter, his talents, his intelligence, his sensitivity. A blind man would guess she was in love with the fellow and doubtless the Australian had done so too. Eloise seemed to have believed his story about his birth ever since he had shown her the theatre programme he had in his possession.

Turning his attention back to the road as he neared the outskirts of London, slowing to avoid the coaches and wagons they encountered in the streets, Hunter realized how tired he was. He'd travelled down to Kenilworth at daybreak and it was nearing midnight by the time he had seen his horses safely installed in their mews stable in the care of the groom and had returned to his club. When finally his valet helped him into bed, he determined not to give further thought to Chislestone, Kenilworth or the Australian imposter. He told himself that he was not going to worry either about Storm's highly unconventional behaviour, allowing herself to be kissed. He had the uncomfortable impression that she would not have objected if her Scottish admirer had kissed her again. But why, he asked himself, should he mind what the unpredictable girl got up to?

SIXTEEN

Italy. Spring, 1857

S till holding his paintbrush which he had been cleaning, David Carter surveyed the canvas on the easel in front of him. He had just completed the portrait of the contessa, but as always happened when he decided a painting could not be improved upon, on reviewing it the following day he would see some small improvement or change he should have made.

Yesterday he had allowed the contessa to see the nearly finished portrait of her, only the hem of her embroidered gown to do. She had been ecstatic. It was *perfetto*! *Magnifico, bello.* He had caught the autocratic expression in her eyes. She would show it to her friend, the Marchesa Angelica Morandodi Cingoli, who she was in no doubt whatever would want her own portrait done. The Marchesa Angelica was very beautiful and the contessa was certain Signor Carter would be inspired.

Gratified as he was by these compliments, David was far from sure he wished to remain any longer in Italy. In spite of their intention not to write to one another, he had received a letter from Eloise which had caused him great unease – it contained many references to 'Cousin James', and although he realized that it made him miserably jealous to think that another companion had taken his place at her side, it was her casual references to her sister's and Hunter's mistrust of the man that concerned him. He knew exactly how soft-hearted Eloise was; how quick she was to offer help, sympathy, assistance; but most of all, how gullible she was. Once, when the estate manager Mr Jenkins had evicted one of the farmers for some serious misdeed, Eloise had insisted on hearing the man's explanation of the events leading to his eviction and had counteracted the agent's decision. David, who loved Eloise so dearly, could well believe how easy it would be for her to be taken in by this imposter she called 'Cousin James'.

He replaced the paintbrush on the table beside the easel and was silent for a moment. Then he said, 'I have been considering returning to England. There is a matter that has arisen of some concern to me, and I may well have to look into it.'

He was far from sure that he could be of help, should it be necessary to intervene. At best it would be to add his voice to those already concerned for Eloise, and that could not possibly be done by letter.

The contessa now tried to convince him that delaying his return by a few weeks could surely not be of such seriousness as to warrant the loss of such an excellent commission.

'Forgive me for being so blunt, dear Signor Carter, but I have to say that I understand you are not a gentleman of means, or putting it more frankly, that the money I have agreed to pay you is by far the largest sum you have ever earned. Well, my friend, the marchesa would not even question your fee if she wanted her portrait painted by you. In fact, if you trebled my own payments, it would not be of the smallest consequence to her. You really must delay your departure, and I shall send my footman to invite her to tea this afternoon. Her *castello* is not all that far from here.' She stood up and went towards the door. Turning back, she smiled. 'Think about what I have said.'

It was on the tip of David's tongue to stop her but the sum of money she had spoken about was almost beyond his imagination. Not only could he vastly improve his family's future, but he might be able to find a small property from which he could venture out to paint the spectacular and historic Italian scenery.

When the contessa returned an hour later, her face was wreathed in smiles. She patted David's arm and said, 'My man has just returned from the *castello*. The marchesa is coming this afternoon to meet you and she will have no trouble judging the degree of your talent when she sees my portrait. I think you can count on a commission, Signor Carter and, as I thought, your fee is for you to name.'

Later that afternoon, David sat down in the *salotto* of the beautiful suite of rooms the contessa had put at his disposal and wrote to Eloise. He told her proudly of the offer he had received from the marchesa that day; of the success of the portrait he had completed for the contessa; and finally, that he would refuse the commission should she have need of him. It worried him, he wrote, that Eloise had offered the visiting Australian the use of the dower house while his claim to be recognized as the rightful heir was not yet established.

Having more faith in Hunter's judgement than in that of his sweet-natured Eloise, David decided he must return to England. However, arranging his passage was taking time and before it could be finalized a short letter arrived from Eloise saying, *Do not refuse the marchesa's commission. I am in no need of assistance. Please reassure me.*

The contessa too was still pressing him to give the marchesa a positive reply before she capriciously changed her mind. After a sleepless night, David decided to agree to paint the portrait. The following day, having thanked the contessa for her generous hospitality and for the introduction to the marchesa, he informed his new client that he would be happy to accept the commission. As it happened, although she was by no means beautiful, the marchesa had fine aristocratic features and exceptionally large liquid brown eyes with interestingly arched brows. Her black hair, glimpsed through the lace cap she chose to wear, made her an intriguing subject, and before long he had moved into her medieval *castello* and was totally absorbed in his task.

England. Spring, 1857

Back in England, Hunter sat in the drawing room of Kenilworth House in Mount Street facing Eloise and Storm, who were seated side by side on the settee. They were in London for a few days in order to make one or two purchases so as to be ready for their intended stay after Easter for the season. The spring sunshine was streaming in through the large windows together with the faint sound of horses' hooves as a large brewer's dray rumbled by. Eloise and Storm were staring at Hunter anxiously.

His handsome features were distorted by a look of severity as, frowning, he forced himself to tell them the truth about James's real identity – that he had received unofficial confirmation that Lord Kenilworth's marriage to the Australian's mother was likely to be genuine.

'I still don't understand how he could have married our mother when he already had a wife,' Eloise said.

Hunter hesitated as he wondered how he was going to continue. After a moment, he said, 'Eloise, I am telling you and Storm what I have established so far. This was many years ago and for all we know your father may have been able to have the marriage dissolved.'

He did not mention his earlier feeling that it was highly unlikely that Lord Kenilworth had divorced his wife; that would have had to take place in the High Court, with all the attendant publicity. After the 'Lord Divorces Chorus Girl' headlines he would never have been able to marry their mother.

Storm was regarding him with a strange look in her eyes. 'So Cousin James . . . are you saying that he really is Father's child?'

Hunter nodded. 'He showed me his birth certificate with Lord John Kenilworth named as his father. He was born in Australia, where he told me his mother had gone to live after she and your father parted company.'

Eloise's face was now white with shock. Almost in a whisper, she asked, 'When was he born, Hunter? Was it before any of us? Before Andrew, John . . .?' She broke off momentarily and then resumed, 'If he is Father's eldest son he might well have left the estate to him, a man, rather than to me. Could I be disinherited?'

'That is something we don't know,' Hunter told her. 'We must wait until the fellow's birth certificate has been verified – and I am still waiting for a reply from Australia. When I receive it I will hire a first-class barrister to refute any claims that James might make. I have to admit that I am not too hopeful that we shall discover any discrepancies in the certificates – the fellow seemed so confident. It worries me that if the certificates were forgeries they would not have that authentic look; the paper would not be as old and discoloured as it is.'

Seeing the abject look on the girls' faces, Hunter added, 'Cheer up, both of you, and permit me to take you out for ice creams at Gunter's. Meanwhile, don't forget that we are talking about events which happened very many years ago. I find myself questioning why a genuine son living in very modest circumstances would not have contacted his family for assistance after his mother's death. James insisted it was because he promised her never to do so; yet when he read your father's obituary he had no hesitation in coming to England.'

He drew a deep sigh. 'I am unable to believe that Lord Kenilworth – a most honourable and law-abiding man – would have married your mother unlawfully.'

Storm was now regarding him intently, her face flushed. 'So if Cousin James is Father's son and Father was never divorced, then we, the Kenilworth children, must be illegitimate.'

Hunter stood up and went to put an arm around her shoulders. 'We don't know the facts yet, and in any event it all happened so long ago that people will have forgotten, if they ever knew about your origins.'

Storm pushed his hand away with a gesture and gave a harsh little laugh. 'It will make a difference to Douglas McKillock if he finds out! His family are frightfully snobby.'

Hunter looked down at her sharply. 'You never mentioned that your relationship was serious, that you are in love with the fellow!'

Storm's chin lifted and her eyes narrowed as she shrugged. 'For one thing, Hunter, I didn't know I was obliged to keep you informed about my private life, but since you ask, no, I am not in love with Douglas, but I don't need to be, do I? I might marry him and go and live in his Scottish castle. Perhaps I could ask him to rush me off to Gretna Green so we could be married before I'm made illegitimate!'

'Storm!' Eloise burst out in a shocked tone of voice. 'How can you even think of such a thing! Hunter, tell her she is behaving like a tiresome child.'

For a moment Hunter was silent, then he said quietly, 'We must face the fact that your sister disapproves of most people these days: you and Mr Carter, who she tells me is still writing to you; Cousin James; and not least, me!' He looked as if he was about to reach out and shake Storm angrily, but he remained standing, his fists clenched. 'Storm, understand that people can be swayed by passion or, indeed, love and it is not their fault if their feelings are misdirected. One should sympathize with poor Mr Carter, not blame him as you do.'

He broke off, his voice husky, as he turned to put his arm round Eloise, who was now weeping. 'Don't cry, my darling, sweet Eloise!' he said, stroking her hair. 'Storm doesn't mean to hurt you. I'm the one she can't forgive . . .' He looked at Storm's white, anguished face, his voice suddenly tender as he continued, 'Please try not to carry your grudge against me. I'm sure that in your heart you know I would never do anything intentionally to hurt you. I have loved you as much as I love my darling little sister and when you reject me it hurts me as much as if Cissy were to do so.'

It was several minutes before Storm said in a choked voice, 'I'm afraid I wasn't born with Cissy's sweet nature, but I will try to be more accepting – less critical of what life offers me. I'm sorry, Eloise. I love you very much and I didn't mean to hurt you. I apologize to you too, Hunter, if I was rude. Now, if you will both excuse me, I must go and write to Cissy. She is so happy, Hunter, knowing she will be going back to live in her own home as soon as the sale of the estate to our family is finalized.' All thoughts of the tantalizing outing to Gunter's forgotten, she left the room.

Eloise sat down again heavily in her favourite chair and, her expression downcast, said with a sigh, 'I have come to the conclusion, as you know, Hunter, that it has been the ongoing restrictions of mourning these past months that have caused Storm's behaviour, her restlessness. I'm not sure what she would have done if the Fothergillls had not been so welcoming, encouraging her to spend so much time with them. They are extremely social, you know, and their house is always full of young people, friends of Thomas and Petal and Daryl.' She attempted a smile. 'I'm not too happy about this friendship between her and Douglas McKillock. Until recently, I had no idea they had been alone together.'

'You should put a stop to it immediately, Eloise!' Hunter said forcefully. 'Storm is no longer a child and is now a very attractive girl. A young man could not be blamed for kissing her if she made it clear that she wished him to do so.'

Momentarily, he was reminded of how he had held her in his arms during the dance. He had never admitted to himself until now how his body had reacted to hers that night at her coming-out ball. Had she not been so young and innocent, he might have believed she was feeling the same desire as his own. He'd quickly put such an idea from his mind, reminding himself that from the time she had learned to walk she had always flung herself into his arms, hugged and kissed him and told him playfully that one day he would marry her. His darling Cissy actually believed it and the two little girls often played at 'pretend weddings'.

During his adult life he had been attracted to a number of different women but there had never been anyone who would leave him devastated, in despair, if they were suddenly to vanish from his life. Was his discomfort, the anxiety he had been feeling ever since Storm had made it clear he was no longer the most important person in her life, an indication of an underlying love for her? Of course, he loved her; had done so since she was a very young child, lifting her pretty face for his kiss. But as an adult he had often felt irritated by her moods and sulks rather than loving.

With a sigh, he crossed the room and kissed Eloise's cheek before departing to meet the Chislestone land agent who had come up to London, Hunter intending to inform him that he had come to an arrangement with the owner of the Kenilworth estate to amalgamate their lands. Such a move would mean that the family retained Chislestone Manor, in which Eloise had no interest.

Eloise had stated (which a stranger would not have done) that all the Chislestone farmers, villagers and employees would retain their jobs as if there were no change in ownership – something which had been a huge relief to Hunter, whose family had for generations ensured their welfare.

No doubt there would be people who would question why he was not doing the obvious thing and marrying Eloise. They knew nothing of her love for the tutor, nor indeed that although he himself loved her as a sister, it was not with the kind of emotion one should feel for a wife.

I've been very lucky, he told himself as he walked down

Mount Street towards his club, to have such a fond friend as Eloise to buy the land. He had always found it difficult to imagine strangers owning Chislestone Manor. Then why, he wondered, now this major issue was resolved, was he still feeling uneasy? It was a question to which he had no answer.

SEVENTEEN

Spring, 1857

Eloise and Harry the coachman had taken the pony and trap in order to visit all the farms on the estate that afternoon. She liked to do this at least three times a year to ensure that the farmers' families were not in need of any kind. Sometimes she would take some of her unwanted garments, or some of Storm's, for the farmers' wives to make over for their children, of whom there were usually at least half a dozen. Although she insisted the farmers were paid for any produce they brought to the house, with such large families nearly all found it difficult to manage to buy any more than the barest of necessities. Therefore Eloise usually took a cake, a pie or sweetmeats as well for the children. Kind-hearted as she was, she would see that Cook sent baskets of food for them in the severest of winter weather. Eloise, as a consequence, was much respected by the men, women and children alike.

There was over a week to go before she and Storm were removing to London for the season, and now Storm, with Eloise out and time on her hands, decided to ride over at lunchtime to the Fothergills where she knew Petal would be. It would be slightly more interesting than sitting by herself with nothing but a book or her embroideries to occupy her. Meanwhile, she went into the conservatory where the sun's rays were blazing cheerfully through the window.

Flinging herself down on one of the big wicker armchairs and settling her skirts around her, she caught sight of a brown and green woollen scarf which had fallen behind Andrew's glass cabinet containing his collection of butterflies. No one had removed them after his death. Nor, apparently, had any of the servants noticed Hunter's scarf. Assuring herself that no one was about, she got up, retrieved the scarf from where it lay and carried it back to her chair. She lay there with it pressed against her face as she breathed in the faint scent of horse, and of Hunter himself.

Tears sprang to her eyes as memories flooded through her of the days when she was young and he took her riding on the saddle in front of him. She would discard her hat and her hair would lose its ribbons and fly back into Hunter's face and, laughing, he would scold her, then urge his stallion into a fast gallop to scare her. Not that she was ever frightened of anything if he were holding her.

Inevitably, her thoughts now went yet again to the night of her ball: her dreadful disappointment when he had failed to get to the dinner; her distress when he had not arrived afterwards; and then the wonderful, blazing joy when he was there, holding her in his arms, waltzing with her, his body pressed to hers. She would, she thought now, have been happy to die there in his arms.

Angry, she brushed away the gathering tears, thinking for the thousandth time that she'd thought then that he loved her as she loved him; that at last he had discovered her as a woman, realized she was no longer his favourite child, Cissy's little friend.

Then that hateful woman had arrived uninvited and literally claimed Hunter as if she owned him. She should not have been surprised, Storm thought, if that horrible female had seduced him.

Sitting up, she threw Hunter's scarf on to the tiled floor, at which point she caught sight suddenly of the man they called Cousin James leaving the dower house. It flashed through her mind that when Hunter had visited them in London he'd told them that he had still received no definitive confirmation from Australia about the validity of his birth certificate. Several times, the Australian had said that his return home was overdue and that he should be ensuring that the neighbour he had left in charge of his ranch was willing to stay on longer, but he had still made no definite plans to depart.

Her eyes followed the distant figure of the interloper on the mare, Firefly, which Eloise had lent him for the duration of his stay. Almost certainly, Storm thought, he was on his way to the village inn, where he usually went for a meal if he were not in their company. Apparently he liked to drink the local beer and listen to the villagers gossiping about past events which often included accounts of the late Lord and Lady Kenilworth in what they called 'the good old days'.

Storm now stood watching until the man was out of sight and wished fervently that he would never come back. She knew Hunter shared her dislike and distrust of the visitor, and wished there were some way she could assist him in his attempt to disprove the Australian's claims. Now, suddenly, she realized that there was at least one way she could attempt to do so: she could use the spare front door key to get into the dower house and look through the man's belongings.

She made her way down the drive, urged on by the faint hope that she might find something incriminating there. The front door opened easily, and there was no sound inside. In the bedroom there were only a few personal effects. The clothes were surprisingly few, both unfashionable and of poor quality, and there was a heavy walking stick which looked as if it might have belonged to a farmer rather than a gentleman.

After searching the other rooms, which were devoid of his belongings, she left the dower house dispirited, carefully locking the front door behind her.

She made her way back to the hall and rang the bell for Mabel to tell her that she was ready to leave for the Fothergills'.

'You take that look off your face, Miss Storm!' Mabel declared as she came into her bedroom. 'Else the wind will change and you won't be able to look no different!'

The maid's warning did have the effect she wanted and Storm's unhappy expression gave way to a smile. Mabel was full of old wives' sayings and ever since Storm was little she would come up with one on every occasion, as often as not causing Storm's mood to change.

'None of Miss Petal's friends will be there this afternoon,' she said. 'They have all gone back to London and I can't wait for the next week to pass.'

She knew that Douglas McKillock was waiting anxiously to see her again. He'd told her he wanted to take her to the Tower of London to see the Crown Jewels, and to make up a

party to go to Richmond Park for a picnic. In fact, it seemed
he wished to monopolize her time. She supposed he was in
love with her and momentarily, while Mabel handed her her
bonnet and reticule, she wondered what it would be like living
in Scotland. Although her father used to go up there for grouse
shooting before his deteriorating health put a stop to it, neither
she nor Eloise had ever accompanied him. Everyone said it
was cold, so living in a castle would probably be even colder
than Kenilworth in the winter.

'Come on, Mabel!' she told her maid. 'It's time we were
on our way. Eloise is using the pony and trap so we will go
in the gig.'

It was early afternoon before Eloise was on her way home
having completed her round of visits. She was chatting with
Harry about one of the farmers' wives who had just had twins
– two healthy-looking boys who would eventually be able
to assist their father on the farm.

Miss Eloise, Harry thought, was probably the kindest, most
sweet-natured female he had ever come across. She had a
smile and a good word to say for everyone, and if very occasionally a reprimand was necessary, it was delivered and dealt
with in a fair way.

His thoughts went back to the week before Mr Carter had
gone to live in London. All the staff had, of course, heard the
rumours about Miss Eloise and the former tutor and there was
a great deal of gossip in the servants' hall. Mr Roberts, the
butler, had finally called a meeting, and after luncheon, when
they were all gathered together, he had informed them that
there was absolutely no truth in any of the rumours. If Mr
Carter had been seen to have his hand on the mistress's arm,
Mr Roberts said, that was because he was guiding her
paintbrush; if anyone had noticed him gazing at her with an
admiring expression, well, she was a lovely woman and it was
a natural thing for women as well as men to do. Moreover,
the mere fact that Miss Eloise had ventured out of doors
without a chaperone was an indication of her innocence – she
had not considered that a painting lesson with her tutor required
chaperonage.

Jed, the boot boy, had started giggling and had been promptly dispatched by Mr Roberts to clean out the privies – an adequate punishment, since the lad had been hoping to spend the afternoon out of doors in the sunshine cleaning the mud off the boot scrapers and polishing them with blacklead – something old Lord Kenilworth had always insisted upon.

Harry and Eloise were now driving along the pathway beside the lake where pink and yellow water lilies were in bud. As they passed the boathouse, Eloise said, smiling, 'That's where Miss Storm fell in and Mr Hunter had to jump in and rescue her!'

Harry nodded. 'Right little mischief she were when she were little!' he said with a laugh. 'Reckon that weren't the first time Mr Chislestone got her out of trouble!'

He turned the horse's head into the long drive leading to Kenilworth Hall. Reaching the front door, he hitched the reins, jumped down and helped Eloise from the trap at the front door before driving round to the kitchen to unload the empty baskets.

As Roberts opened the door for her Eloise caught sight of Cousin James coming up the drive. Roberts, too, had seen him.

'Shall I tell Daisy to bring tea to the drawing room, miss?' he asked.

'Yes, please, Roberts!' Eloise said.

Storm, learning from Roberts on her arrival home that the Australian was in the drawing room, hurried upstairs to her bedroom, her eyes drawn together in a deep frown. Had she known that Cousin James was at the house she would not have returned home for tea, but supposing Eloise would be without company, she had deliberately left the Fothergills' early. Turning to Mabel, she said furiously, 'Oh, Mabel! How could she! How *could* Eloise invite him here *again*? Mabel, go down and tell her . . . what shall I say? Tell her I've got a headache!'

Mabel lifted her eyebrows and sighed. 'Surely Miss Eloise won't believe it!' she said. 'She knows you've taken against the visitor something awful.'

'Well, I'm not the only one to think him an imposter!' Storm retaliated. 'Mr Hunter thinks so too. Anyway, I'm not going down to tea.'

Mabel sighed again, well aware from her mistress's tone of voice that she meant what she said. She left the room and went down to the drawing room to do as Storm had instructed. Opening the door, she saw Miss Eloise was pouring tea for the visitor from the big silver teapot; the foreign gentleman was standing with his hands clasped behind his back, gazing up at the portrait over the fireplace.

'Can that be my grandfather?' he was asking Eloise. 'Do you know, I can see quite a family likeness.' He turned and sat down opposite Eloise, reaching for his teacup as he added, 'It is strange, is it not, how family resemblances can pass down to later generations!'

Excusing herself for interrupting, Mabel delivered her message. Eloise looked far from pleased, and as Mabel left the room she heard her saying, 'I'm so sorry my sister won't be joining us, Cousin James, but she has been a little under the weather these past few days and I fear she may be contracting one of those tiresome summer colds!'

Mabel's dour expression gave way to a smile as she made her way back upstairs. Her young mistress was the epitome of good health and very rarely caught a cold. Her smile broadened as she found herself hoping that the stranger would know that this was only an excuse. Did he realize, she wondered, that he was disliked not only by Miss Storm but by all the staff too?

Entering the bedroom, Mabel saw Storm standing by the window, her arm raised as she shaded her eyes.

'It's Hunter, Mabel!' she said huskily. 'I know it is. I recognize his horse!'

She swung round, her face glowing as she said to her maid, 'Quick, Mabel! Get my muslin dress with the crimson ribbons, and my shawl, and I'll wear my new garnet pendant.'

Miss Eloise had no idea that her sister had accepted this necklace as a Christmas gift from the Scottish gentleman, and Mabel was well aware that if she had, her young mistress would have been obliged to return it. Until now Storm had never shown any inclination to wear the gift.

Mabel opened her mouth but shut it again. When Storm had finally finished dressing, Mabel very reluctantly fastened the delicate chain round her neck and handed her the shawl. She knew only too well how her strong-willed mistress felt about Mr Hunter, and in some ways she didn't blame her, but at the same time she knew that Mr Hunter still considered her a child.

When Storm entered the drawing room she went first to the Australian, greeting him cordially, because she knew Hunter would prefer her to remain polite. Then she turned with a feigned look of astonishment. 'Hunter, what a nice surprise!'

She lifted her face for him to give his customary kiss on her forehead, making certain that her necklace was unavoidably visible to him. 'Oh!' she exclaimed. 'Were you noticing my pendant, Hunter? I was given it at Christmas by the Fothergills . . . well, not by them, exactly, but a friend.' She gave a little self-deprecating laugh. 'I suppose I shouldn't have accepted it, really, but Mrs Fothergill thought it would do no harm if I kept it.'

Seeing Eloise's expression, she hurried to her side and apologized for being so late for tea. 'I wasn't sure if the medication Mabel gave me for my headache would enable me to join you after all.'

She smiled prettily, fingering the delicate chain around her neck. 'I don't think I ever showed this to you, did I, dearest?' she asked innocently. She took care not to look at Hunter, who she was now hoping might be guessing that the necklace was a present from Mr McKillock rather than the Fothergills, and that it was for this reason it had not previously been drawn to Eloise's attention. He would, she knew, object strongly to the breach of etiquette if he suspected that anyone other than a relative had given her a gift of jewellery.

She said, 'I expect you know that Eloise and I will be back in London next week. Mr McKillock has promised to take me to the Tower of London. Have you ever been there, Hunter?'

For the space of a single minute, Storm thought he was going to strike her, such was his expression. His hazel eyes were full of anger and he was clearly making an effort to control his voice as he said, 'I seem to recall you had your debut not long ago, Storm. I know you like to be independent, but now you are a young woman it's time your sister taught you some of our adult conventions. It is not appropriate for you to let any young man monopolize your time in such a way, and you should certainly not accept jewellery as a gift.'

He crossed the room and accepted a piece of shortbread from the plate Eloise was offering him, first stooping to kiss her cheek. Only then did Hunter acknowledge James's presence.

'I have received a reply, sir, regarding the certificate you gave me of Lord Kenilworth's first marriage. If you would care to come to the study with me after tea, I will show you the letter I have received.'

Watching the Australian's reaction, Storm saw his face grow pale, his expression one of anxiety. Then he forced a smile as he replied casually, 'Splendid news, sir! Taken enough time, hasn't it?'

Hunter's voice was quiet, noticeably chilly. 'Yes, it has, and I'm afraid we shall have to wait a very great deal longer for a verification of your birth certificate to come from Australia, but we shall get it in the end.'

Storm's eyes were now fastened on Cousin James and her heart sank as she saw nothing but confidence there. It now seemed more likely than ever that the man did not doubt the authenticity of his birth certificate, and that it would be verified.

As far as he was concerned, it didn't matter how long that might take. With Eloise now covering all his expenses and even having his household necessities from the village put on the house bills, he could continue to live in the dower house however long he had to wait.

His only concern was that Mildred would grow tired of waiting for confirmation that his plan had been successful.

EIGHTEEN

Spring, 1857

I t was Monday and Eloise was upstairs in her dressing room supervising her maid, who was packing the last of her summer dresses ready for their removal to London on Wednesday in time for the season. Storm, who had preferred to leave her packing in Mabel's capable hands, had decided to go out to the garden to pick some flowers to brighten the rooms in Mount Street.

Placing the last of the roses she had just gathered carefully in her large oval-shaped flower basket, she was surveying the beautiful blooms when she saw Dick, the post boy, trotting up the drive. She waved her hand to the boy, a freckled, tousle-haired youth she had known since childhood. She stepped off the lawn on to the drive and walked towards him as he pulled his horse to a halt.

Reaching into his leather satchel, he said, 'Afternoon, Miss Storm! Gotta letter here wiv a foreign stamp on it. Postmaster says it ain't for you or Miss Eloise so it must be for one of the servants.'

Certain this must be a mistake because it was only rarely that any of the household staff received letters at all, let alone from a foreign country, Storm reached up and took all the letters from him.

'I'll save you a trip up to the house, Dick,' she said. 'I'm on my way there now.'

With a cheerful grin on his face, the boy turned his pony and headed off back down the drive. Storm looked down at the bundle of letters Dick had given her. The foreign one was on top. Its large stamp with its picture of Queen Victoria was bordered by the words 'New South Wales'. Her heart missed a beat. Surely, she thought, New South Wales was in Australia? Australia, where their so-called cousin, James, lived.

Her heart now racing, Storm hurried across the lawn to the summerhouse where she knew she would have privacy. Pushing open the door, she went into the dusty interior and, moving the box of croquet hoops, mallets and balls off the wooden bench by the window, she put down her basket of flowers and sat down to read, placing the other mail beside her.

The foreign letter was addressed to 'Mr Daniel Collins, Kenulworth House' (misspelled), 'Chiselstune' (misspelled), 'Sussex'. Storm's hesitation lasted only half a minute before she prised open the envelope and removed the two sheets of cheap notepaper inside. She could hardly believe what she was reading.

> *Dear Daniel,*
>
> *I know you said I wasn't to write no matter what, but it's now nearly six months since you've been gone and I'm all but out of the money you left. There's bills I can't pay and you saying it was only a few weeks afore you'd be a rich Lord don't help pay what's owing nor give me no credit at shops.*
>
> *I've borrowed money from my sister so if you aren't on your way home right now, please send me some as quick as you can.*
>
> *From your wife, Mildred*

Storm's hands were trembling as she put the two badly written pages back in the envelope. Her immediate reaction was to go straight to the dower house and accuse the man claiming to be James Kenilworth of being an imposter. She now had no doubt that his real name was Daniel Collins. How then, she asked herself, had he James Kenilworth's birth certificate in his possession? They were waiting now for confirmation of James's birth in Australia. The man called Daniel Collins must somehow have stolen that child's identity.

Storm took a deep breath and slowly revised her first impulse to challenge the interloper with the truth. If she showed him his wife's letter he might try to wrestle it from her – possibly even harm her – to prevent her from exposing him. On second thoughts, she decided first to show the letter to Eloise.

As she walked down the steps of the summerhouse and made her way towards the house, Storm changed her mind once more. Eloise was far too sweet-natured to tackle someone so devious, so evil as this interloper. He might harm her, too. No, she decided, she would say nothing to her sister and, when they were in London, she would hand the letter to Hunter. He would know how best to tackle the man.

It was only by the merest chance later that evening that Daniel discovered that a letter from Australia had been delivered by the post boy that morning. Dusk was falling and the trees on either side of the bridleway through the wood were casting dark shadows which caused his horse to dance nervously on the way to the village. It had become his habit to visit the Bell, the village inn, and enjoy a few pints of ale with the local inhabitants. As was usual, there were several villagers already sitting at the taproom's tables when he arrived. With a brimming pewter mug in his hand, seated on one of the wooden benches by the unlit fire, he overheard two of the locals' conversation. One was Jacob, the village carpenter, the other George the postmaster who, with his wife, ran the tiny post counter and village store. They were discussing an unusual letter Dick had delivered that morning to Miss Storm up at the big house. The carpenter was requesting a more detailed description of the Australian stamp George had said was on it. At the mention of his country, Daniel felt a sudden, painful sharp stab of fear.

'Excuse me interrupting sirs,' he intervened, 'but it wasn't by any chance for me, was it? Mr James Kenilworth?' For months past the locals had known that a distant relative of the family, a Mr James Kenilworth, had come to stay at the dower house.

The postmaster shook his head. 'Weren't addressed to you, sir,' he said. ''Twere for a Mr Colwyn, I think. No, t'were a Mr Collins.'

With the greatest difficulty Daniel managed to keep the look of horror from his face and the shock from his voice. He shook his head, saying, 'So none of my six wives have written to me! What a shame!'

The men laughed.

'Reckon you be lucky at that, sir!' the carpenter said. 'One alone complaining you be away from home too long is nuisance enough, let alone six!'

Hurriedly, Daniel ordered them another ale and finished his own before quickly riding home, a hundred different questions whirling in his brain. Who was the letter from? Mildred, despite the dire warnings he had given her before he'd left? 'I'll write to you, but *on no account* are you to write back!' he'd instructed her.

Had Storm opened the letter? Had she shown it to Eloise, and had the two of them guessed that he was this Daniel Collins? What did it say? Was his carefully worked-out plan to be scuppered just when it was about to succeed? It was inconceivable that he had taken the terrible risk of killing James to no purpose.

That night, after settling his horse in its stable, he let himself into the dower house and realized that he was trembling.

He ordered the manservant Eloise had allocated to the dower house to bring him a large brandy, and to leave the decanter on the side table. As for food, he was not hungry and would not require an evening meal.

Ten minutes later, having drunk the first brandy, he reached for the decanter and poured himself another. As he paced the room his thoughts turned to the interfering Mr Hunter Chislestone who had taken it upon himself to be the girls' guardian. If they showed him the letter, he would without any doubt make enquiries about Mildred. Even if she were astute enough to deny any knowledge of him the neighbours would supply the necessary details, and his name would be on local records.

Daniel was now sweating as his fear increased, and he tried to work out what would be best to do. There was a chance that neither of the two young women had yet opened the envelope and read the letter. If that were the case, he could go up to the house and with a bright, cheery look on his face ask if by any chance a letter addressed to a Mr Daniel Collins had been delivered to them by mistake. He would tell them the letter was for an Australian friend who was planning to visit him.

It was a brilliant idea, he thought, but then his relief vanished as he reminded himself that there was still the danger that one or other of the Kenilworth daughters might in fact have opened and read the letter. It could only have come from Mildred since no one else in New South Wales was aware that he was in England, and there was no way of knowing what the silly woman might have said.

Several minutes passed before Daniel made up his mind to take no immediate action that evening. Tomorrow morning he would watch for the post boy and, after he had left, he would wander up to the house and enquire casually if they happened to have received a letter from Australia addressed to his 'friend', Mr Collins.

Daniel would have had a far more sleepless night had he known that Storm had indeed opened and read the letter.

Sitting on the side of her bed that night, she reread the untidy, misspelled words a second time. If this man was Daniel Collins, how was he in possession of the real James Kenilworth's certificates? Were they forgeries? Did such a man ever exist? She put the letter back in the envelope and placed it on her bedside table. Climbing into bed after ten more minutes' deliberation, Storm realized this was an instance when she really had no alternative but to ask Hunter for his advice.

The next morning, her mind made up, she was able to greet Daniel when he called after breakfast with a casual indifference.

'Letter?' she echoed, as she heard him ask Eloise if one had arrived for his friend when she joined them in the hallway. 'No, I haven't seen any such letter, have you, dearest? Don't worry, Cousin James, I'm sure we will get it. As soon as we do, you shall have it.'

He nodded, even further convinced that, in spite of her denials, Storm had the letter in her possession. She would be leaving the following morning for London with her sister and he would have no possible hope of recovering it. If she did indeed have it in her possession, she would without doubt show it to Chislestone when they reached London, with all the fatal consequences that would entail.

Although he had managed to appear indifferent when the fellow insisted he checked up on the validity of the certificates, he had resented Chislestone's interference. He had hoped that checks would be carried out by a simple clerk or minor legal assistant who would do no more than ask for verification of their existence in the records.

Returning to the dower house, Daniel's mouth was set in a tight line as his resolve hardened. Storm must not be allowed to show the letter to Mr Hunter Chislestone. Should he, he wondered, tell Eloise that he had had a change of mind and would go to London with them after all, after previously turning down Eloise's suggestion that he should accompany them? He could use the pretext that he needed a lighter coat for the summer. It would at least mean he would remain close to Storm – perhaps affecting a robbery, or thinking up some other means of getting the letter back.

It was not long, however, before he devised a far better plan which would, he hoped, ensure that the incriminating letter was soon safely in his hands. He would tell his manservant that he had decided to spend the day at the annual horse fair at Harmsworth Common and instruct him to have his horse ready for his departure the next day. This would adequately explain his absence.

His heart beating with excitement, Daniel realized he had now found a way open for him to retrieve the letter, which he felt sure that Storm had in her possession. Certain as he was of her intention to involve Chislestone, he had only to obtain the letter before she reached London. All he had to do was to disguise himself to ensure that she would be unaware of who had robbed her.

His thoughts now concentrated on the gossip in the village inn about the highwaymen who had recently held up the mail coach and successfully made off with all the passengers' possessions as well as the parcels the mail was carrying. Robberies were not unusual, it was agreed, but in this instance, the highwaymen had shot and killed both the driver and the guard. The men had not been caught and descriptions of them by the mail coach passengers were so vague, night having fallen, that they were still at large.

It was the perfect plan for him to impersonate the fellows and hold-up the Kenilworth coach.

Daniel now told his servant he could take the rest of the day off. As soon as the man had departed it did not take Daniel very long to find what he needed. His own cloak, a dark, almost black one, would suffice to cover his body. But it lacked a hood. In the nearby gardener's shed he found a grubby brown felt hat, shapeless and so well worn it could be pulled down over his forehead. He did not have a mask to cover his mouth and eyes but was confident his scarf would serve the purpose.

By now, Daniel had travelled the road from London on several occasions and was moderately familiar with the countryside through which it passed. He had twice stopped at the Pig and Boar, the coaching inn on the edge of the forest known as The Beeches where the recent robbery had taken place. Nobody, he told himself, would expect a second hold-up in the same place.

Back indoors, fortified by a glass of brandy, Daniel set about planning an itinerary for the following day. After the best part of an hour, he had decided that if he was to cover his tracks, he must depart as soon as possible after the Kenilworth coaches had disappeared down the drive. There would almost certainly be two coaches – the second a carriage containing the luggage and servants apart from Storm and Eloise's maids. This, he supposed, would set off first so as to be in London in time to have the house ready for their employers' arrival.

For a moment, Daniel allowed himself to relax. Then he stiffened as he realized he had forgotten something important. After the hold-up inevitable enquiries would be made and no doubt Chislestone would check on his movements. He would, therefore, go straight from The Beeches to Harmsworth Common for the horse fair, where he would make it his business to be seen.

Half an hour and another brandy later, Daniel had devised what he believed to be a foolproof scheme. He would go back up to the hall that afternoon and tell Eloise he had decided to spend the next day at Harmsworth Common, as he wanted to see what happened at a renowned English country horse fair.

A faint smile spread across Daniel's face as, with a feeling of great satisfaction, he reviewed his plan. Certain that the Kenilworth coach would stop for a change of horses and refreshment at the Pig and Boar, he decided to leave in time to conceal himself in The Beeches forest, don his disguise and await its arrival.

After the hold-up it would take him only a few minutes to discard his disguise and be on his way to the fair.

Congratulating himself on having found a solution to the dangerous problem of the letter, he rose to his feet and went up to his room to perform one last task – namely, to clean the pistol which was concealed in the box under his bed.

NINETEEN

The next day.

Fuller, the elderly caretaker of Chislestone Manor, opened the door and regarded the smartly dressed man who had rung the front doorbell, and who was now smiling at him.

'Come now, Fuller! Don't say you have forgotten me?'

The caretaker stared at the stranger he judged to be in his thirties. He did look familiar, surprisingly like his young master, Mr Hunter, yet older with more lines about the eyes. He had a beard which was streaked with grey, as was his dark hair, which was now visible as he removed his hat and handed it to him.

Fuller's lined face suddenly turned white as he recognized the visitor, who was clearly enjoying his confusion. 'Mr Percy!' he gasped. 'But . . .'

'Yes, I know, I'm supposed to be dead!' Percy Chislestone replied, patting the old retainer on the shoulder. 'Don't look so horrified, Fuller, old chap. I'm not a ghost!'

Still trembling but now with a look of joyful surprise on his face, Fuller stood back to allow the hired coachman to bring in his passenger's trunk. Fuller looked apologetically at Percy.

'I'm afraid the house is shut up, sir!' he said. 'So there aren't no provisions to feed you or your driver.'

'Don't worry yourself, Fuller,' Percy interrupted. 'He can get a meal and a bed for the night at the Bell. If I recall, they used to dish up a really tasty game pie there! And I am happy to have whatever you are having . . . whatever the kitchen can provide.' He turned to the coach driver he had hired in Southampton when he'd docked and took out his purse. Withdrawing some coins, he said cheerfully, 'That should cover the hiring and a decent meal and a bed for the night.'

The coachman, grinning happily as he pocketed the generous number of coins Percy had given him, touched his hat, thanked his passenger and disappeared out through the front door.

Fuller now followed Percy into the drawing room, hurrying ahead to remove the holland covers shrouding the furniture.

'Family on holiday?' Percy enquired cheerfully. 'Her Ladyship? My sister?'

'Her Ladyship and Miss Cissy are holidaying in Lancing with Lady Clarice Witton,' said Fuller, as he drew the heavy curtains to shut out the darkening sky. 'Mr Hunter lives in London but comes here time to time to check that everything is in order. There's only me and Mrs Fuller as lives here now, and we don't see no one else.'

'Visitors?' Percy queried as Fuller bent down to light the fire.

'Yes, sir! People as want to look round if they was thinking of buying—'

He broke off as he saw the look of disbelief on Percy Chislestone's face. He said hurriedly, 'Maybe t'would be best if Mr Hunter explains, Mr Percy. You see, things haven't gone well for the family ever since . . .' he hesitated once more and then said quietly, '. . . ever since your father died, Mr Percy.'

Percy looked shocked.

'The master had a heart attack, sir. It was on Miss Cissy's sixteenth birthday – a dreadful shock for us all.'

Seeing how distressed Percy was now looking, he offered to send Bob, the stable lad who took care of the few remaining horses, to ride up to London first thing next morning to inform Mr Hunter of his brother's miraculous reappearance.

Percy hesitated for a minute or two and then shook his head. 'I'll go myself, Fuller. All I need now is something to eat, if Mrs Fuller can find it: bread and cheese will suffice, and if the cellar still contains some of my father's claret, I could do with a bottle of that!'

'Mr Hunter locked up the cellar when he closed the house, sir, but he left me the key,' the old man said, smiling. 'Is there anything more that I can do?'

'You could ask Mrs Fuller to make up a bed for me and put a couple of warming pans in. Ever since those weeks I was buried in the mine, I seem to have felt the cold in a way I never did before.'

Fuller looked concerned. 'At the time, Mrs Fuller and I said there was naught worse could happen to a man than to be buried alive. When we heard the mine had collapsed we was told there were some survivors, but then there was a letter came saying you hadn't been found and must be presumed dead after so long.'

Percy was standing warming his legs in front of the now blazing fire. He nodded, his eyes thoughtful as he recalled the frightening moment when he could no longer hear the noise of digging which had represented his only hope of survival.

'That was when I resigned myself to the fact that I was going to die down there in the dark,' he said in a tone of voice so low it was almost a whisper. Then, his voice strengthening, he continued, 'I was lucky, Fuller, very lucky! I'd been buried in quite a large pocket of air. Not only that, there was a steady drip of water within reach of where I was lying. That helped me survive although, by the time I was found, I was too weak to reach for it.'

He gave a faint smile as he patted the elderly caretaker on his shoulder.

'Don't ever let anyone tell you there isn't a God, Fuller,' he said. 'I never stopped praying, even when I could no longer hear the rescuers and knew they must have given up. Days and nights passed as I grew weaker and weaker. In my few conscious moments, I prayed for delivery.'

Fuller was looking on the point of tears as he murmured, 'God be praised, Mr Percy! He answered your prayers!'

Percy nodded, then continued, 'Unbeknownst to me, a young lad had arrived and had begun searching for souvenirs in the mounds of rubble which had once been the entrance to the mine. The son of a farmer some miles away, he had been given a day off for working hard and decided to explore. He had not intended to take his dog with him, but the animal had persisted in following him. While the lad searched for souvenirs among the rubble left by the rescue parties, the dog began frantically digging far above my head.'

He stopped for a moment and went and settled himself in

the fireside armchair, gesturing to Fuller to do the same on a smaller chair by the door as he continued, 'Although the boy called him and finally tugged at his collar when he decided to return home, the dog refused to leave and eventually the boy went home without him. There the dog stayed for two days, at which point the farmer decided to alert some of his neighbours to the fact that there might be someone still alive whom the dog was trying to reach.'

Percy now paused, his eyes half closed as he allowed his memories to surface again.

'I was told the authorities were asked to resume their rescue attempt, but they refused on the grounds that even if the dog had sensed a body, whoever it was would certainly be dead, which made a further search by busy hard-working men unwarranted.'

Fuller was now beaming happily. 'But they changed their minds?'

'No, but that dog knew I was alive and would not give up. If the farmer put him on a lead so he'd stop digging long enough to eat and drink, he'd go straight back to the same place and start digging again when he was freed.' He paused, smiling, and then said, 'The men had no special equipment, only their farm tools, and progress was slow, but by then there wasn't a man among them not prepared to follow the direction the dog was taking. He'd realized they were trying to help him and stood quietly while they removed a boulder or shored up a roof, and with the dog leading them, after three days they dug their way to me.'

Percy's smile broadened. 'Copper, his name was: part hound, part sheepdog, and there's no doubt he saved my life. I dare say some folk will think me silly, but I'm going to arrange for my bank to set up money for a home for dogs like Copper – he was once a stray, you see, and only survived because of my rescuer's kind heart.'

Hearing the grandfather clock in the hall strike seven times, Fuller stood up slowly and straightened his shoulders as best he could, saying, 'It's time I asked Mrs Fuller to get some jugs of water heated, Mr Percy, as I don't doubt you'll be wanting a bath.'

Percy gestured his thanks.

Thirty minutes later and with an effort, Fuller contained his impatience while he poured hot water over Percy's back, dried him with a large fluffy towel and helped him into some of the smart new clothes Percy told him he had purchased in New York before he'd boarded ship.

Mrs Fuller had joined her husband in the drawing room as he enjoyed a simple meal and three quarters of a bottle of claret on a tray in front of the fire. She sat tut-tutting as Percy continued his story.

'The dog's owner, a farmer by the name of Wilbur Fox,' he told Fuller, 'took me into his home, where his wife nursed me. I regained consciousness two days later but I had completely lost my memory. I had not the slightest idea of my name, my age, my nationality, my home, even whether I had brothers, sisters, parents . . . Sometimes I spoke in French, as if I were back in school.' He shook his head at the memory, and after a brief pause continued. 'I had been part-owner of the mine, and when I did not appear on the scene I was presumed dead and that was when my poor mother would have been told of my demise.'

He broke off and then added with a smile, 'I continued to live with my rescuer – a truly godly man who had taken pity on me.'

'May God bless him!' Mrs Fuller muttered as her husband put another log on the dwindling fire.

Percy smiled. 'Then gradually, to everyone's amazement – not least my own – my memory began to return. I had been living as one of the family, learning to turn my hand to whatever tasks needed attending to, be it milking the cow, cleaning out the stables, even ploughing the fields. I regained my health and was physically strong, missing only my senses, and when they began to return the farmer drove me into the nearest town to see the local doctor. The doctor was a wise man. He told me not to try to recollect my past too quickly, that it would all return to me in time. Meanwhile, he suggested it might be best for all concerned if I did not notify my family until I was well enough to return to them.' Percy took a sip of his wine and continued, 'Now it's time for you to bring me up to date with the family's fortunes, Fuller. I hope there is better news than that of my poor father's death.'

While Fuller replenished his glass he outlined briefly the misfortunes of both the Chislestones and the Kenilworth family. He made only the briefest reference to the Chislestones' financial situation, saying that Hunter would be far better able to explain it.

So much had happened, Percy thought, in the missing years of his life. Not only to his own family but to their neighbours, the Kenilworths, who had always been like a second family to them. He grieved especially for John, who had been his closest childhood friend, killed in an avalanche with Lord Kenilworth. The news about the astonishing success of the self-effacing Kenilworth tutor amazed him, as did the sudden appearance of an Australian gentleman who was said to be a long-lost member of the Kenilworth family.

Pouring Percy the last of the bottle of claret, Fuller noted the look of exhaustion on his face and said, 'You must be tired, sir, after all that travelling. Let me help you up to bed now, and tomorrow before you leave for London, I will tell you what Mr Hunter said to us about why the manor has to be sold.'

Percy would have liked to be further enlightened right away, but the wholesome meal, the claret and the long, tiring day were suddenly too much for him. Such was his exhaustion that Fuller, old as he was, had to half carry him upstairs, undress him and lift him into bed.

Percy was woken by the sun streaming through his window. In America he had fallen into the habit of sleeping with his curtains open ever since his time trapped in the mine. Now he could also hear the familiar noise of birdsong on this lovely early summer morning. Throwing back the covers, he got out of bed and for several minutes remained standing at the window reflecting on what a truly beautiful country he lived in and how grateful he was to be home after these lost years. Not for the first time since he had set off for home, he felt an overwhelming wave of gratitude to the man who had saved his life and who had cared for him for so long as one of his own family. It was Wilbur Fox who, once he knew who Percy was, had also discovered the whereabouts of his best friend, the co-owner of the derelict mine.

When Fuller arrived with his breakfast, Percy informed him that as soon as he had eaten and was dressed he would leave at once for London.

'I have such wonderful news to give the family!' he told him, as Fuller placed a laden tray on a table by his bed. 'I was too tired last night to complete my story, but I wish to waste no further time before letting you and Mrs Fuller hear of my good fortune.'

While the old man did his best to act as Percy's valet, Percy said, 'There is no longer a necessity for Chislestone Manor to be sold: I am a rich man, Fuller, and likely to be even richer in the future!'

Seeing the look of astonishment on the man's face, he laughed. 'It's true, my good fellow, and if you will now help me put on my shoes I will further relate my good fortune. When I had fully recovered my memory, I told my host how I and my best friend at university, a fellow called Mihailo Milanovic, had decided to invest in one of the new gold mines which we'd seen written about in an article in the newspaper. Our parents were horrified when in due course we set off to America to inspect the mining prospects in which we intended to invest our money.'

Percy smiled once more at the expression on Fuller's face. 'Yes, our fathers were right to warn us we had no guarantees and were in all probability going to be disappointed.' He sighed at the memory of those anxious times when he and Milanovic had risked their money buying from a disappointed prospector a tunnel which was not producing the promised amount of gold. They had been overjoyed when they finally found the promised veins and then, without warning, the mine tunnel had collapsed.

'After many enquiries I was able to find out that my friend had survived the accident,' Percy related. 'He had been told that my body had never been found and I was presumed to be dead. While I was being cared for, my friend was suddenly approached by a wealthy prospector offering him an extra-ordinary sum of money for the right to our mine.'

Percy stood in front of the looking glass and carefully tied the knot of his cravat. Satisfied with its appearance, he continued, 'Milanovic was no fool. He made enquiries and learned that the anxious buyer had had some searches made in the ruins and discovered an extended vein of gold which had been made visible by the rockfall during the tunnel's collapse.'

He reached for the trousers that Fuller was holding out to him and pulled them on. Once his shoes were on, he patted Fuller's shoulder. 'Milanovic did not sell despite the fact that he was penniless. He borrowed money and reactivated the mine, discovering a vast deposit of gold within the first months of tunnelling. Milanovic, an honourable fellow, immediately transferred my share to a bank account in my name, and this he intended to send to my family once the mine's future prospects were established.'

For a few minutes, Fuller did not speak. Then he said, 'It's like one of them fairy tales what Mrs Fuller used to read to our little 'uns when they was bairns.' He paused again before adding, 'Mr Hunter's been that sad having to sell an' all. Her Ladyship and Miss Cissy was that upset, and of course them servants 'as had to lose their jobs. Mrs Fuller and me and the gardeners was lucky to be staying.' He sighed. 'Young Bob were in tears the day most of the estate horses were sold.'

'Well, the staff can all come back now!' Percy said, as Fuller helped him into his fawn waistcoat and immaculately cut dark brown jacket. 'The sooner I get to London to see my young brother, the more quickly we can all get back to normal and get this house up and running again.'

Glancing at his pocket watch, he added, 'I'd best make haste, Fuller, if I am to catch the stage coach in Chislestone. The sooner I get a replacement horse for old Pegasus, the better.'

Fuller smiled to himself and followed Percy downstairs with his overnight bag and a spring in his step.

'Miss Kenilworth and Miss Storm went to the sale of the estate horses and bought Firefly for themselves. Much too big for them, but folk in the village who've seen Miss Storm riding her says she manages her like she were a Shetland pony!'

Hours later, it was already dark as Percy alighted from the stage coach. Retrieving his bag from the coachman, he made his way among the bustling crowds to his family's London home in Upper Brook Street. Tired, hungry and stiff from the journey, he was deeply disappointed to hear from the porter that Hunter had left for Lancing two days previously to see his mother.

Nor, it seemed, was he the only person wishing to see Hunter urgently. Miss Storm had also left a message asking his master to visit her as soon as possible at Mount Street, but Mr Hunter had already left London by then, the man informed Percy. The porter also related the shocking news that on the previous afternoon the Kenilworth coach had been held up on its way to London and one of the young Kenilworth ladies had been shot.

With a sinking heart he realized that, far from being able to announce the good news of his survival, he might instead have to learn that one of his childhood friends was dead.

Checking his watch, Percy realized it was too late for him to call round to Mount Street to see if his help was needed. In the morning, he told himself, he would hire a coach to take him to Lancing, but before that he would stop off at the Kenilworth house. Overcome by weariness, he went to bed.

TWENTY

The same day.

As the day drew to a close, Eloise sat back in the chair that had been placed by Storm's bedside and closed her eyes. It had been a terrifying and exhausting day. That afternoon when she had heard the two gunshots and seen Storm fall to the floor of the coach, she had feared the highwayman had killed her sister. It was a huge relief when they had reached the sanctuary of the Pig and Boar where a passing midwife had been lunching. She had attended to Storm's wound, and reassured Eloise that the bullet had passed through the fleshy part of Storm's left arm. Provided she kept it clean, the worst she might expect would be an unsightly scar.

By the time they reached London, the street lamps had been lit and the staff at Mount Street were filled with anxiety at the delay in their arrival. It had taken Harry the groom some time to quieten the horses and find a replacement from the Pig and Boar staff for the guard, who had been shot and badly wounded during the ambush. Eloise and Mabel had sat either side of Storm in the coach doing their best to calm her as she slowly recovered from the shock.

'I know him! I know who it was and what he wants!' she kept saying. 'His horse, it knew me. Eloise, you must listen to me . . .'

Believing Storm to be delirious, Eloise had done her best to calm her. Her one concern had been to get her sister to London where she could call their family doctor to visit her. They had reached the haven of their London house without further delay and, refusing to rest, Storm was sitting up in bed confronting Eloise once more.

'I *have* to see Hunter before it's too late! I've got to see him, Eloise. I have evidence which proves James is not our brother. I've got to talk to Hunter, I've got to. Don't you see? I can't explain now. Please trust me. This afternoon that man tried to kill me. But I can come to no harm on the stage coach with other people around me if I travel to Lancing tomorrow. Mabel will look after me too.'

Eloise was still adamant in her refusal – Storm should not travel on the stage coach to Lancing. For the first time in their lives, to Mabel's dismay, the sisters had quarrelled, their voices raised. When finally Eloise left Storm's room, both young women were in tears. Eloise resolved that she would ask the doctor to forbid Storm's proposed journey when he called in the morning, and Storm secretly determined she would slip out through the gate in the walled back garden into the narrow mews street behind, wearing Mabel's black mantle and bonnet if necessary.

Next morning, unaware of her sister's intention, Eloise was in the kitchen discussing the day's meals with Cook when the front doorbell jangled loudly. Peering through the window up the area steps, Cook said, 'Seems you have a visitor, Miss Eloise. Will we finish the menu later?'

Unaccustomed to receiving callers before eleven at the earliest, Eloise supposed this must be a senior officer from the constabulary wanting information about the previous day's hold-up. She went upstairs, where Roberts informed her that he had put the visitor in the morning room.

When Roberts opened the door and Eloise saw David Carter standing by the window staring out into the garden, she nearly fainted. 'Thank you, Roberts! That will be all!' she said weakly. The door closed behind the butler and David turned to face her.

'Forgive me for not advising you that I would be calling to see you,' he said.

Although his clothes were, as usual, slightly untidy and outdated, he was different in a way she could not at first define. There was a look of confidence in his stature, a stronger tone to his voice, as he stepped forward and helped her into a chair. Then, looking down at her, he said quietly, 'I know we agreed not to see one another again, but circumstances have changed.'

His voice now deepened with emotion as he said huskily, 'Eloise, I have come to ask you to marry me!'

For a moment, Eloise looked up at him disbelievingly, her heart beating furiously from the shock of his announcement. Then he reached down and took one of her hands in his, holding it gently as he continued, 'You know I have always loved you, and I dare to think that you have discovered the same feeling for me. Had I been in a position to do so, I would have declared myself many years ago, but I never once imagined that such a thing might one day be possible. Now I feel able to say: Eloise, I love you! I want to be married to you, and at long last the miracle has happened and I am in a position to ask you to be my wife.'

For several minutes while David had been declaring himself, Eloise wondered if she was dreaming. He had changed. There was a new look of authority about him she'd only ever seen when he had been discussing art. Even in her wildest dreams, she had never imagined he would one day arrive on her doorstep and ask her to marry him.

Correctly interpreting Eloise's thoughts, David drew up a chair next to hers and, now holding both her hands tightly in his, he continued, 'I arrived back in England yesterday. I thought you might be down at Kenilworth. My plan was to hire a carriage to take me there. Then, on my way to my lodgings, I saw your carriage outside this house and knew I would find you here.'

He lifted one of her hands and kissed the back of it tenderly as he spoke in a low voice. 'I can now tell you that my life . . . it has changed in the most miraculous way. I am now not only a rich man but the owner of a very beautiful house.' He paused and then said, 'I am now in a position to support you if you will consider marrying me.'

Yet again, Eloise thought she must be dreaming. There had been so many times over the years when she had sat by her bedroom window at Kenilworth Hall watching David Carter leaving the house at the end of a day's tutorials, weak with longing for him to stay with her for ever. She daydreamed of a well-born relation appearing from David's past who would make him acceptable as her husband. She would happily disregard any difference in their backgrounds, but she understood why it would be impossible for David to do so. Apart from knowing he would be responsible for her being struck off society hostesses' invitation lists, he would be far too proud to permit her to support him financially.

Consumed now with the need to know that this was not all an impossible dream, Eloise said urgently, 'Tell me! Tell me, David! What has happened to you?'

His grip on her hands loosened as he stood up and drew her gently to her feet, his eyes shining. 'I told you in my letter that I had accepted the commission the marchesa had offered me to paint her portrait; well, I finished it recently while staying as a guest at her beautiful home. She was extremely pleased with my painting, and knowing I was a great admirer of beautiful artefacts, she offered to show me round the *castello*.'

David paused for a moment, his eyes now thoughtful as he recalled that afternoon.

'In the marchesa's bedroom – a magnificent room I will one day describe to you – there was a framed pen and ink sketch of a prettily dressed small boy perched on a wall. The card it was drawn on was no bigger than a postcard so it was difficult to distinguish the child's features. The marchesa saw me staring at it and said in a voice I can only describe as tragic, "That is my beloved son, Carlo. He was three years old when a friend sketched that picture. It is the only likeness I have of him".'

David's face was now sombre as he recounted the marchesa's story of the great tragedy of her life. Her husband had taken the little boy for a ride in his yacht. The sea was very calm and there would normally have been no danger. The marchesa had been waving to them from the terrace when, without warning, a dark object surfaced in front of them. It turned out to be a lobster pot which had broken loose. It became entangled in the rudder, there was a sudden squall of wind, the boat overturned and the marchesa's husband and child both drowned.'

'What a terrible thing for that poor woman to have witnessed!' Eloise exclaimed.

David nodded.

'She led me to understand that she never spoke of the tragedy or showed little Carlo's likeness to strangers as it was too painful for her to do so, but she was now telling me because she wanted to know if I would be able to paint a full-sized portrait of Carlo which she could have framed and hung beside her own in the big salon.'

'David, you managed to do it?' Eloise asked urgently.

He shook his head. 'Not at first; the likeness was no more than a sketch. But then the marchesa started telling me about the child – everything she could recall about his charming little ways, his laughter, his loving nature, his enthusiasm for the life around him which he was discovering. Without making any promises, I told the marchesa I would try to recreate the likeness she so badly wanted.'

Eloise's eyes were shining. 'So you succeeded!' she whispered.

'Not immediately. But then the marchesa decided she should take me down to the harbour. Her husband used to moor his boat there in the summer months, in the boathouse attached to their summer villa. The house is built right on the edge of the bay, with steps leading down to the sea, and is overlooked by the *castello*. It was there that the tragedy happened. She had not been back there since. Nor, she informed me, would she ever live there again, despite its beauty.'

'I can understand that,' Eloise said. 'I am surprised she took you there.'

David hesitated. 'I, too, was surprised when she suggested it,' he continued, stroking her hand as she talked, 'but her instinct was right. From the stories she told when we were there I was gradually able to picture the little boy in far greater detail: his mischievousness, his curiosity, his adoration of his parents, his fascination with the sea and its underwater life. I almost felt I had known him.'

Eloise's eyes were alight with anticipation. 'So you were able to provide the marchesa with the portrait she wanted?'

David nodded. 'I had not once considered that she would wish to show her gratitude further after her generous commission, and at first I could not believe she was serious when she insisted I should accept the ownership of the beautiful villa as a thank-you present in return for the joy I had given her.'

He smiled at Eloise. 'No matter how hard I tried to explain that I was more than satisfied with the fee she had paid me, she steadfastly insisted that I accepted the villa as a gift. She did not feel inclined to sell to a stranger a place which held so many memories for her. She felt I had managed somehow to connect spiritually with her beloved child and would remember him there as strangers would not.'

David gave an embarrassed laugh and looked down at Eloise with a questioning expression. 'Perhaps I should not have done so, but I finally accepted her offer. I had indeed fallen in love with the house, perched as it is on the edge of the Mediterranean. Maybe it was the atmosphere of the place: the changing colours of the sea and the cry of the birds; maybe it was because the marchesa had told me so much about the child she brought him back to life, and his happy spirit seemed to be everywhere.'

David's voice thickened with emotion as he added, 'I want to take you there to live with me. We would be happy, I know we would. We could make a home there, paint together, raise our children there. Storm could visit us . . .'

Eloise caught her breath as he now put his arms around her, saying, 'Marry me, Eloise, my love, my only love. I am no longer in need of money and my income can support us both. I already have several rich clients waiting for me to paint their wives' portraits. I love you! Please, please tell me you will marry me.'

It was on the tip of Eloise's tongue to cry out, 'Yes! Yes, of course I will marry you!' but she bit back the words in time. She stepped away from him, took his hand and held it to her cheek.

'David, I can't! I want to, but I can't! I have to live here in England where I can take care of the family estate. I must also look after Storm.' She told him briefly about the previous day's frightening hold-up and her worry for Storm's wellbeing.

'I suppose there may be a tiny ray of hope for us,' she said finally in a quiet voice, adding that if the man they were calling

Cousin James was indeed their half-brother, it was possible the estate would have to be passed legally to him. If that were to happen, and if he learned how best to look after the estate at Kenilworth, and if by then Storm were married—'

She broke off, choked by her words and on the verge of breaking down as she saw and understood the look of dismay on David's face. All she was promising him was a possibility of happiness many years ahead. She looked at him with eyes filled with tears. 'I'm so sorry; so very sorry!' she whispered. 'I love you, David. I cannot think of any greater happiness than to go to live in Italy with you. Maybe some women could put love before duty and be happy, but I could not do so. Please, please try to be happy without me. I am so very proud of your success and I have not the slightest doubt that you will achieve even more. Wherever you are, whatever you are doing, I shall be with you in spirit.'

Doing his utmost to hide his cruel disappointment, David drew Eloise back into his arms. 'There will never be anyone but you,' he said. 'You will be in my thoughts day and night, and I shall live for your letters.'

They kissed one another passionately for several minutes, and then David drew reluctantly away from her. 'If I stay longer I will never find the strength to leave you, my dearest!' he murmured. 'Please take the greatest care of yourself – and write to me!'

He kissed her once more and then hurriedly left the morning room. He picked up his hat and gloves from the table in the hall, and went out of the house as quickly as he could without a backward glance. Eloise remained alone in the room, her heart aching too strongly for her to stem the tears. Every part of her body longed to run after him; to stop him leaving; to tell him that she couldn't bear the thought that she might never see him again. She struggled to control the sobs choking in her throat as her sadness and despair engulfed her. It was several minutes before she managed to stop weeping, knowing that when she visited Storm upstairs in bed her sister would want to know the reason for her despair. She was still standing by the window when Mabel found her there. Had it been Storm weeping, Mabel would have put her arms round her and soothed her as if she were a child again, but this was Eloise, the brave, stoical, proud young mistress who had over the years earned the respect of her staff. She would not want her moment of weakness to be seen.

'Dearie me, Miss Eloise!' she said in a cheerful voice. 'Sounds like you've caught one of them nasty colds what's going around. I'll give Violet that bottle of embrocation to rub on your chest tonight, and it wouldn't do no harm to inhale some tincture of benzoin. Now, I almost forgot to tell you that Miss Storm is ever so much better since she woke up and is demanding to see you!'

Somehow Eloise managed a smile. Grasping Mabel's suggestion of a head cold, she wiped her eyes with her handkerchief and blew her nose. 'Thank you, Mabel! Tell Miss Storm I will be up to see her shortly – and Mabel, however improved she may be feeling, she is to remain quietly in bed and obey the doctor's orders, whether she likes them or not!'

Mabel was smiling as she trundled back upstairs. No one knew better than she did what a self-willed child Miss Storm was. She'd do whatever took her fancy no matter who said what to the contrary. At least it now looked as if the wound was not infected after all. The swelling had gone down and the ugly redness had all but disappeared.

As for Miss Storm's insistence that she knew the identity of the highwayman, Mabel was far from sure that it was not her imagination playing tricks. She herself had neither seen nor recognized the man and thought it beyond belief that the Australian visitor – whom, in spite of his well-mannered behaviour, the staff had all disliked – was wicked enough to be capable of such evil.

TWENTY-ONE

The same day

Opening the door Roberts was, for the first time in his life, left standing open-mouthed and speechless as he stared disbelievingly at the bearded figure. He knew nearly every one of the family's friends, relations and neighbours, and thought at first that this man was not one of them. Then, for the first time in his impeccable career, he clapped his hand to his mouth and his eyes widened in shock.

'Mr Percy Chislestone!' he whispered. 'We thought you were—'

'Dead!' Percy finished for him, smiling. 'I'm no ghost, Roberts, so there's no need to look so alarmed. I very nearly died when the mine collapsed but eventually I was rescued. I lost my memory, or I would have been home long since.'

The butler had now recovered his equilibrium. Percy allowed him to take his hat, gloves and walking stick and asked anxiously, 'I do hope neither of the young ladies was badly injured? I spent last night in our London house and the caretaker there told me that one of them had been shot.'

Roberts nodded. 'Yes!' he said. 'It was poor Miss Storm. Fortunately the bullet the blackguard aimed at her was wide of its mark and only pierced her upper arm. The doctor has been and I am told he announced she was not in any danger provided the wound did not become infected.'

'A highwayman?' Percy queried.

Roberts nodded. 'He was, I understand, masked. Unfortunately, the guard Miss Eloise had hired for the journey who sat next to our coachman Harry was shot before he could fire his weapon and so the fellow got away. Miss Eloise is in the drawing room, sir. Shall I break it to her gently that you are here?'

'There is no need, Roberts!' Eloise was standing in the open doorway staring in astonishment at the familiar figure of her childhood friend and neighbour, long presumed dead.

For a moment she wondered if she had not in fact woken up this morning – could she be dreaming? First there had been the unbelievable surprise of David's visit and his proposal of marriage; now here was Percy Chislestone, whom they had all believed to be dead.

Still unsure she was not dreaming, Eloise led Percy into the drawing room where, after hugging one another, they sat down side by side on the sofa. Percy told her a much abbreviated account of his survival as he was impatient to hear the details of their terrifying ordeal the previous day which Eloise then described.

'It happened no more than half a mile from the Pig and Boar coaching inn,' Eloise said. 'The highwayman was waiting on horseback as our coach was passing through The Beeches. We were horrified – and very frightened—'

She broke off to catch her breath, and then resumed in a whisper, 'The man didn't say a word but beckoned us out of our carriage. Then, with his gun trained on us, he reached down with his free hand and snatched my reticule containing my jewellery. He was about to take Storm's when suddenly she turned and slung it back through the open door of the carriage. He let off a shot at her; I was terrified he had killed her, but his aim must have been deflected by Storm's movement because the shot pierced her raised arm, which mercifully stopped the bullet from reaching her heart. At that point, the guard raised his gun to shoot the man, but he was too late and he himself was shot.'

Eloise broke off, now smiling tentatively at Percy.

'Storm was so brave! And I think she might even have tried to strike him if he had not galloped off into the forest. Although a search was made by some of the men in the coaching inn when they heard the news, he was not found.'

'And poor little Storm; she is in no danger?'

Eloise smiled. 'Storm would not like you to refer to her as if she were a child!' she said. 'She is a very pretty young woman now, Percy. As far as her arm is concerned, it is only a minor wound and is not causing her too much pain. I am worried about her nonetheless. She keeps saying she is convinced she knows the identity of the highwayman and that he wants to kill her because she has vital evidence against him. In fact, she is insisting that when she is up and dressed she is going to Lancing because she has something important to tell your brother, Hunter. She won't explain what it is! She is in no condition to travel alone and no doubt the doctor would forbid it. Frankly, Percy, I don't know how I can prevent her leaving the house unless I lock her in her room.'

Percy frowned. 'This sounds very much like the self-willed young girl I used to know,' he said, smiling briefly. 'Eloise, maybe I can solve this dilemma for you. Storm can travel in my carriage with me, if she is well enough. I planned to leave immediately after I had seen you were both all right. You can be reassured that she will come to no harm with me.'

Eloise hesitated. 'I can tell you, Percy, that my darling sister will be well enough to do anything she wishes to! Although . . . I can't understand the urgency about her seeing Hunter; in fact, for some time she has been avoiding him whenever she can.'

Percy looked astonished. 'But she absolutely adored him when she was a child! And he was fond of her. Ah well, no doubt I shall hear about it on our way to Lancing! Do you not wish to come with us, Eloise?'

She shook her head. 'We have only just come up here from Kenilworth,' she said reluctantly, 'so I have many domestic duties demanding my attention. I will go now and ask Storm if she would like to travel to Lancing with you.' A smile lit up her face. 'She is going to be so elated when she hears that you are alive. I can't think of a more agreeable surprise than your appearance this morning.'

Storm was delighted that Eloise now agreed to her travelling to Lancing with Percy Chislestone, who had so miraculously reappeared. Despite Mabel's disapproving protests, she began to plan for the journey.

Storm had slept fitfully the previous night, alternate visions of Firefly and the highwayman tormenting her dreams. She had woken knowing, without a shadow of doubt, two important facts: the highwayman's horse, despite the black discolouring of her mane and tail, was Firefly, the horse that Eloise had allowed their visitor to use – she would recognize the build of the well-loved animal anywhere; and the masked highwayman was the man purporting to be James Kenilworth, prepared to kill her if that was the only way he could recover the incriminating letter from Australia.

Eloise was answering Percy's many questions as to what had happened to his family while he had been away. He already had a vague idea of the financial disasters from Fuller's limited knowledge but was now shocked to hear from Eloise how truly serious his family's situation was. It was a wonderful moment for him when he saw the happiness flood Eloise's face after he reassured her that Chislestone Manor could now remain as it had always been in the past, their much-loved family home.

Meanwhile upstairs, Mabel, grumbling under her breath, was hurriedly packing a valise for her young mistress. 'You should be staying here right in your bed!' Mabel muttered angrily. 'Goodness knows what the doctor will say. And don't you pretend that wound ain't hurting,' she added.

'Stop fussing, Mabel,' Storm said with an excited glitter in her eyes. 'I am perfectly all right.' She was unusually quiet and Mabel guessed it was the discomfort from her wound.

'You won't be saying that after we've bumped along the road all the way to Lancing!' Mabel muttered. 'I can tell you this much, Miss Storm, I wouldn't be going to Lancing with you were it not for Lady Chislestone and Lady Witton there to take responsibility for you. I'm that surprised Miss Eloise is letting you go . . .'

Storm became uncomfortably aware of her injury during the journey. As the afternoon wore on and the surface of the road deteriorated, she realized that Mabel had been absolutely right. Her arm ached almost unbearably as it was jolted in the confines of the carriage, and it was with a tremendous sigh of relief that she saw the familiar signpost to Chislestone village come into view.

She tried to divert her thoughts from the painful throbbing by relating to Percy the series of unfortunate events that had evolved since his supposed death. It gave him great satisfaction that the fortune he had accumulated in the past few years would be so helpful in re-establishing the family's security.

It was Mabel who suggested that her young mistress was not fit to continue the journey and that Percy should leave them at Kenilworth.

Despite the pain of her arm, Storm's mind was as sharp as ever. The letter, that vital piece of evidence, was too precious to be entrusted to anyone but Hunter. She would, however, she decided, scribble a note for Percy to give to Hunter, explaining how it came to be in her possession and asking him to come immediately to Kenilworth to see it. Meanwhile she would retain the letter, which she could hide safely in her father's study until Hunter arrived, and retrieve the pistol from the locked drawer in his desk as a precaution.

Storm's thoughts were not on the passing countryside as Percy's hired coach took her and Mabel along the familiar main thoroughfare to Kenilworth Hall. It was only five o'clock in the evening and the farm workers were still busy in the fields.

Beside Storm, Mabel sat silently, resigned now to the fact that they might well be heading into trouble. She was now beginning to believe her young mistress that the foreign visitor was indeed an imposter, and that it was he who had held up the coach and shot Miss Storm. Although Miss Storm's condition necessitated this change of plan, it struck her as the height of madness for the young girl to stay at Kenilworth Hall, with the fraudster possibly back in the dower house, before Mr Hunter knew of the situation.

'Mabel, will you take that look off your face?' Storm whispered as her maid helped her down from the carriage. While Percy alerted the few remaining household staff to their unexpected arrival and oversaw the change of horses, she went straight into her father's study. Sitting down at the desk, she wrote the note for Percy to give to Hunter.

It was only with difficulty that Storm had managed to persuade Percy to continue his journey without her. While he was on his way to Lancing with her precious note safely in his pocket she would, she insisted, be perfectly safe with

Mabel. In any event, she expected Hunter would arrive the next day to deal with the problem. She would allow Mabel to put her to bed as soon as her room was prepared, and Percy had no cause whatsoever to worry about her.

After eating a hurried meal of Cook's skilfully prepared jellied pig's head, potted meat from the store cupboard and warm bread and cheese in the welcome warmth of the kitchen, all washed down with a glass of claret, Percy finally departed once he had heard from Mabel that Storm was safely tucked up in bed.

As the sound of the carriage wheels diminished down the drive, Mabel came into Storm's bedroom to bring her a tray of soup and some bread. Storm sat up in bed.

'Fetch me that old peignoir, Mabel!' she instructed. 'I don't need food. I want to go down to Papa's study again to make sure the pistol is still there – and don't argue with me. To be on the safe side, you must check the windows and doors are locked. I give you my word my arm is not paining me unduly.'

Her many years of attending Storm had taught her the folly of trying to divert her once she had made up her mind to do something and Mabel now went in search of the warm garment, wondering if her young mistress could actually be expecting the dower house occupant to come up to the big house and attack them. Realizing he might have seen the carriage leaving and guessed that they were alone with only a few servants in the house, she understood Storm's request that she see that the building was secured against intruders. She helped Storm into her dressing gown and accompanied her downstairs.

Lord Kenilworth's pistol was exactly where he had left it, complete with bullets. The drawer was locked and the key was hanging beneath the mahogany desk top. With a contented smile, Storm removed the case and replaced it with Mildred's letter. She closed the drawer and locked it once more.

Watching her from the doorway, Mabel sighed again, her frown deepening as she muttered, 'Should be a man, not a young lady like you, Miss Storm, to be doing this. Isn't even as if I was young and strong like I used to be and could defend you if you was attacked. You should wait until Mr Hunter comes and can deal with things proper.'

Impulsively, Storm put her arm round her faithful servant. 'Darling Mabel, I shall not allow that man to come anywhere near us. I am not in the least afraid of shooting him; when Mr Hunter used to allow me to do target shooting with him, he said I had a naturally good aim.'

Mabel looked thoughtful. ''Tis to be hoped Mr Percy will reach Lancing quickly.'

'Quite right, Mabel. That's why I have Papa's pistol.'

Mabel nodded. 'I'll go now and make sure all the doors is properly locked and no windows left open.'

So certain was Storm that Daniel Collins would grab this unexpected chance to get the letter from her that she slept only fitfully after Mabel had retired for the night. Although partially reassured, knowing that all the doors and windows were locked, she was instantly alert when, after an hour or so, she heard the faintest sound of footsteps in the passage outside her bedroom door. She reached for the pistol on her bedside table but missed her handhold in the pitch darkness. The case containing the weapon and bullets fell to the floor with a clatter as the door creaked open. The next moment, she felt a hand cover her mouth.

A voice she recognized immediately, no longer refined but harsh, sounded by her ear. 'Don't make a sound and you won't get hurt!'

There was no mistaking the rough accent and Storm felt a stab of fear as she whispered, 'I don't have the letter you want.'

She could not see his face in the darkness but there was an unmistakable sneer in his tone. 'Don't lie to me. I intend to get it back no matter what harm I do you. So are you going to be sensible and hand it over?'

'I give you my word, I don't have it,' Storm declared, trying hard to keep the tremor from her voice.

For a moment the man did not speak, but his grip tightened on her arm and she could not withhold a small cry of pain. Immediately he clamped his hand over her mouth again.

Storm might have been less frightened had she known that at that moment Percy had arrived at Lancing.

*   *   *

Cissy stared at her elder brother in disbelief as he recounted his story. It was some years since he had left home with his university friend Mihailo Milanovic, both young men in their twenties and she still a child. She had been saddened when Hunter had told her of Percy's death, but his life and hers had been so far apart when they were children, she had not really mourned Percy's passing. As the servants removed the last of the dishes from the late celebratory supper Lady Witton's cook had hurriedly prepared for them, Cissy glanced at Percy's broad, smiling face, partly covered by a thick beard, and felt a rush of affection for him. Not only was his reappearance a wonderful surprise, but she was also delighted by his announcement that his gold mine was now flourishing and that there was no longer the horrid prospect of her home being sold.

Percy was laughing. 'So you see, Mama, you should never have doubted me when I left home that day promising I would return, no matter how many years passed before I could do so!'

Lady Chislestone dabbed at her eyes and smiled once more as Hunter stood up from the table and went to put his arm round her shoulders. Grinning, he looked across the table at his brother. 'That old proverb about the bad penny always turning up hardly applies in your life, Percy, old fellow! From what you have been telling us, it sounds as if you are swamped in gold!'

Percy nodded. 'We don't even need to count it. Milanovic has been saving my share of the proceeds intending to send them to you at the year's end, so not only have I a very large capital sum to give you, Hunter, which I hope will pay off those debts poor Father left, but the money should also enable us to safeguard the estate. Milanovic tells me the mine is expected to go on producing gold for many years to come, so if we invest wisely, we should have no further concerns about the future.'

Hunter crossed the room and patted his brother's shoulder. 'You could not have timed your return better, Percy. I nearly sold the house to an American who – luckily, as it turns out – changed her mind at the last minute. As for the land, Eloise is arranging to purchase the estate. I am certain she will be perfectly happy to relinquish the plan, which I know she devised purely to help our family.'

'Has she plans to marry, then?' Percy enquired.

Hunter shook his head and, encouraged by Cissy, related the sad story of Eloise's feelings for her former tutor. 'Carter is now on the way to fame as an artist!' he concluded. 'But there is no possibility that he, a potter's son, could take the place of the custodian of the Kenilworth estate if he married Eloise. Eloise has always taken her responsibilities as her father's heir very seriously.'

Percy told them how he had called in at Mount Street earlier to see Eloise and Storm. 'They had been in a hold-up on their way up to London. It's all right, they are shaken but not seriously hurt, although Storm did sustain a glancing wound on her arm.'

There was general consternation, and Cissy was especially disturbed until Percy reassured her that Storm was now much recovered. 'Tell Percy about the stranger, Hunter!' Cissy said, having heard about Cousin James from Storm in one of her many letters.

Percy had heard something of the man from Fuller the caretaker, but Hunter now told his brother the story of the Australian's claim to be Lord Kenilworth's firstborn son from a previous marriage.

'Of course, it may well turn out that the fellow is an imposter, and the papers he has produced are forgeries. I have been making enquiries on Eloise's behalf, but have not yet had a definitive reply from the Australian authorities,' Hunter said. 'I'm sure Storm has told Cissy how much she dislikes the stranger, but unfortunately Eloise is quite taken with him and has actually offered him the use of their dower house for the duration of his stay, while the enquiries are going on.'

'Storm absolutely hates him!' Cissy broke in. 'She says he spends his time trying to ingratiate himself with Eloise and—' She broke off as the grandfather clock in the hall resounded eleven times.

Lady Chislestone pushed back her chair and, standing, said, 'It's long past your bedtime, Cissy dear, and you, Percy, look exhausted. It has been a truly memorable evening and I think we should now retire for the night.' She turned to Lady Witton, who had also risen from her chair, and together they walked from the room with Cissy reluctantly following in their wake.

Once the women had left the room and the brothers had shared a final drink together, Percy clapped the palm of his hand over his mouth. Putting his other hand in his coat pocket, he drew out Storm's scribbled note and handed it to Hunter. 'So sorry, old fellow!' he said. 'With all the excitement I'm afraid I forgot to give you this. Storm gave it to me to give to you when I dropped her off at Kenilworth Hall earlier. I think you should go there tomorrow. I can come with you if you like.'

In a state of shock at this unexpected news and with a strange feeling of apprehension, Hunter unfolded the sheet of paper and started to read Storm's erratic writing. The colour left his face and he was aware of a thudding anxiety in the region of his heart.

> *Hunter, I know the identity of the highwayman who held us up. It was Cousin James.*
>
> *Eloise doesn't believe me, but I recognized his horse. He knows I have a letter proving he is an imposter (I saw it was from Australia and opened it secretly), and he will go to any lengths to retrieve it. I have locked it in Father's desk so it will be safe until you can come and confront him with it.*
>
> *I have Father's pistol but please come to Kenilworth with great haste.*

Hunter was horrified. There was no doubt that Storm had put herself in appalling peril if it was true that she had proof of the man's real identity. What lengths might he go to in order to retrieve this letter? He was filled with dreadful anxiety; it was becoming apparent that 'Cousin James' might well be a dangerous character. It worried him to the very core of his being that Storm might be in danger – in serious danger – and could even lose her life.

Such was the extent of Hunter's unease that he decided to waste no more time and travel immediately to Kenilworth. Once Pegasus was saddled, Hunter turned to Percy.

'I hope to be back tomorrow with Storm, but take care of Mama and Cissy. I will send word if I need your help.'

He wasted no more time and in his haste to get to Kenilworth quickly, he decided to leave the main thoroughfare after an hour and take a shortcut across the countryside through the woods.

It was a silly choice he had made, he reprimanded himself, to leave the main road where he could have kept to a steady speed. His sense of urgency as time was passing was increasing. Now, as his horse picked his way through the trees, he was travelling at little more than a walking pace.

It was at this moment that he realized for the first time how much Storm meant to him. The wilful, argumentative, tempestuous child had now looked to him to be her protector, her defender; someone on whom she knew, without doubt, she could depend.

All he could think of now was the sound of her voice appealing to him for help.

TWENTY-TWO

Kenilworth Hall, the same night

The servants' rooms on the attic floor in the east wing of the house were too distant, Storm realized, for any of them to hear her if she called for help. As if reading her thoughts, Daniel removed his hand, gagged her with a handkerchief and blindfolded her with a scarf. Despite her struggles, he tied her wrists firmly together behind her back.

He was breathing heavily and she tried to twist her face away from his to avoid the fumes from his brandy-laden breath. Her mind was working furiously as she tried to anticipate the likely outcome of this assault. Clearly Daniel Collins was determined to retrieve the letter he knew she must have. She thought of it now safely locked in the drawer of her father's desk; there was no way the man could get hold of it unless she told him of its whereabouts. She had no doubt he would disbelieve her were she to tell him she had destroyed it, and now she wondered whether he might go to the length of killing her if she did not produce it.

For the first time since she had left London, Storm's determination to outwit this man was wavering. With hindsight, she should not have delayed giving Hunter the letter when it first came into her hands. She was now overcome by a sudden, all-consuming desire to see Hunter, hear his voice, feel his arms round her. If fate was now decreeing that her life was to end at any moment, she would not mind if only she could believe that he loved her and she could hear him tell her so.

Such thoughts quickly vanished as she heard Daniel by the window wrestling with the curtains, and then she felt his rough hands tying her ankles together with one of the curtain cords. With her wrists already bound, her mouth gagged and her eyes blindfolded, Storm knew she was powerless to object to her helplessness. Her only hope of survival, she now realized, was if Hunter came to her rescue. Percy, she told herself, should have reached Lancing by now and if Hunter had set out at once for Kenilworth, he should be arriving soon.

Storm would have been in far greater terror had she known that Percy had not yet given her note to Hunter.

With total disregard for the tears now trickling down his victim's cheeks, Daniel wrapped her tightly in a bedsheet and lifted her over his shoulder. Opening the bedroom door, he confirmed that there was no one about and carried her down the back staircase and out of the unlocked door to the big store room where a large copper sat waiting for the household laundry. An hour or so earlier, he had watched and noted where Mabel had put the key after closing the door to the kitchen garden. Three floors above them in their attic bedrooms, the servants heard nothing as Daniel nudged the door shut and hurried down the cinder pathway to the greenhouses where he had tethered his horse.

Slinging Storm's body none too gently on to the saddle, he walked the horse as quietly as possible down the back drive. There was not a soul to be seen and although they were making slow progress in the darkness, it was not long before they were in the relative seclusion of the forest. Aching now in every limb, Storm was fighting against the desire to offer to give her captor the letter once he took the gag from her mouth and set her free, but before she could make up her mind, the horse stopped abruptly and she realized it was being tethered to a tree. From far away in the distance she heard the faint sound of Chislestone village church clock striking once. Daniel now lifted her unceremoniously from the horse and carried her into a shelter. She could tell from the musty smell that it was one of the derelict huts previously used by charcoal burners. Pushing her roughly down on to a rickety wooden bench, he removed the blindfold and pulled the gag from her mouth. With a length of greasy rope lying on the floor, he tied her ankles to the bench, saying, 'One last chance, my fine lady. Tell me where the letter is. Once it is in my possession, I will disappear to a place where I cannot be found. I will not be able to release you immediately, but I will send word to your sister to say you are safe in this hut.' He gave a caustic laugh, adding, 'Save both our lives, eh?'

Weak as she was now feeling, Storm knew instantly that she must not fall into the trap her abductor had set: namely, that if she let him have the incriminating letter he would leave her here to die. The chances of anyone finding her were minimal. Gathering the remnants of her strength, she said, 'If I were to help you escape justice, I would be guilty too.' She added righteously, 'Our family motto is "Honesty" and since early childhood we always had to repeat it after our prayers.'

For a fraction of a second Daniel did not speak, then he said angrily, 'Enough of this nonsense. Perhaps you will think more sensibly when I come back tomorrow.'

Storm looked about the shadowy room in horror. Other than the bench on which she was sitting, there was no furniture. The end of the rope he had used to tie her to the bench he now tied to one of the few remaining posts supporting the damp, moss-covered roof. No one, she realized, could have used this hut for several years. There was no covering on the earth floor and the half-open door hung sideways on its hinges.

She felt a stab of real fear for her life.

'You can't leave me like this!' she said. 'I may well die from the cold, besides which I don't have the salve that the doctor gave me for my arm . . . where you shot me!' She continued, 'I recognized you – and Firefly! The doctor said I must have the wound dressed four times a day and gave my maid the medication she is to use. If you leave me here, I shall almost certainly die . . . and you will be hanged for my murder,' she finished defiantly.

Daniel's hesitation was only momentary. He had not known Storm would be coming to Kenilworth Hall that day or he would have had more time to prepare the hut – to put provisions in, and bedding of some sort. That would have been the sensible course of action to take, since he knew that unless he left her alone in her cold prison to think it over for a while she was highly unlikely to surrender the letter he so badly needed. Seeing the coach arrive that evening, he had had no time to work out a satisfactory plan for forcing her to give it to him. Of course, he did not know the contents or how damaging they were, but it was enough that the envelope was addressed to 'Daniel Collins'; that name would link him to the murder of James Smithers.

A cold shiver of apprehension caused him to catch his breath. The girl was right. He could not allow her to die; not before he had the letter. The chance of her being found here in the woods far from any of the many paths through the trees was a risk worth taking. After one or two days in isolation with no company or creature comforts, she would almost certainly give in and hand it over. The moment he had it, he would disappear – get a passage on any craft going to a distant country where he would make a new life for himself under an assumed name. He would be safe, though admittedly without the prize he came for.

'I'll go back to the dower house and get a few supplies for you,' he said. 'Then you will realize I wish you no harm and all I want from you is my letter. Now, I'm afraid I shall have to replace your gag as I cannot risk you calling for help.'

With her hands still tied together, Storm had no chance of preventing him pushing the handkerchief once more into her mouth. Exhausted, and perilously close to tears, she watched him leave the hut, heard his movements as he mounted his horse, then the sound of the animal's hooves fading away. Almost simultaneously, the moonlight became fitful and cast an eerie light inside the hut. Before too long, Storm tried to comfort herself; it would be daylight and Mabel would go to her bedroom and find her missing. There would be a search for her and maybe someone would find her, though that seemed unlikely since no footpath led to or past the hut.

Such was Storm's physical exhaustion that now both her courage and her hopes deserted her. Frightening thoughts criss-crossed her mind: Hunter might be busy and have other claims on his time; he might think that she had become paranoid about the Australian and that there was no point trying to investigate his past until he'd had a reply to his enquiries; he might decide not to come to Kenilworth for several days, and by that time she might not be alive . . .

With a last call upon her usual reserves of courage, Storm forced herself to believe she would survive this present ordeal.

Her decision was made. She would never allow the threat of death to force her to surrender the letter, and sooner or later Hunter would come and find her while there was still time.

Meanwhile, Hunter had turned off the grassy lane on to the footpath through the forest which was a shortcut to Walgreen, a village close to the Chislestone and Kenilworth estates. His stallion Pegasus was a strong, good-natured animal which had once belonged to Percy. He was the only horse he now owned, kept at Chislestone for local use. As he had anticipated, Lady Witton's groom had been none too pleased to be asked to saddle up the horse at such a late hour; he had recovered his usual good humour, however, when Hunter told him he was not expecting to be accompanied.

Although his speed was limited by the vagaries of the clouds drifting across the face of a full moon, both he and his mount were familiar with the shortcuts around Kenilworth and Chislestone. So now he was more perturbed by memories of Storm's untidily written appeal to him for help. It was the first time he had received such a request from her for herself, though she had asked him to do something about Cousin James and Eloise's relationship with David Carter. Yet the note she had entrusted to Percy was a direct appeal for his immediate assistance. Although sharing her doubts as to the man's real identity, until this evening he had been prepared to leave the status quo and not urge Eloise to dismiss the man from the dower house. Instead he had done his best to persuade Storm to withhold judgement until after he had received the results to his enquiries in Australia. Not fully convinced that the man was an imposter, he had not taken seriously Storm's wild accusations. Her insistence now that she could prove that she was correct would indeed put her in great danger, and the thought of her alone with her maid at Kenilworth, the dower house not a hundred yards away, added to his growing anxiety.

To Hunter's dismay, as he turned his horse's head to follow the shortcut that led through Kenilworth woods, the moonlight became spasmodic and he had to slow to almost walking pace. All around them, the night life of the forest startled the

horse: the sonorous hooting of owls; the shadow of a frightened deer crossing their path; the screech of a vixen or the
bark of a dog fox. It was when they had slowed to a hesitant
walking pace that the horse suddenly stopped in its tracks
and neighed – a sound Hunter instantly recognized as his
stallion's call to a mare whose scent he had detected – and
then there was a distant answering neigh. Astonished that there
could be another horse in these woods in the middle of the
night, he waited until the animals' calls to one another ceased
before moving on.

Luck was not on Hunter's side. Less than five minutes later
he felt Pegasus stumble, and dismounting he discovered that
his stallion had cast a shoe. He now had no alternative but to
walk beside the horse. It was therefore a considerable time
before they reached Kenilworth Hall. The house was visible,
a black shape silhouetted against the slightly lighter sky.
Securing Pegasus to the post and mounting the stone steps,
he grasped the wrought-iron bell rope, the ensuing noise such
that the roosting pigeons flew up into the air in terror.

It was several minutes before Simms, the senior valet left
in charge while the family was in London, opened the heavy
door. A cloak was hurriedly flung round his shoulders, covering
his nightshirt, and he stood staring open-mouthed, astonished
at the large figure standing impatiently in front of him.

Hunter stepped forward and, putting his hand on the elderly
man's shoulder, he shook the confused servant impatiently.
'Miss Storm!' he said urgently. 'Is she here?'

Bewildered, the man informed Hunter that, as far as he
knew from Mabel, Miss Storm was tucked up in her bed.

Hunter paused. 'Go and wake up Mabel and tell her she is
to go to Miss Storm's room and make sure she is all right.'

Meanwhile, the stable lad was to take his horse to one
of the stables and see he was made as comfortable as
possible. The farrier was to be called first thing in the morning
to re-shoe Pegasus.

With a worried frown as still no one appeared, Hunter's
apprehension grew. Five minutes passed before, standing in
the hallway, Hunter heard Mabel's screams as she came flying
down the stairs, her nightcap and grey flannel dressing gown

awry, and flung herself unceremoniously into his arms. She was sobbing hysterically.

'I locked up everywhere, he can't have got in . . . She knew he wanted the letter . . . She locked it in Lord Kenilworth's desk. She was safe in her bed when I left her . . . nine o'clock it was . . .'

She broke off as Hunter took hold of her shoulders and shook her.

'Calm yourself, Mabel!' he said firmly. 'We have no reason to fear she has been abducted.'

'But we have, sir!' Mabel wept. 'Her room looks a terrible mess – the curtains falling which-a-way, the bedsheet missing and—'

She broke off, tears falling down her cheeks once more. 'It's that dratted letter. She says he wants it and she won't let him have it!'

At first, Hunter believed that at any minute one of the servants would appear saying they had found Storm in a different bedroom, where she had wandered in a feverish sleep. But this hope was dashed. White-faced, he despatched Simms to make haste to the stables to saddle another horse for him.

'I'm going down to the dower house,' he announced. 'If Miss Storm is not there, I'll need my mount ready immediately. Meanwhile, keep searching – the garden, the sheds . . . everywhere.'

It took Hunter no more than ten minutes to search the dower house, where a nightshirt-clad servant had opened the door to him. Bleary-eyed, he told Hunter that his employer had told him he'd been invited to a dinner party some distance away and that since he was likely to be late back, the man need not wait up for him.

His anxiety now seriously increased, Hunter hurried back to the house. The village clock was striking three as Simms greeted him with the news that Storm had not been found. Momentarily speechless with anxiety, Hunter stood by the front door. He was still wondering what could now be done when Starlight the carriage horse broke the silence with a loud, impatient neigh. The stable lad holding its reins grinned.

'Reckon she's wanting back to her warm stable!' he muttered, earning himself a sharp reprimand from Simms for being cheeky. As if in sympathy, the horse neighed a second time.

Before Simms could chastise the boy again, Hunter said quickly, 'No, no, don't be angry, Simms. The horse has given me an idea . . .'

He broke off, his mind whirling. The last time he had heard a similar neighing, he had been in the woods; had heard his stallion whinnying and the mare's answering reply. He'd been so eager to get to Kenilworth he had not stopped to find out what a horse was doing in the woods so late at night, away from the footpaths. Unless a charcoal burner was using a horse and cart to ferry his sacks of charcoal back to the town, there would be no reason for a horse to be off the path. The trees and undergrowth were dense where the charcoal burners had obtained their fuel and built rough temporary shelters for themselves. He and his brothers and the Kenilworth boys had used them as camps when they were young.

Was it possible, he thought, that the Australian really was evil enough to kidnap Storm who, according to Mabel, had locked away the incriminating letter? What better place to conceal her than in this forest which was seldom frequented except by travellers to the south coast? It was unlikely that he would have killed her without getting hold of the letter he wanted, but he could well have hidden her there where nobody would think to search for her.

Starlight neighed for the third time and Hunter no longer hesitated. Remembering the extraordinary occasion an hour or so ago when Pegasus had received an answering call from a mare in the forest, he had the strangest feeling that he must go back there and check to see if he could possibly be right, improbable as it seemed. It would take less than fifteen minutes to reach the area and reassure himself that Storm was not imprisoned in a former charcoal burner's hut.

With instructions to the servants to keep searching for Storm, he mounted Starlight and cantered off down the drive. The moon was now giving adequate light for him to find his way back to the part of the woods where the huts were. A slight wind was rustling the tops of the trees and Starlight's hoof-beats on the dry forest floor were the only sounds he could hear. He was totally unaware of Daniel riding along an adjacent footpath on his way back from the dower house. He had delayed entering the house until he was sure his servant would be asleep and there were no signs of light in the upstairs windows. Now he was retuning with the supplies he had collected.

Exhausted but unable to sleep, Storm was lying awkwardly against the wooden post to which she had been tied. Vaguely, she heard the sound of a horse's hooves and supposed her abductor had returned. With an effort she tried to pull herself upright, but by now the wound on her arm had become pain-fully inflamed. The figure of a man she supposed to be Daniel appeared in the entrance of the hut, and such was the degree of her pain that she gestured to him to release the rope round her injured arm. The shadowy figure came closer, and suddenly Hunter's arms were encircling her and he was murmuring huskily, 'Thank God you are safe, my dearest girl.'

He removed her gag and then he was kissing her, telling her he loved her, and Storm realized she was not hallucinating, that it was really Hunter holding her, Hunter who had said that he loved her.

'Hunter, he's coming back, he's keeping me here until I give him the letter he wants. You must go! Hunter, please go! Don't let him find you here. He might kill you if he thinks I have told you where the letter is.' She broke off as she realized that Hunter was not listening to her. He was holding a finger to his lips as he moved quickly to the far side of the door. Only then did she, too, hear the sound of a horse approaching.

For a moment there was complete silence. Outside, Daniel saw Hunter's horse tethered to a tree and there came the sound of an oath as he realized someone had found his prisoner. Quickly, he removed his pistol from the pouch on the saddle and, with a look of fury on his face, strode towards the open doorway of the hut, his pistol in his right hand.

Storm saw him approaching and only after a gasp of horror did she obey Hunter's signal, with his finger to his lips, to stay silent. But Daniel had seen the direction of her gaze and swung round to face Hunter. Before he could raise his pistol, Hunter fell on him, knocking them both to the ground.

Now fearing for his life, Daniel used all his strength to free his right arm and smash the pistol into Hunter's face. Despite the excruciating pain of the blow, Hunter retained his grip on Daniel's body. By far the sturdier of the two men, he managed to manoeuvre his weight gradually on to Daniel's chest so that the man began gasping for breath. Quickly, Hunter unfastened Daniel's leather belt and secured the man's wrists together.

Getting to his feet, he now hurried over to Storm and started to loosen the cords securing her to the post. She was silent now, very close to exhaustion, and was unable to support herself on her feet when Hunter finally freed her.

'I'm going to secure the fellow to this post,' he said, 'and then take you back to the house. I'll send one of the servants down to the village to alert the magistrate and the local constable in charge of the lock-up.' He glanced scornfully at Daniel's inert body. 'I can't imagine what the penalty is for kidnap and for claiming to be someone else, but he'll certainly have a few years behind bars!'

As quickly as he could, he secured Daniel firmly to the wooden post. There was now a look of such extreme terror on Daniel's face that Storm almost felt sorry for him. What she did not know, of course, was the terrible degree of punishment he was now about to face. She did not know what was contained in the damning reply to Hunter's enquiry, already on its way from Australia – the news that Daniel Collins was a murderer.

Held securely on the saddle in front of Hunter on the way back to the hall, Storm found herself wondering if she was dreaming. The pain from her arm and her utter exhaustion had vanished as Starlight walked them gently home. She half believed she was a little girl again: dishevelled hair, grubby dress, tucked on the saddle in front of Hunter, held tight as his stallion cantered back to the house so she wouldn't be late for tea. Many were the times he would get her out of trouble, laughing off Eloise's or the governess's disapproval of her adventurous escapades. 'How's my wicked little princess?' he would greet her.

Now, as they approached the house and Mabel, tears pouring down her cheeks, rushed out of the front door to greet them, Storm could think of only one thing – Hunter had kissed her and told her he loved her. He was saying it again as he carried her upstairs and laid her gently down against the pillows.

'I love you!' he said yet again as he bent to kiss her. 'When you have had a good sleep, we will talk about the future. I need to hear you say you love me and that you will marry me.'

Those were the last magical words Storm heard before exhaustion overcame her and she fell into a deep, refreshing sleep.

EPILOGUE

Kenilworth Hall. May, 1857

'It's beautiful . . . really lovely, Storm,' Cissy declared as she stroked the ivory silk wedding gown Storm was showing her. 'That design is gorgeous and I love the way your dressmaker has gathered the lace edging so it falls over your shoulders, and the bodice with the embroidered roses just nestling in the lace.'

Storm smiled happily. 'Only three more weeks and I'll be Hunter's wife!' she said as she stood up to hang the wedding gown back on the wardrobe door before resuming her seat on the chaise next to Cissy.

The younger girl drew a long, contented sigh. 'Do you remember how we used to play pretend weddings and we always chose you and Hunter to be the bride and groom! Oh, Storm, darling, I am just so, so happy. Now we are truly going to be sisters . . . real ones!'

Smiling, Storm put her arm around her friend and hugged her. 'And you shall be godmother to our first child!' she said. Then she added: 'And Cissy, I haven't told you yet, but Eloise has chosen the prettiest bridesmaid dress for you in a stunning apricot colour.'

Cissy smiled. 'I just hope I don't have one of my asthma attacks!' she said. 'Although I've been so much better lately, haven't I? Mama says it's because Percy has come back and brought good luck with him, and of course it's so wonderful being home at Chislestone again, nice as Lady Witton is. Mama looks ten years younger and smiles all the time!'

Storm nodded and then sighed. 'I wish my darling Eloise was happier. Sometimes when she doesn't know I am looking at her, I see such a sad expression on her face. I know she misses Mr Carter and it saddens me that she can never have someone to love her the way Hunter loves me.'

Cissy nodded. 'Mama thinks his portrait of Eloise is really beautiful and says she'd have liked him to paint me if he hadn't gone to Italy.'

As the two girls went downstairs for luncheon, Hunter and Eloise emerged from the study where, they had told them, they had been discussing the possibility that they might jointly provide the village with a hall for community activities. Hunter greeted the girls at the foot of the wide staircase and, putting an arm around each of them, said, 'Eloise and I have just had a most satisfactory meeting and reached a conclusion which we will tell you about in due course and at the appropriate time: that is to say, after our wedding, my love.' He smiled at Cissy as she tucked her arm through his, and they followed Eloise and Storm into the dining room. 'And what have you two mischief-makers been planning?' he asked.

'Whether or not we can be bothered to come to the wedding,' Cissy said, giggling. 'We thought it might be more fun to get that handsome Scottish admirer of Storm's to take us to London to see the wild animals in the zoo at Regent's Park on that day!'

'That's the third time you have mentioned that man this week!' Hunter said, pretending to scowl. 'I don't mind if he has turned his attentions to you, my darling, but I'll not have him sending flowers to Storm, even on the pretext that he thought it was her birthday!'

They were all smiling as they sat down at the dining room table. After the meal was over Hunter took both girls in his curricle for the short drive to Chislestone Manor.

They found Percy sitting in an armchair, watching his mother with amusement as she happily supervised the fitting of new curtains for the drawing room.

'I've not seen Mama looking so content for heaven knows how many years!' Hunter whispered to Cissy.

When Lady Chislestone was satisfied, she sat down with her two sons and the girls and listened with genuine interest while Percy, his face glowing with enthusiasm, outlined his plan to become involved in the growing local railway industry.

'At the rate they are progressing, there will soon be train

routes to every corner of the country!' he said. 'It's simply a matter of sufficient investment and, as you know, money is the one thing I now have.'

His face alight, he announced he was going north next week to meet some investors to see if he could join their syndicate and play an active part in their plan to develop a new direct route to the south coast.

'As you know, Mama,' he said, 'I used to think mining was the most exciting thing in the world, but railways! I don't doubt that soon people will be able to travel wherever they want by rail. Just think, Mama, you could ride on a train from Chislestone to London, do your shopping and be home in time for tea!'

They all laughed at this improbable excursion. But Lady Chislestone looked doubtful.

'If you are right, Percy, it would in some ways be a great advantage, but I am far from sure that I want our beautiful countryside polluted by smoke and defaced with the ugly trenches which will be dug for the rails the trains will need to run on.'

'Personally, I'd rather travel on horseback!' Hunter said. 'Even if it does take so much longer. Do you agree with me, Percy?'

'Maybe in the summer when the sun is shining and the trees and flowers adorn the roadside. It's a different game in winter with rain, snow, mud and cold winds to hamper you,' Percy replied.

Eloise ended the discussion by reminding them that they were promised to attend the village school prizegiving at three o'clock.

After the event ended to much applause they returned to the hall, where Petal's father Admiral Fothergill was joining them for tea. He had been asked if he would officiate at the wedding by giving Storm away since she had no male relatives. It was something Percy would have done but for the fact that he was Hunter's best man. Eloise was to be Storm's matron of honour, and Cissy and Petal her bridesmaids. The wedding was to take place in the Chislestone village church and the entire population

to be invited back to Kenilworth Hall gardens for refreshments.
This was no mean task, bearing in mind that the village and
outlying farmsteads had a large number of inhabitants to be
catered for. Mrs Barnes, the Kenilworth cook, had already
started baking a rich, fruit-filled wedding cake which could
be safely stored for the necessary month before being iced
and decorated just before the wedding.

Lady Chislestone had politely informed Hunter that she
really felt strongly that he and Storm should have a proper
London wedding, which she would gladly host and to which
their personal friends could be invited. However, Hunter and
Storm agreed it would be a great deal more fun to have a
village wedding rather than a conventional society one. This
delighted Eloise, who had no wish to relinquish the responsibility of organizing Storm's special day. It would be up to
their personal friends whether or not they wished to travel so
far for the wedding.

Storm knew that a number of Hunter's bachelor friends and
several of her own and Petal's schoolfriends would attend.
Among the guests would also be 'Old Porky' – Mr Samuel
Turner, the Chislestones' long-suffering bank manager, who
declared openly that Percy's survival and the restoration of the
Chislestone fortunes pleased him almost as much as if he
himself had been the beneficiary.

Two days before the wedding, from her bedroom window,
Storm could see four of the gardeners erecting the huge tent
normally used for village fêtes. Eloise, with Storm's and
Cissy's help, was going to decorate it both inside and out with
some of the garden flowers. Barrels of beer and cider had been
brought up from the village inn and placed in the cellar
to keep cool until needed. Although she was not supposed to
know about it, Cissy had told her about the magnificent iced
wedding cake Mrs Barnes had made and allowed her to see,
along with the mountain of cheese scones, meat pies, fruit
tartlets and spun sugar pastries.

Storm felt a wave of happiness as she watched the activities
in the garden and thought of Mabel's remark that morning
when she had dressed her. Her maid had commented on how

enthusiastically the entire village had welcomed the forth-coming union of the two families.

Now, unexpectedly, she saw Hunter ride up and dismount by the tent where he signalled to the gardeners, presumably indicating that they could stop work and take a brief respite in the early summer sunshine.

She smiled, and her heart filled with love as she watched her future husband laughing at a joke one of the men had made. Her mind returned, as it often did, to the night he had rescued her from the charcoal burner's derelict hut and the unbelievable magical feeling of his arms around her and his voice saying he loved her. While she had been recuperating Hunter had barely left her side. As for the man who had kidnapped her and might have killed her, Hunter had waited until she had fully recovered before telling her and Eloise that the Australian calling himself their half-brother was not only an imposter but a murderer, although he was still protesting his innocence. It had come to light that the unfortu-nate James Smithers had recently been found dead at his farmstead and there had been no trace of his birth certificate or the other relevant documents. Daniel Collins, who was now in possession of the certificates, had known Smithers, and the Australian authorities now believed that he had murdered him and attempted to steal his identity.

But almost of more importance was the news that brought comfort and great relief to Eloise and Storm. The whole question of their father's possible first marriage need never come to light. When investigated by their solicitor, the parish records in Scotland were found to be incomplete. There was no record of a marriage between their father and an actress named Lily. The marriage certificate James Smithers' mother held was found to be a forgery, created by whom no one knew. So there was doubt on the veracity of the whole story.

Daniel Collins was in prison in London waiting to be shipped back to Australia where he would stand trial for his actions and, if found guilty, would almost certainly be hanged – a fate he richly deserved. But as Storm had told Eloise, she would never regret his appearance in this country because it was the danger that she had been in that had made Hunter realize he loved her.

Everything in her life was now perfect, with only one exception: Eloise. There were times when her sister looked so sad; times when Storm feared her beloved sister was thinking how lonely she would be.

There had recently had been several discussions between Eloise and Hunter. There was no need, Eloise had said, for Storm to be present, because they were about the management of the two estates. After their most recent meeting, when she, Storm, had joined them for tea, Eloise told her that she had invited them both to reside at Kenilworth after they were married; that Hunter would help her manage the estate, for Percy would now be resuming his rightful place as head of the Chislestone family and thus managing the Chislestone estate. Their mother would remain as chatelaine of the manor and Hunter would in effect be master of Kenilworth Hall.

It was an unorthodox arrangement but, as Eloise pointed out, Hunter's help would be invaluable to her and Percy was more than capable of managing the manor by himself. His brother had, Hunter told them, already hosted a weekend party for the partners in the new railway company in which he intended to invest some of his wealth.

Storm was surprised by Eloise's plan that Hunter should become the virtual Master of Kenilworth, a solution which pleased her; she would far prefer to live with him at her home than at Chislestone Manor.

With this future arrangement agreed, Eloise would have their company and not be alone. Was there a possibility, she wondered, that one of Hunter's bachelor friends, meeting Eloise at Kenilworth in the future, would be attracted by her beauty and sweet nature and decide he wanted a wife after all?

As she left her bedroom and went downstairs to go out into the garden, Storm's thoughts returned happily to her own wedding. It would be more like a joyous garden party than a formal wedding reception, she told Hunter when he asked if this arrangement pleased her. It was a constant surprise to her how thoughtful, how caring, how loving he could be. He was not only verbally but also physically

passionate, holding her hand to his lips or stealing hungry
kisses whenever he could if no one was in sight. He would
talk of the honeymoon he had planned, in France, Spain,
Italy and Greece. Not, he had whispered, that she would have
a chance to see much of their famous sights and artefacts,
because he intended to spend most of the time making love
to her. He did not want her to have children too soon, he
had declared; he wanted her all to himself. Cissy, however,
told Storm she could not wait for them to produce a little
niece or nephew for her. She most definitely did not want
ever to get married, she confided, but she would dearly love
to have lots of little ones to whom she could read stories
and with whom she could play games and act plays, the way
she and Storm had done all those years ago.

Cissy's asthma attacks were now few and far between, and
she was in the best of health when the wedding day finally
arrived and she and Petal followed Storm down the aisle of
the lovely old village church. It was far too small to accommodate all those who wished to attend the wedding, but those
who could not get in gathered outside in the warm summer
sunshine.

It was a day everyone in the village was to talk about for
years to come. Storm looked radiant in her ivory spangled
dress with its lace neckline and wide skirts, the overskirt held
up in scallops round the hem with embroidered rosebuds and
cornflowers, showing the flounced underskirt of layers of
deeper cream gauze. She stood outside the church door after
the ceremony gazing up at Hunter, who looked incredibly
handsome. He was standing with his hand possessively
covering hers where it lay on his arm, in his black frock coat
and pale grey trousers and a striped grey and gold silk waistcoat. The villagers lining the path showered them with rice,
wishing them good luck and happiness with genuine emotion.
Behind them, Cissy and Petal, in their matching apricot silk
dresses and straw bonnets decorated with apple blossom and
matching silk ribbons, framed with lace under the brim, were
gathering up the flowers thrown by the children. Percy and
Eloise were standing by the lychgate where the Kenilworth

horses pawed the ground, waiting impatiently to pull the decorated carriage with the newly married couple back to the hall.

By four o'clock the garden party was in full swing and by seven o'clock the last of the guests had departed.

Exhausted, but immensely happy with the success of their informal wedding celebrations, the two families went into the welcome peace and quiet of the house. Eloise, thoughtful as ever, told all the staff they could tidy up the next day as they, too, had been working so hard to make the day a success.

Together with Percy, Cissy and Lady Chislestone, Hunter, Storm and Eloise sat down to a light supper, after which the Chislestone family went home. Taking Storm's arm, Hunter led her and Eloise into the drawing room where, seated beside his bride on the sofa facing Eloise in her chair by the window, he complimented her on the success of the day. Eloise was smiling but Storm looked downcast.

'Yes, it was wonderful, Eloise, and there is only one thing which prevents me believing this will always be one of the happiest days of my life.' She looked across at her sister, her expression sad. 'I would so much have liked you to enjoy the same wonderful happiness Hunter and I have shared today—' She broke off as Hunter took her hand in his and clasped it tightly.

'Storm, my darling, I think this is the moment when your sister wishes to divulge the plans she and I have been making.' He looked expectantly at Eloise.

Eloise looked at Storm, her expression slightly anxious. 'I didn't want to tell you this before, dearest, as I did not wish anything to upset you, but I have to tell you that tomorrow I am leaving to join David in Italy.' Ignoring the expression of stunned astonishment on Storm's face, she continued, 'The marchesa has given him the beautiful villa below her castle. It overlooks the sea and when David and I are married we shall be able to paint the wonderful scenery there – and, indeed, all over the world, since David is now so famous. He is meeting me tomorrow in London and we will be leaving by boat from Southampton the next day.'

Seeing the look of amazement on her sister's face, she continued, 'I expect you wondered why dear Hunter and I spent so much time recently alone together in the study, supposedly discussing estate matters. We were in fact discussing the future. Now Percy is home and can take care of Chislestone Manor, I have handed over the management of Kenilworth to Hunter, as you know. This will now be your marital home and I have every faith in Hunter's ability to care for everything – and you, my darling. I am sure you will be a wonderful help to Hunter and I have no doubt that the pair of you will be happy.'

She leaned forward, holding out her arms in supplication.

'Tell me you don't mind my leaving you, dearest. I know you are aware of how long David and I have loved one another. Please tell me you understand.'

Storm jumped to her feet with tears in her eyes and, crossing the room, flung her arms round her sister. 'Of course I understand! I couldn't be more happy for you. In fact, it makes this day absolutely perfect for me.' They kissed one another and Eloise rose to her feet.

'I must leave you both now; Violet and I still have some packing to do.' She was smiling as she blew a kiss to Hunter before leaving the room. 'I will see you both in the morning before I go.'

Hunter stood up, walked over to Storm and put his arms round her waist. 'Now you know the reason why I postponed our honeymoon,' he said. 'There were two important considerations. First, that Eloise would not leave you until after our wedding, and second, that you would almost certainly wish to be at hers. Eloise's one concern was at being parted from you, and your loving sister was overjoyed when I suggested we went to Italy for part of our honeymoon and were with her and David for their wedding.'

'Oh, Hunter! What a wonderful idea. I am just so happy and so grateful to you for your thoughtfulness.' She reached up and gently touched his cheek. 'I never thought it was possible to be so happy, to love someone as much as I love you.'

Hunter kissed the palm of her hand. 'Now that I know my plan pleases you,' he said tenderly, 'I think the time has come for us to be truly wed. Come to bed with me, my darling, and I will show you just how much I love you.'

* * *

As the night drew to an end and the faint glimmer of dawn crept through the casement windows, Storm finally closed her eyes. Exhausted as she was by Hunter's passionate lovemaking, she felt overwhelmed with happiness. She had never imagined that anything could be as wonderful as the last few hours when Hunter had claimed her body as well as her heart. She had absolutely no doubt whatsoever that their married life was going to be unimaginably happy.

Beside her, on the brink of sleep, Hunter found himself wondering how he could possibly have let so many years pass before discovering that his love for Storm was much more than the deep affection he had always felt for the tempestuous little girl. The young woman lying now in his embrace was more precious to him than anything else in the world could ever be.

'I love you,' he murmured as he drifted into sleep.

Smiling softly, she whispered, 'I love you too.'

Lightning Source UK Ltd.
Milton Keynes UK
UKHW011831130920
369846UK00001B/18